TARA TAYLOR QUINN

The Moment of Truth

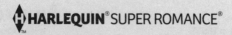

Recycling programs
for this product may
not exist in your area.

ISBN-13: 978-0-373-71889-4

THE MOMENT OF TRUTH

ABOUT THE AUTHOR

With sixty original novels, published in more than twenty languages, Tara Taylor Quinn is a *USA TODAY* bestselling author. She is a winner of the 2008 National Readers' Choice Award, four-time finalist for the RWA RITA® Award, a finalist for the Reviewers' Choice Award, the Booksellers' Best Award and the Holt Medallion, and she appears regularly on Amazon bestseller lists. Tara Taylor Quinn is a past president of the Romance Writers of America and served for eight years on its board of directors. She is in demand as a public speaker and has appeared on television and radio shows across the country, including CBS *Sunday Morning*. Tara is a spokesperson for the National Domestic Violence Hotline, and she and her husband, Tim, sponsor an annual in-line skating race in Phoenix to benefit the fight against domestic violence. When she's not at home in Arizona with Tim and their canine owners, Jerry Lee and Taylor Marie, or fulfilling speaking engagements, Tara spends her time traveling and in-line skating.

Books by Tara Taylor Quinn

HARLEQUIN SUPERROMANCE

*Shelter Valley Stories
**Chapman Files
***It Happened in Comfort Cove

Other titles by this author available in ebook format.

SINGLE TITLE

MIRA BOOKS

For my mother, Penny Gumser,
my aunt Phyllis Pawloski, my sister-in-law,
Kim Barney, and my husband, Tim Barney, who all
understand that my fur babies are family, and love
and care for them accordingly.

CHAPTER ONE

"COME ON, JOSH, it's only a few weeks before Thanksgiving, please stay until after the holiday...."

Joshua P. Redmond III, heir to a conglomeration of holdings that spanned the globe, replayed his mother's words as he stood alone in the elevator of the Rose Garden Residential Resort, watching the floor lights blink their way upward.

Two, three, four.

"My presence is a detriment to Father's firm, and a source of incredible pain to the Wellingtons." His stilted response followed his mother's plea in his replay of that morning's breakfast table conversation.

"You are our son, Josh. Your father cares more about you than he does about the firm."

Six, seven, eight.

"And you are more important to us than the Wellingtons, too, you know that."

And if tradition provided for a small family gathering at the Redmond mansion, Josh might have stayed—to please his mother who'd done nothing but champion him since the day he was born.

Nine, ten, eleven.

But Thanksgiving at the Redmond estate had always been a highly coveted social affair among Boston's elite. To uninvite the Wellingtons would be in poor taste. Beyond indecent.

It wasn't anything that would have crossed his mind six months ago.

Twelve, thirteen, fourteen.

"I'm leaving this evening, Mom. It's for the best."

She'd nodded then, blinking away tears. He knew she'd given in because his going was for the best. And because she'd already pushed him as far as she could in getting him to agree to relocate to the godforsaken desert town of Shelter Valley.

As godforsaken as he was, he should fit right in there.

Seventeen.

A bell dinged gently, followed by the almost imperceptible glide to a stop that preceded the opening of the doors in front of him.

Plush beige carpet greeted him. Stepping out, he hardly noticed the cream-colored walls with maroon accents, or the expensive-looking paintings adorning them. Michelle Wellington's suite, one of four on the floor, was to the right. He headed in that direction.

Who would ever have believed, two months ago, when they'd arrived in separate cars for their combined bachelor/bachelorette party, that the vivacious and sexy, gracious and gorgeous twenty-seven-year-old brunette would be reduced to living in a long-term care facility? An expensive and elegant one, to be sure, but still a home for those who couldn't function on their own.

Michelle should have been lounging on a private beach on an island off the French coast, enjoying her honeymoon—their honeymoon.

"Hi, sweetie." He announced himself the very same way every time he visited.

Her vacant gaze continued to stare forward.

Approaching the maroon velvet-upholstered chair, he held out the sprig of colorful wildflowers in his hand.

Michelle loved natural arrangements, colorful arrangements, not hothouse or professionally raised blooms. Something he'd learned from her mother while they were both sitting in the hospital waiting room two months before.

Dressed in a silk blouse and linen pants, she showed no reaction to the flowers he'd placed in her direct line of vision. The ties holding her upright and in the chair were discreet—and all that he saw.

"I brought flowers," he said. He'd have brought chocolate, too, if she'd been able to taste it through the feeding tube that administered all of her nourishment these days.

No more decadence for Michelle Wellington.

No more sushi or expensive wine, shopping, traveling or any of the other things she'd loved.

And he, Joshua P. Redmond III, descendent not only of the Boston Redmonds, but also, on his mother's side, of the even more influential Boston Montfords, was largely to blame.

"HEY, LITTLE FELLA, where's your family?"

The soft, feminine voice floated through the balmy Arizona night, seemingly out of nowhere.

Stopping on the path behind the Montford University library, a shortcut to the parking lot where she'd left her car, twenty-five-year-old Dana Harris listened.

"It's okay, little guy," Dana heard the woman say. "I won't hurt you."

Dana hardly took a breath as she strained to pinpoint the direction the voice came from.

"Come on, it's okay. See? I won't hurt you. Where do you belong?"

The voice came from the right, and all she could see there was a huge desert plant of some kind. Still fairly new to campus, Dana didn't know what lay behind the large desert bush that stood well over her head. She didn't usually park where she'd parked that evening, didn't usually take this route to her car and had never studied at the library this late before.

"You're all right," the voice crooned. "We're a pair, aren't we? Both of us out alone in the dark and cold? Don't worry, little buddy, I'll take care of you."

Rounding the bush slowly, Dana caught sight of a small figure leaning against a cement wall that matched all the others that surrounded trash Dumpsters on campus, with what looked to be a ten- or fifteen-pound dog in her arms.

"Hey," she called out softly. "I don't want to startle you, but I couldn't help overhearing…"

The owner of the voice glanced up, and with the help of the security light shining behind the Dumpster, Dana recognized her.

"You're in my freshman English class," she said, in case the younger woman was nervous, being approached in the dark.

The other girl studied Dana for a second. "Yeah," she said after a moment. "I'm Lori Higley. And you're the woman who always sits in the front row."

"Right." Drawing the sides of her sweater around her, Dana moved closer. "What have you got there?"

"A dog, or rather a puppy, I think. I'm not sure what kind. But his paws are pretty big for his size so I'm thinking he's young and going to be big."

Reaching out, Dana stroked the dog's back. "It's okay, little fella," she said gently when she felt the animal quiver beneath her touch.

"He's scared," Lori said, adjusting the dog in her arms so Dana could get a better look at him.

"And hungry, too, I'd guess," Dana replied, scratching

him lightly under the chin, near the throat. "His back is too bony."

"Do you think he's abandoned?"

"He has a collar."

"I couldn't read the tag."

Moving together, Dana and Lori approached the security light and Lori held the dog aloft as Dana studied the tag on his collar.

"He's had his rabies shot, which means he's probably at least three months old," she said. "But there's no name or ID other than the rabies registration number."

The dog shivered, and shoved his nose against Dana's hand. "We can call the vet in the morning and see if we can have this tag traced," she said, lightly massaging the top of the dog's head with her fingers. The more good feeling they could bestow on the little guy, the better chance that he'd relax.

She was also checking for mats or scabs or any other sign of disease or abuse.

"He was cowering in the corner over there by the Dumpster," Lori said, rubbing the dog's side as she held him. A bit huskier than Dana, Lori took the little guy's weight with one arm.

"Probably looking for something to eat."

"I've got tuna in my dorm…" Lori's voice faded away, and Dana remembered overhearing the girl say something about being alone in the cold.

"I've got a kitchen full of food at home," she said quickly. "Why don't the two of you come with me and we'll get a better look at this guy while he eats."

"You live off campus?" Lori's gaze matched the envious tone in her voice.

"I have a duplex about a mile from here. You can ride with me in my car if you'd like. That way you can hold him. And I'll bring you back whenever you're ready. Do you have a curfew?"

From what she'd heard, the dorms at Montford were still old-school—separated by gender and under pretty firm house rules. Dana started slowly walking toward her car.

"It's not until midnight, and I'm in no hurry to go back." Still cuddling the puppy, Lori fell into step beside Dana.

"Problems?"

"A roommate who was great until she met some guy that she can't live without. We have a suite and right now he's in the living room part of it with her and they'll do it even if I'm there."

"I thought the dorms were segregated."

"They are."

"So he's not supposed to be in the room?"

"Right. But if I tell on them, I'll have made a couple of enemies for life. They don't care if I'm around so it's not like I can act all put-out, like they're keeping me from my room or anything. And I don't want them to get kicked out of school."

"Did you know her before you came to school?"

"Yeah. Forever. She's my best friend. Or she was until she met him. She started drinking with him, and I wouldn't be surprised if she's doing drugs, too."

"Montford's not the place to start screwing around with that stuff." Dana crossed behind the library and headed toward the parking lot in the distance. Her little used Mazda was the only vehicle there. "From what I've heard, they've got zero tolerance for substance abuse. You're caught, you're out."

"Yeah, but that doesn't stop kids from partying. It goes on even here, trust me," Lori said. "Kids are more cool about it, and keep it quieter, but college is college, you know? I just never expected Marissa to get into that scene.

We were like the nerds in high school because we were the only two in our class who didn't party. It's one of the reasons we chose Montford."

They'd reached Dana's car. Unlocking the passenger door, she held it open while Lori, puppy in arms, slid inside.

"Where are you from?" she asked the pretty blonde beside her as she started the car.

Dana had always wanted blond hair—naturally blond—instead of the mousy brown she'd been born with. Her younger half sisters both had blond hair. At least she had their blue eyes.

"I'm from Bisbee. It's a little town in southern Arizona. How about you?"

"I'm from Richmond, Indiana. It's on the Ohio border." She gave the dog a reassuring scratch and put the car in gear. "My folks own a small chain of furniture stores there."

"Indiana is days away from here!" Lori said. "What brought you all the way across the country? You have relatives here?"

"Nope." Dana shook her head, feeling a tug as her long ponytail caught between her back and the seat. "I'm here on scholarship."

"What made you apply to Montford?"

It was just talk. A normal conversation between fellow students who'd just rescued a dog.

And it was excruciating as far as Dana was concerned—the explaining, answering to and thinking about her past. Shelter Valley represented a new start for her. A life where she could just be Dana Harris, a person who wasn't second-best, who didn't wear Cinderella clothes and live a Cinderella life. A woman who'd accepted a scholarship she hadn't applied for, to embark on a life she hadn't planned on, because she hadn't been able to bear the thought of doing as her father had demanded and marry a man she didn't love.

But then, Daniel Harris, for whom she'd been named, the man she'd always called "Dad" and thought was her biological father, wasn't really her father. And no matter how far away she roamed, or how hard she tried to be good enough, that fact was never going to change.

CHAPTER TWO

"YOUR MOM AND DAD are well and send their love." Sitting in the chair opposite Michelle, a chair identical to hers except for the restraints, Josh looked from the still-beautiful woman to the day's fresh flowers in the vase on the coffee table directly in front of them. He'd replaced yesterday's bouquet. Opened the sheers that had been pulled for the night across the window opposite them, giving Michelle a skyline view of the harbor she loved.

He'd turned on the sixty-inch flat-screen television hanging on the wall next to the window. And, when she'd frowned, turned it back off again, although he knew her frown probably had nothing to do with the TV.

Michelle comprehended little, if any, of what went on around her. According to her doctors, frowning—and smiling, too—were simple reflexes that came and went. Sometimes her eyes filled with tears—a physiological reaction to medication, dry eyes or something in the air. Her gaze would land on something sometimes, but there was no connection between visual stimulation and a thought process that would translate the view. Permanent vegetative state was the diagnosis—and it was the same according to all four specialists Josh and her family had called in from around the world to see to her. She couldn't move of her own volition. Or speak. Or even think.

But somehow she breathed on her own. And as long as that was the case, Josh's inheritance would be providing for her care. Every dime of it. From a trust account he'd established in her name.

Her parents had more than enough wealth to care for her. Insurance covered basic expenses. But as far as Josh was concerned, his money would be dirty if he spent it on himself.

"I'm going away, Michelle." He said what he'd come to say. "I'm on my way out of town now." He'd waited until nightfall so there'd be less traffic.

It seemed fitting that he'd slink away into the night.

Leaning forward, he grabbed a tissue from the box beside her and wiped a drop of drool from the side of her mouth, catching it before it could roll down her chin. "I don't know when I'll be back," he told her. It wasn't right, him leaving her like this. But staying wasn't right, either. His presence in town was hurting his father's business, creating strife for the Wellingtons and embarrassing his mother's family, the Montfords. The Montfords had worked hard to rebuild their reputation of decorum after his distant uncle's scandalous marriage and desertion many decades before. They'd dedicated all the decades since to reestablishing themselves as a family of conservative do-gooders, whose purpose on earth was to contribute to and better the world and whose behavior was always above reproach.

Josh's behavior, his selfishness and lack of awareness, had caused a scandal.

So he'd had to choose between further hurting Michelle, who, by all accounts had no idea he was even sitting there speaking with her, and hurting all of the people who loved him, who'd supported him and given him everything he had. People whom he'd taken completely for granted. People who still had work to do and much to contribute, to better the world in which they lived.

The choice had been a no-win. Hell. Just like the life his years of cavalier unawareness had created for him.

"It's taken the Montfords three generations to gain back the respect my great-great-uncle lost," he told Michelle, something he never would have mentioned to her in the past. Truth be told, he couldn't remember ever having a meaningful conversation with her, period.

Even his marriage proposal had been made on the fly. They'd been skydiving that day. He'd been filled with the adrenaline of having conquered the air—coupled with his newly resolved determination that it was time for him to marry. His marriage would be good for the family name. Good for business.

And because, in all of his travels across the United States and abroad, he'd never found that one woman who stood out above the rest, he'd chosen the most beautiful one he knew.

One he'd dated on and off for years.

"Let's get married," he'd blurted over a glass of celebratory champagne in the back of the family limo on the way home from the airfield.

He would have driven his Mercedes convertible but hadn't wanted to stay sober after the great event....

The sky outside Michelle's window was a purplish hue, aglow from the lights of the harbor. Earlier that day, when he'd left his mother's house, that sky had been a vivid blue. As blue as it had been the day, two years before when, without hesitation, Michelle had accepted his proposal. And thrown her arms around him, confessing her undying love for him.

He'd had no idea she'd cared so much. Then, or after.

He was one of the blessed ones. The privileged. He was too busy to care....

Busy upholding his reputation, keeping up appearances, studying and, later, working even harder than his ancestors

had in order to ensure the continuation of the family name
and financial success. And when his work was done, he'd
been busy partying.

"My great-uncle a few times removed, Sam Montford,
married a black woman and brought her to live in the family mansion downtown," he told Michelle. Back then, the
scandal had nearly ruined the Montfords. It was old his-
tory now, something people knew but didn't talk about
much anymore.

"And if that wasn't bad enough," he continued softly,
"he fathered a child with her who was to be raised among
the privileged society kids, equal to them."

Michelle's expressionless face gave proof to the seriousness of her condition. If she'd had any mental cogni-
tion at all, she'd have shuddered at that one. Not because
of the child's mixed race, but because of the societal scandal such an act would have caused back in his great-great-
uncle's day.

People of his family's social class absolutely did not
cause scandal. At any cost. To the Montfords and Wellingtons, Redmonds and people like them, appearances and
reputations were every bit as valuable as their financial
net worth. Sometimes more so.

In today's world, his distant uncle's actions might have
produced a raised eyebrow in their conservative society,
but generations ago, mixed marriages, particularly among
the elite, were unheard of. Blasphemous.

Michelle offered him a steady stream of drool.

"Hard to believe, isn't it?" he asked, wiping her chin and
slowly running one finger down Michelle's linen-clad knee.

Her therapist had already been there that day, and would
be in again before bedtime, to massage every muscle in
her body and move her limbs, to keep her as toned as they
could for as long as they could.

Because he'd deemed it so. He wanted her to be as comfortable as she could be.

And the irony was not lost on him. If he'd paid even a hundredth of the attention to Michelle then that he did now, none of this would have happened. It was an inarguable fact—and the reason Josh took full blame for the probable attempted suicide that had left Michelle in her current state.

What kind of fool left his deliriously drunk fiancée alone to sleep it off while he went back to party some more? True, he hadn't known that Michelle had consumed enough liquor to make alcohol poisoning a risk. He hadn't even paid enough attention to know she had a low tolerance for alcohol. He knew she drank with the rest of them; he hadn't bothered to notice how much. Or, in her case, how little. As her future husband, he should have noticed. And if he'd stayed with her that night, tended to her, paid even a little bit of attention to the symptoms of alcohol poisoning that she'd already been exhibiting, he could probably have saved her.

"Remember that New Year's party we went to at the Montford mansion the year I turned twenty-one?"

He'd been there with a blonde whose name he couldn't remember—someone he'd brought home from Harvard to show his father he was his own man. Another woman he'd treated kindly but had callously used for his own end. Michelle had had a date, too—a pompous ass a few years older than them who'd looked down his nose at all the alumni from their elite high school. Forty-eight of the fifty kids he'd graduated with had been there. And many from Michelle's class, two years behind his, had attended, as well.

"A bunch of us got drunk and my date threw up on the porch steps," Josh continued, sparing himself nothing—telling her something she already knew. "Thank goodness it was the back porch steps and Bart liked us enough to get it cleaned up before anyone found out."

Bart—his maternal grandfather's live-in help. A man who'd run the Montford city estate since before Josh had been born.

Josh had escaped besmirching the Montford name that time. But he hadn't learned his lesson.

Michelle's head tipped forward, and with his fingers around her chin as he'd been shown, Josh righted her. And rubbed her cheek.

On some level, he told himself, she had to know that he was there. That she was surrounded by tenderness. By anything and everything money could provide.

She had to know that the only thing she'd wanted—his attention—was hers.

"One day when Sam Montford was away from the mansion on business, his wife and baby went out and found a lynch mob waiting for them on the front steps outside their home," he said, looking out in the distance, to the harbor seventeen stories down and about a mile over from them. Unlike his shame of ten years ago, that long-ago event had taken place on the front porch—not the back.

"The mob killed them both," he said evenly, hardly feeling anything at all. Just like Michelle. They were alike in that way. Dead to any kind of real living. "Hard to picture Boston's elite in any kind of a mob, isn't it?" he said. "But things were more primitive then. People took matters into their own hands. And didn't stand calmly by when others tried to change the rules by which they lived."

Michelle's gaze was turned on him and his breath caught in his throat. Until he remembered that he'd repositioned her head.

"But to kill a woman and an innocent baby…"

If only Michelle would recover, even a little bit, if he

could talk to her, find out what she'd been thinking the night she'd nearly drunk herself to death, to know for sure that he'd been the reason she'd consumed such a dangerous level of alcohol the night of their prewedding party.

He hadn't loved her. Her heart was breaking.

And he'd been too self-absorbed to notice that anything was wrong.

Alcohol poisoning, loss of oxygen and a careless fiancé had all contributed to Michelle's predicament. He'd been the only one who could have saved her.

"When his wife and baby were killed, Sam Montford left town," he blurted. "He took up residence with an Indian tribe out west. And later, after marrying the daughter of a missionary he met on the reservation, he founded a little town in the middle of the Arizona desert."

It had just been in the past couple of years that his mother had developed an interest in genealogy, helped along by the readily available resources on the internet. That research infused her with the need to get to know her distant relatives—relatives she'd heard about but never met. Being able to look them up, learn details of their lives, made them seem real to her, although she hadn't contacted any of them yet. The two branches of the family had not been in touch since old Sam Montford left Boston. After his sojourn with the Indians, he'd founded Shelter Valley. But he'd never reconnected with the Boston part of his family.

While researching her family tree, Josh's mom had discovered the names of cousins several times removed, as well as birth dates, marriages and deaths. The need to meet them intensified.

And because Josh had agreed to make his home there, she'd finally given her blessing to his plan to move away—at least for a while—rather than travel for an extended period until the news of Michelle's tragedy and his subsequent broken engagement died down a bit. "It's a town that welcomes losers," he added.

Not quite what his mother had said. She had framed it as a town that would welcome him.

Because she thought he was going to arrive in town a Montford. Or even a Redmond. She thought he'd been in touch with the newfound—and long-estranged—branch of her family. He'd never told her so. It was just what she'd have done—and expected him to do.

He wasn't moving to Shelter Valley as a Montford.

He was going as Josh. To accept the junior-level position his Harvard business degree had qualified him to have in the university's business operations office.

"That's where I'm going, sweetie," he said. "Out to Shelter Valley, Arizona."

He wiped away more saliva. And could hardly remember what it had felt like to kiss her lips. Wished they stood out from all of the other lips he'd kissed.

Or even that he could remember the last time he'd kissed her.

"We didn't get to the altar, to exchange our vows." He bowed his head. "But I'm promising something to you now. I will change my ways, become more aware of those around me and do what I can to make this world a better place."

He wasn't actually sure if Michelle was into the whole bettering the world thing as much as the Montfords were. They'd never really gotten around to talking about it. Still, she'd been involved in charity work. He wasn't sure how much. But during their two-year engagement, he'd accompanied her to several black-tie affairs for different causes.

He'd written generous checks.

And spent most of the evenings making business contacts. Or doing other things like planning the mountain-climbing expedition he and several of his friends had taken over Christmas the previous year.

"I've got a few thousand dollars with me to get started," he told her. "I sold the Mercedes. And the 4x4. I bought a used SUV with a hitch and loaded a trailer with stuff, and that's all I'm taking. The rest of the stuff I sold with the condo, and that money went into your trust, too. My monthly stipend will also go into the trust. It's there for as long as you need it.

"My mother's agreed, for the time being, not to get involved," he said, thinking of the days ahead. "I told her I'd handle the first contact with the Arizona Montfords on my own—or I wouldn't go. If she interferes with my life while I'm there, I'll just move on. The point is for me to get away from here. It doesn't matter where. *She's* the one who wants me in Shelter Valley, and this is the only way I'll do it." There wasn't going to be any big family reunion in the near future.

What his mother didn't know was that his "visit" with the Montfords was going to be short and sweet. He wasn't one of them.

He was starting a new life. Not going on vacation. He was going to live like a regular guy. One who had to work and sweat and save. One who was humbled enough to pay attention to the people around him. He couldn't do that if his old life followed him. Making things easy for him.

"Sweetie? Michelle? Is there anything I can do, or say, anything that…"

His voice broke. Looking down, Josh breathed and waited for the emotion to pass. It always did. One of the many things he'd learned over the past couple of months.

He hadn't meant anyone any harm. Hadn't meant to ignore the needs of those around him. He just hadn't noticed.

"Oh, I'm sorry, Mr. Redmond, I didn't realize you were here. I'll come back later...."

Sara, one of the three full-time caregivers he employed to see that Michelle had everything she could possibly need, stepped back through the archway leading to Michelle's bedroom.

"No, it's okay, Sara," he said, standing. "You can come in. I was just leaving."

"I hear you're leaving town, that you won't be coming by here anymore," the middle-aged widow said. He knew Sara best. She lived in the suite with Michelle.

"That's right." She could castigate him for his callousness. All Michelle had left was his visits. Her parents couldn't bear to come. Couldn't bear to see her this way.

And her sisters, all their friends...they considered Michelle dead and buried.

But Michelle didn't need him there as much as the rest of them, her family included, needed him gone.

"It's about time," Sara said, smiling at him with a warmth he wasn't used to seeing. People in his world banked their emotions, their expressions, showing the world a blankness that preserved their ability to walk in and out of rooms, do the business they'd come to do, without drama.

Or shame.

Without anyone getting one up on them—or being able to manipulate them.

Their walls protected their reputations.

And they protected the money.

The gray-haired woman moved quietly to Michelle's side, running her fingers tenderly through the young woman's hair. "We'll be just fine without you," she said. "Missy here has no idea you're killing yourself over something you didn't do. She ordered those drinks and she drank them. You wasn't even in the same room as her.

And she gets no benefit from these visits. But you…you've got a whole life to live. Things to do and people to help. It's time for you to let go."

Let go?

Michelle had taken that last irrevocable step—she'd drunk herself into a stupor, but she'd done so because of his negligence.

And she'd been without oxygen for so long because he'd left her alone in a nearly comatose state. If he'd been committed enough, devoted enough, even aware enough to stay with her, they'd be on their honeymoon now.

Let go? Never.

No matter what Sara said, Michelle had lost her life because of him. It was a fact that couldn't be denied. Or changed. And her family had made that plain to him.

His friends, too, had blamed him, even as they commiserated with him. He'd have to live with the aftermath of guilt, and the whispers that condemned him for having left her alone that night.

But Sara was right about one thing. He had to get out into the world. To live among those he'd spent his entire life ignoring.

To find something human in the selfish bastard he'd become.

CHAPTER THREE

DANA AND LORI fed the dog.

"We should name him," Lori said as they watched him gulp down a bowl of instant rice with canned chicken mixed in.

"Uh-uh." Dana shook her head. "You name him, you take on ownership—and he's not ours."

She couldn't keep him. He wasn't house-trained, as they'd already discovered. And as he grew he was going to need more space than her little duplex would give him.

They bathed him. And fed him again.

Or attempted to. As soon as Dana put down the second bowl of chicken she'd boiled for the puppy, Kitty Kari darted out from behind the refrigerator and over to the bowl.

"You have a kitten! How cute." Lori grinned, watching the tiny calico put her front paws on the bowl and dip her head inside until she reached her goal.

The puppy, easily five times her size, cowered back and watched as the kitten ate his food. And Dana felt a kinship with him.

"Kari, that's not yours," she said, reaching over and plucking the cat out of the bowl. "Little Guy's a lot hungrier than you are," she explained.

"Did you bring her with you from Indiana?" Lori asked, reaching over to pet the kitten.

Shaking her head, Dana watched the puppy, hoping he'd

head back to the bowl on his own. It was best if siblings could find a way to coexist.

Not that he was, or would be, a member of their family. Still, while he was in their home...

"She was left on the side of the road in Missouri. I'd stopped for the night on my trip out here and saw the box on the entrance ramp to the freeway. There were three kittens inside, but only Kari survived." Holding the cat up to her face she said, "And you're doing just fine, aren't you, girl? Healthy and sassy as can be."

Kneeling, Lori coaxed the puppy slowly to the bowl and told Dana that she'd never had a pet, which led to a conversation about the younger woman's life in Bisbee living alone with her miner father after her mother died.

Dana had no idea who *her* real father was. But she didn't offer up that information.

Over a glass of iced tea, while they sat on her back patio waiting for the little guy to do his business, Dana offered the younger woman her spare bedroom for the night. And any night that her roommate had her boyfriend over. Marissa couldn't get away with sneaking a boy into an all-girls' dorm too often. And Dana understood Lori's predicament. Sometimes you had to choose to look the other way for the greater good.

TWO DAYS AND TWELVE HOURS later, on Friday morning, Dana was almost late for her freshman English class because she'd had to clean up two puppy messes left by Little Guy in the fifteen minutes between taking him outside first thing in the morning and getting out of the shower. Lori, who'd caught a ride with her back to campus in time for their English class on Wednesday hadn't been over since, but had offered to babysit the dog over the weekend.

Dana was hoping she wouldn't need her. After class on

Friday, she headed straight home to the bathroom where she'd been locking up the puppy while she was away, groaned at the toilet-paper-strewn floor, scooped up the unrepentant offender, and the jarred sample she'd collected from the backyard that morning. Leaving the mess, she headed back out the door.

Cassie Tate Montford, owner of the Shelter Valley animal clinic, was waiting for them and she didn't want to be late.

Zack Foster, the only other veterinarian on Cassie's staff, had taken care of the kittens for her when she'd arrived in town, and she'd called him first thing Wednesday morning only to find that he was out of town. The clinic's receptionist had assured Dana that Dr. Tate would handle their situation.

Driving with Little Guy wasn't easy. Luckily, she didn't have far to go and arrived at the clinic five minutes ahead of her one-thirty appointment. And five minutes after that, Dr. Tate entered the examination room.

The middle-aged redhead wore her long hair piled into a twist. With her white coat and efficient air, she was a bit intimidating, until her brown eyes landed on the creature in Dana's arms.

"Hello, friend, what can you tell us about yourself?"

The gentleness with which the older woman handled the stray, the way she treated him like a person, instead of a lesser being, endeared her to Dana.

"He looks to be in perfect health," the doctor said after a thorough examination. "I'm guessing he's somewhere between four and six months old. Temp is normal, heart sounds good. Gums are healthy. Teeth, too. No fleas or skin infestations, no signs of internal parasites or worms in the sample you brought in. His eyes and ears are clear. His coat's healthy. He's certainly got a good disposition."

Dana could vouch for that. Standing at the table, opposite the doctor, Dana asked, "What breed do you think he is?"

"He's got some Lab in him. And, I think, poodle." Dr. Tate smiled. "Do you have any interest in keeping him?"

"I can hang on to him for a little while. But I live in a duplex. And he's going to get big, isn't he?" *Please tell me I'm wrong, that his big paws are just a fluke.*

"I'd guess at least fifty pounds. Maybe more."

"He's got a rabies tag," Dana pointed out.

"I know," Cassie Tate Montford said. "We're checking on that now, but since no one's called looking for him, my guess is he's been abandoned."

He was too sweet to have been abandoned. Someone loved him. Was worried about him. Probably putting up lost-dog signs all over the neighborhood. She hadn't seen any, when she'd driven around town looking for them after class on Thursday. But she probably just hadn't landed on the right neighborhood. "I have a kitty…"

"Right. Kari. I read Zack's notes on her. And a hamster, too, I saw."

"Some kids in my freshman biology class were talking about having gotten him for their dorm and then found out they couldn't keep him."

"Freshman biology?" the doctor asked. Petting the dog, she said, "If you're in school full-time, and working, it might be hard to take care of a new puppy."

"I don't work," she blurted. "I'm here on a full scholarship, including living expenses. And I've been working in my family's furniture business back home for the past six years. I've got savings…."

When she realized she was babbling, she shut up.

Curiosity flashed across the doctor's expression. "You're scholarship includes living expenses?" The veterinarian sounded surprised by that fact.

"Yes." So? Little Guy was getting restless, and Dana lightly scratched his chest in between his two front paws. It was his favorite spot—as she'd discovered during the middle of the night when she couldn't get him to stop whining in the bathroom and go to sleep. He'd done just fine in her bed.

"Did you apply for the scholarship?"

"No." She frowned. "Why?"

"It's just that…I know someone else…the fiancé of a friend of a friend." Cassie Tate Montford chuckled. "He's also here this semester on a scholarship with full living expenses included, and those kinds of scholarships are few and far between. He didn't apply for his, either, and he has no idea where the scholarship came from. He's convinced his grandmother set it up, but if you got one, too, that's probably not likely. Unless you know him. Mark Heber?"

"I've never heard of him. Is he from Indiana?"

"No. It's probably just some kind of national program set up by a private benefactor. Private meaning whoever donates the money wants to remain anonymous. I've just… no one here has ever heard of this before and now we have multiple recipients in one semester."

"Yeah." She shrugged. Dana didn't really care how the scholarship had come to be—only that it was. "I'm pretty sure my mother applied for it on my behalf," she offered because of the tenderness the older woman was showing to Little Guy. "Anyway, I'm fine, financially, as long as I watch my spending. I can certainly afford dog food and vet bills until we find a home for him."

"We have a pet placement program here at the clinic. If you were to keep him, it probably won't be long before—"

"I, actually…wanted to talk to you about that," Dana said. Zack had mentioned the pet placement program when she'd brought the kittens in to be seen. And again after she'd joined his and his wife's pet-therapy program at school. "Dr. Foster mentioned that you needed someone to temporarily house unwanted pets. Also people who'd be willing to travel to new adoptive homes to make sure the new owners weren't overwhelmed and to check on the general well-being of the pet."

The doctor smiled. "That's right. We're looking for another pet placement counselor. But the job is volunteer only. I'm assuming Zack explained that there aren't any funds to pay you. Are you interested?"

"Yes," Dana said without hesitation.

"Great, since Zack already offered you the position, I don't need any other reference. I'll have our receptionist, Hope, sign you up." Dr. Tate grinned and added, "We have a pet-therapy program, too. It's part of a club through the university. Zack and his wife head it up. I'm guessing he mentioned it to you?"

"He did," Dana said. "I'm already a member."

The doctor nodded. "In the meantime, let's wait until we hear back about the rabies tag and go from there. If you'd like to see Hope about the counselor position while you're waiting, we'll be all set."

Dana was settled in a chair in the waiting room, a packet filled with pet counselor information on her lap. She was watching a rerun of a dog whisperer show on the flat-screen television on the wall, when the door to the clinic opened.

Little Guy jumped down from her lap and darted the full extent of his leash to jump up on the man who was taking off his sunglasses as he walked toward the reception desk. Dana yanked on the puppy's leash just as the stranger stepped back, right onto Little Guy's foot. The puppy squealed and peed on what looked to be a very expensive leather shoe.

Before she had time to react, the inner door opened and Dr. Tate Montford emerged.

"Ms. Harris? We just heard… Oh!" The doctor noticed the stranger. "I'm sorry, I didn't hear the bell and Hope's out back. Can we help you?"

By the time her eyes dropped to the man's shoe, Dana had grabbed a wad of paper towel from the dispenser on the wall and, with the little guy's leash tightly held in one hand, was cleaning up the man's expensive leather with the other.

"I can take care of that," the man said, his voice friendly as he bent down to her level.

She held on to the towel. "I should have watched him better. I'm so sorry." Dana looked up from the shoe and into the most soulful pair of blue eyes she'd ever seen, just inches from her own.

"It's fine," the man said, the warmth of his fingers transferring to hers as he took the towel from her and finished cleaning the toe of his shoe. "It's just a pair of shoes. I have more."

Staring, she couldn't think of a thing to say, so she stood up. And hoped someone would do *something* to break the awkward moment.

"I'm Josh Redmond," the stranger said to Dr. Tate, upright again. "I'm new to town, working at the university, and was hoping to have a word with you, when you're free."

"I've got half an hour for a late lunch, if you can wait for about five minutes," the doctor said easily enough.

Stupidly, Dana experienced a pang of envy. The man was gorgeous, but she didn't give much credence to looks. It was his eyes that got to her. They had a depth to them, as if they were searching. As if he'd lost something.

She was a sucker for strays.

Kitty Kari and Billy the hamster were it for her. Their small duplex had reached its capacity.

"I'm sorry." The doctor turned to Dana as Josh Redmond took a seat. "I was just coming out to tell you that we traced the tag to an address out on the reservation. Sheriff Richards knew the place. It's been boarded up for about a week. The family left no forwarding address."

So Little Guy had been abandoned.

"You want to keep him until we find a home?" Dr. Tate asked Dana. "I'd take him myself but our collie is getting up there in years and her health is failing. I'm afraid of what an energetic puppy would do to her at this point."

Little Guy looked up at Dana. She'd have to buy a dog bowl. And puppy pads. A kennel to keep him in while she was attending class. But she'd need those things on hand, anyway, as the newest pet placement counselor of the Love To Go Around Program.

"I'll give him a home." Josh Redmond stood up. "If you don't already have a permanent home in mind for him, that is. I'm new to town. I…live alone. And would like the company."

Dana knew what it felt like to be alone.

"I'll fill out whatever paperwork you need," Josh said, his gaze moving between Dana and the vet. The earnestness in his voice caught at her emotions even more than the look in his eyes. He seemed to feel he had to convince them.

Dana recognized that note in his voice, almost as if he was trying to convince himself that he was good enough….

"I can do the home checks, if you like," she offered.

And maybe she'd get a puppy for herself, too. One that was smaller and could live happily in a duplex.

Dr. Tate explained to Josh Redmond about the pet adoption program requirements. Adding that Dana would perform periodic home checks for the first month or so, and asking if that was all right with him.

"Absolutely," the man said. He wasn't smiling, but he seemed eager enough to take the puppy home with him.

Dana handed over the leash and, counselor packet hugged to her chest, ignored the sting of tears as she turned to go and leave Little Guy behind.

She'd best get better at turning the unwanted pets over to new families if she was going to be any good to the Love To Go Around program. And really, how selfish of her to think that she deserved all the stray love.

"Aren't you forgetting something?" the man's voice sounded behind her.

"I already paid my bill," she assured him, needing to get outside, to take a breath of fresh air. She'd be fine in a second.

"How are you going to visit him if you don't know where he lives?" Josh Redmond asked.

Oh, right. Turning back, she waited patiently while the man wrote his address on a pad of paper Dr. Tate handed to him. She gave him her cell number, as well, in case he had any problems with the puppy. And she bent to kiss Little Guy goodbye.

"This address is only temporary," he said as he handed her the piece of paper. "Until I can find something more permanent."

Dana's smile, while still shaky, wasn't forced the second time she turned to go. She'd see Little Guy again. Very soon.

CHAPTER FOUR

"ARE YOU SURE I can't get you something to eat?" Sitting outside at a picnic table in the little courtyard behind the clinic, Cassandra Montford was absolutely nothing like Josh had expected.

On the bench across from her, his knees beneath the cement tabletop avoiding hers, Josh shook his head. He'd chosen Cassie deliberately because she was one step away from blood relation. One step away from someone who would be directly affected by what he had to say.

"We've always got fresh veggies and sandwich fixings in the fridge," Cassie said. "For days like today when there isn't time for a proper meal."

"You always this busy, then?"

"Sometimes." The beautiful redhead took a bite of a sandwich and shrugged. "My partner, Zack, is out of town with his wife this week so things are a little more crazy than usual around here."

His mind reeling with the knowledge that he had a four-legged creature waiting for him in a kennel inside that back door, Josh said, "I won't keep you long."

"What can I do for you?" Cassie asked.

She took a sip from a water bottle and offered him a bottle of his own. He declined that, too.

"I have a favor to ask," he said, suddenly conscious of the fact that the pretty veterinarian had limited time to offer him and was already halfway through her sandwich. "Of sorts," he amended.

He'd told himself he wasn't going to ask anything of anyone.

And he wasn't.

Not of material value, anyway.

"You said your place is only temporary. You're new to town?" The doctor's expression was serious.

"Yes."

"Here to stay?"

"For now."

Cassie Montford swallowed her last bite of sandwich and wrapped her hands around the plastic bottle, looking at him expectantly.

"I'm Josh Redmond."

"I know. You said so. Should that mean something to me?"

"I'd hoped not, but I wasn't sure. My mother promised me she'd stay out of things, but I wasn't positive she had. It was also possible someone from here had done the same research she did." Which had been another reason he'd waited to do this in person. He was hoping for anonymity and he wouldn't have had any chance of success at all if his identity preceded him.

Frowning, Cassie's gaze remained open. "Do I know your mother?"

"No! And I'm making more out of this than I should. I need to tell you who I am and why I'm in town, but before I do, I'd like to ask you to keep what I'm about to tell you to yourself."

"I can't promise that. In the first place, I'm not in the habit of keeping secrets from my husband."

"Sam, Jr."

"You know Sam? Were you in the peace corps with him?"

"No." But he was surprised to hear that Cassie's husband, Sam, had been. A stint in the peace corps wasn't typically something you found on the résumés of the sons of the elite.

Curious.

"I'm sorry, I just thought..." Cassie broke off. "Other than Sam's time in the peace corps, we pretty much know all of the same people. We've been friends since kindergarten."

"I wouldn't ask you to keep anything from your husband," Josh jumped in. "Though I'd hope that he'd keep anything you tell him to himself."

"I still can't give you any assurances that either one of us will keep your secret until I know the nature of it."

"Fair enough," he said. "I wouldn't have bothered you at all except that I need you to send a letter to my mother, assuring her that I've arrived and am being properly looked after."

She hadn't asked him to do so. But he knew her. She'd manage to keep her word to stay out of things longer if she had some sort of contact, was involved in some little way.

The other woman's frown deepened. As did the look of compassion in her eyes.

"Are you ill?" Cassie asked.

"No. I'm in perfect health." As fate would have it. Michelle was the one who'd paid for his years of selfish indifference. "And I have absolutely no intention of being looked after." He had to make that quite clear. Whether the Montfords agreed to keep his secret or not was not going to change his plan. It just might change his location.

"Okay, tell me who you are, and I'll tell you what I'm willing to do for you."

"I'm your cousin," Josh said. "Or rather, your husband's cousin. Twice removed, but not so much when it comes to the family fortunes. As near as my mother could tell, Sam and I are currently the only direct heirs, once our parents pass."

Cassie's mouth dropped open. "You're a Montford," she said, as though she'd expected him to show up some day.

"My mother is the sole descendent of the Boston Montfords. Your husband's father is the sole descendent of the Arizona Montfords."

"It's my understanding that the Boston Montfords disowned our Sam and that the two branches of the family haven't been in touch in all the generations since."

Josh's mother was an only child. Josh was an only child. The Boston Montfords just might die out.

"I know," he said. "But my mother, as the only heir to the Boston half of the fortune, intends to change that."

"And she's using you to do so."

"In a manner of speaking."

"So what's in it for you?"

Josh bowed his head.

Cassie Montford, who, according to his mother, had been born and raised in Shelter Valley, had obviously learned a thing or two about the outside world, as well.

He sized up the woman across from him. Like he'd study a client across the boardroom table. To see how far he could push, how much he could get.

He saw a spot of moisture on her lip.

A spot of moisture that, in that second, reminded him of Michelle.

"Peace," he finally answered. "And it's not something you or anyone else can give me," he said, knowing that his life in Shelter Valley depended on his honesty in this moment, because it depended on her full cooperation.

"I don't understand."

"Like Sam's great-grandfather, I'm in Shelter Valley to start a new life," Josh said, looking her straight in the eye. "Also like him, I am choosing to do so without benefit of the family fortune."

"Choosing to do so."

"Yes."

"So you aren't on the run? Or cut off for heinous deeds?" She might have been joking, if not for the dead seriousness of her gaze.

"No. On the contrary. I'm in Shelter Valley because the only way my mother would be at peace with me leaving Boston was to know that I was coming here. My parents think that I'm living off my monthly inheritance draw."

"And that's why you want me to write to her and let her know that you're here and being cared for, for her peace of mind?"

"Right."

"What kind of care do you need, Mr. Redmond?"

"Call me Josh...please. And the only thing I need from you and Sam—other than this one communication with my mother who is, by the way, a wonderful lady who will want to meet you someday—is my space and a promise that you will not say anything to anyone, including family, about who I really am."

"Let me guess, you want your mother to believe you're here as a Montford, but you want no part of the family name and all that goes with it."

"Pretty much. My mother has promised to stay out of my life for a while at least. She agreed not to pursue a relationship with your side of the family until I could get established on my own."

It was the only way he'd agree to live in Shelter Valley.

And maybe it was harsh, but he was only asking her not to get to know people she'd never met.

Cassie nodded. Obviously assessing him.

"You don't seem surprised by any of this."

"I'm not. Seems to run in the family."

Josh remembered her peace corps comment. "From what my mother was able to find out from her searches, your husband, and his father before him, have been upstanding Montford heirs, honoring the family name."

"She must not have looked far enough," Cassie said with a not quite humorous, half grin. "My Sam was more like the man he was named after," she said. "He left town when we were barely out of our teens. He's only been back in Shelter Valley, living as a Montford, for the past twelve years. His father, James, had some health issues several years back. We thought we'd lost him, but he surprised us all."

For the first time, Josh was actually curious about the family he'd come to town to avoid.

But getting to know his distant relatives was not part of his plan.

Neither was a dog.

But he was there to help others. And the little pisser needed a home.

Sam and Cassie Montford didn't need him.

Leaning forward, he put his arms on the table. "I applied for...was offered...and accepted a job in the Montford University Business Affairs department." He told her what he needed her to know. "Acquired only on the basis of my business degree from Harvard, not because of any other connection. Being out on my own...living without the benefit of name or fortune...is something I have to do for myself. To keep my mother off my back, I would like to do it here, in Shelter Valley. But I can't do that without your cooperation. If anyone here finds out who I am, I won't be able to become simply a citizen. From what I've gathered in the short time I've been in town, the name Montford carries weight around here. If I'm going to find some self-respect, I have to live off my own efforts, not the benefits that come with my background."

"Sounds like you have something to prove."

"I need anonymity," he said. "If I can't find that here, I'll move on."

Lips pursed, Cassie studied him for a long moment and then took a deep breath. "I have to tell Sam...."

"Understood."

"And get his cooperation."

Josh nodded.

"As long as my husband doesn't foresee any trouble, I have no problem granting your request."

"Thank you." Josh stood, relieved. "For the time being, I'm renting a vacant house on the west side of town," he told her. "I plan to buy something as soon as I get an idea of where I'd like to settle."

Cassie mentioned some acreage with mountain views and Josh shook his head. "I meant it when I said I'm on my own," he told her. "Any Montford monies I had, or will have in the future, are going in a trust designated for another use."

He didn't elaborate.

"The only house I can buy has to fall within mortgage qualification requirements commensurate with my new salary."

Cassie Montford gathered up the remnants from her lunch and walked with him toward the back door of the clinic. "You're really serious about this."

"Completely."

She reached for the door and stopped with her hand on the knob. "Can I ask why?"

He'd been prepared for the question. Not for the empathy he read in her eyes.

"I was born into a life of privilege, which, as it turns out, I didn't deserve. And I'm terrified of dying with nothing but a wasted life to show for having been here."

She wanted to ask more. He could see the questions in her eyes.

"I think my husband's going to want to meet you."

Not if Josh could avoid it. He couldn't afford to let himself get that close to the life he was leaving behind. Not if he was going to make this work.

Because, like an alcoholic tempting himself with a drink, Josh was scared of what the smell and feel and taste of privilege would do to him after a week or two without it.

His resolve was firm. He just wasn't sure he could trust himself to live up to it. Which was another major reason he'd left Boston, and everything and everyone familiar to him, behind.

"Maybe, at some point," he said. "But not here in town. Not where anyone might see us together."

"I'm sure that could be arranged," Cassie said, grinning over her shoulder at him as they stepped back into the clinic. "My husband could probably fool God if he tried hard enough."

Leaving Cassie his cell phone number, with the understanding that she'd let him know what Sam said regarding the favor he'd asked, Josh let her turn him over to Hope, who gave him a starter pack of something called puppy pads, a plastic container of vitamins and a small bag of dog food—all of which he carried out to the back of the SUV.

When he returned, she handed him a leash attached to the ten-pound mass of jumping and peeing fur he'd just agreed to take home with him.

If only his mother could see him now.

CHAPTER FIVE

"DANA, WHERE SHOULD I put this towel?" At the sound of Lori's voice on Saturday morning, Dana turned from the desk in her little living room where she was typing on her laptop. The girl had called sometime after ten the night before and told her Marissa's boyfriend was spending part of the night at the dorm.

"Just hang the towels on the hook on the back of the door," she told the younger woman. "In case you need them again. I'll wash them the next time I do laundry."

Kitty Kari, who'd been curled up on the corner of the desk, woke, stretched and, when her paw knocked against the edge of the laptop, started patting at the screen.

Lori grabbed her purse, keys and the backpack she'd brought her overnight paraphernalia in.

"You going home for Thanksgiving?" Dana asked.

"I'm not sure. If my dad's going to be there, yes. I'm not leaving him there alone."

"If?"

"A couple of his mining buddies have been talking about taking a hunting trip over the holidays. If they go, he will, too."

"Has he done that before?"

"No, but I think he'd have liked to. He wouldn't have left me home alone, though."

Daniel wouldn't have left Dana home alone, either. He just wouldn't have played video games with her like he had with his two biological daughters. And he wouldn't have asked the other two to help with the cooking or the dishes.

They'd done that on their own. Her half sisters, Rebecca and Lindsey—twenty and twenty-two, respectively—were good girls. Good sisters. To a point.

They just didn't go to bat for her. Not that she blamed them. Her mother hadn't, either.

And Dana didn't blame Susan Harris for that choice. For an earlier one, yes, but not that one.

"Well, if you're in town, you're welcome to come over here. I'm getting a big turkey and making dinner for anyone at school who can't make it home for the holiday." She loved cooking Thanksgiving dinner. And even though the holiday was still three weeks away, she'd already started buying groceries as they went on sale.

"If I'm in town, I'll help you cook," Lori said and, thanking Dana for letting her crash at her place, let herself out.

Eight o'clock in the morning and she had her whole day ahead of her. As soon as she got her English paper done, that was. The five-hundred-word essay was due on Monday. And while Dana had an *A* in the class—straight *A*s in all of her classes, actually—she wouldn't be able to maintain her grades if she didn't turn her work in on time.

She was two sentences farther along when her phone rang.

It was Jerome, from her English class. He'd lost part of his grant and was low on cash. He'd shown up for class one day in jeans that were wrinkled and had a stain at the knee and she'd made a joke about a rough night. He'd replied that he didn't have enough money for laundry and was wearing things until they stank—at which time she'd offered him the use of her washer and dryer.

He'd been over every Saturday for the past three weeks. And was calling to ask if he could use her facilities again.

She told him that he was welcome, took a break from her laptop to clear her as yet unwashed clothes out of the washing machine and went back to work. Another paragraph, rewritten four times, and Jerome was at the door. She let him in and returned to her desk.

She heard him in the kitchen, settling at her kitchen table with his own laptop and thought to call out, "You going home for Thanksgiving?"

"No," he answered back. "My folks and I decided to save the money so I could fly home for Christmas break instead of driving. It'll give us four more days together."

Jerome was from Missouri.

"I'm making dinner here for anyone who can't get home," she said. "You're welcome to join us."

"Cool. I'm there," the eighteen-year-old said. "I'm no cook, but I know how to load a dishwasher."

"Then dishwasher loader you are," she said. Kari pounced on her keyboard, typing a series of *A*s, just as Dana's cell phone rang. "Hello?" she answered.

"Dana Harris?"

She recognized the voice. There was no reason to—she'd only heard it briefly—but she did.

"Yes."

"This is Josh Redmond. I met you—"

"I remember you, Josh. I was going to call you in a little while to see how you and Little Guy are doing. I didn't want to call too early." With it being Saturday and all.

"The middle of the night wouldn't have been too early," the man said with a tired-sounding chuckle.

Dana remembered her own sleepless state a few days before. "He whined all night?" she said. She should have warned him. But why borrow trouble? The puppy might not have whined at Josh's place.

And Little Guy needed a home.

But they needed it to be a good home, so that he would have a permanent home. And that's where she came in.

"He whined. And then yelped. And pooped and peed. And whined some more."

"Did you bring him into bed with you?" Most pet lovers knew how to solve separation anxiety issues. Or resolved to put up with the whining for the little bit of time it would take to train the animal to sleep alone.

"Hell, no, I didn't bring it to bed with me!" Josh sounded affronted. "Why would I do that?"

"To get some sleep," she said calmly, not sure they'd made the right choice in a home for Little Guy. Some animal shelters gave animals away to pretty much anyone who stopped in. A home was better than no home. But...

"I'm not sure how you think I'd sleep any better with him whining next to my ear than I did with him howling from the kennel in the bathroom," he said. "I started him out with a pet bed in the kennel, but he chewed on that and left foam everywhere. So I tried a blanket. He peed on it. He ripped up the puppy pad and..."

The man was clearly beside himself. If she hadn't been worried about Little Guy's future, Dana would have smiled.

"Have you ever had a dog before, Josh?"

She'd assumed, since he'd been at the veterinary clinic, and seemed eager to take the dog, that he was an experienced pet owner.

"No."

"You're a cat person, then?"

"No."

"Horses?"

"I've never had so much as a goldfish."

Dana's heart sank. She could hear Jerome in the tiny laundry room off the kitchen, moving clothes from the washer to the dryer.

"You've never had a pet?" She'd grown up with a kennel of them. Literally. And had made more than one road trip with her mother to deliver one of Susan's purebred poodles.

"No."

"And you're there alone?"

With a growing and teething puppy who was going to get huge?

"I live alone, yes."

He sounded tired. Frustrated. But he hadn't asked her to take Little Guy back. Or called the clinic and dropped him off there.

He'd called her. His pet counselor.

Anyone who owned pets had to start somewhere....

"How about if I drive out there," she heard herself suggesting before she'd fully thought about what she was saying. Her paper was three-quarters of the way finished. She had another day and a half before it was due. She could still make the movie she'd been hoping to see that afternoon. And the hair appointment she'd scheduled, if she was quick about it. "Puppies are a lot like two-year-olds...."

"I have no more experience with those than I do dogs," he inserted.

Her curiosity flared. Josh was easily a year or two older than she was. At least. He wore expensive shoes. Was new to town and single. Where had he been before he'd relocated to the middle of nowhere in the Arizona desert?

And why did he choose Shelter Valley?

It was absolutely none of her business. She'd spent too much time with her nose in books. Wanted to know everything about everyone.

"He's testing his boundaries," she told the slightly desperate-sounding man. "And probably suffering some anxiety, too. As soon as he feels secure, and knows what's expected of him, he'll settle down."

"How long does that normally take?"

"Could be a week, could be months." She had to be honest with him. For Little Guy's sake. As much as she wanted the puppy to have found a home, she didn't want him to stay if it wasn't the right place for him. "But there are some things you can do to make the process a lot easier on both of you," she added. "How about if I do your first house check this morning and see what we can do?"

"Would you?"

"Of course."

"We aren't taking you away from something important, are we?"

"Just homework," she told him. "And I'm almost done." Or she would be. Soon. "I'll be there within the hour."

Right after she showered and told Jerome to lock up after himself when he was through.

JOSH WASN'T READY for company. He'd hauled a rented trailer behind the SUV for the trip out to Arizona with his brown leather sofa and recliner, his sleep mattress and bed frame and the solid wood dresser he'd had made in Spain during a weekend jaunt with Michelle and another couple. He'd brought the butcher-block kitchen table because it was the one he'd grown up with and had snatched from his mother when she'd been redecorating after he left for college.

He had linens—more than he needed. And the kitchen things his mother had hired her housekeeper to outfit him with when they'd given him his condo in Boston as a gift for graduating from Harvard.

His housewarming gift had been a housekeeper of his own.

He'd brought his bicycle, with a promise to himself to get back to riding it. His business books, a flat-screen for his bedroom and one for the front room, his stereo. And very little else.

Not even a trash can, or trash bags, he'd realized during the night when he'd had no place to put the puppy's soiled towels.

He hadn't brought paper towels, either. Or cleaning supplies. And he'd found that while toilet paper was good enough for human waste, it didn't stand up to the messes his new housemate made.

An early-morning trip to the big-box store outside of town had taken care of the basics. He'd already used up a full roll of paper towels. Filled two trash bags with smelly and destroyed goods and hadn't made his bed.

Or showered, either, for that matter. There'd been the little issue of soap. He'd had the toiletry bag he'd used on the road, the one he always traveled with and that he'd kept stocked with the supplies his housekeeper bought for him. He'd just never had to stop and think about such things as soap before. It was embarrassing to realize that he was a grown man who'd never done a thing to take care of himself. Including buying a bar of soap.

He *definitely* wasn't ready for company, but neither could he afford to turn away the help from Pretty Pet Woman, who was giving up her Saturday to help him. Remembering her homework comment, he wondered if she was a student at the university. She'd seemed older to him.

He heard her car in the driveway and watched through his uncurtained front window as she climbed out, hooked a big brown satchel on her shoulder and shut the door of the old Mazda behind her. Mazdas weren't bad cars. He'd never ridden in one but he'd read reviews. Their engines were decent.

The woman, Dana, looked even better this morning. Her jeans weren't designer, by any means, but they fit her snugly and accentuated her long legs. Josh wasn't swearing off women. But he'd sworn off commitment—relationships where someone was going to count on him. He wasn't going to risk letting someone else down.

"Where's Little Guy?" she asked after he let her into the modest, three-bedroom, two-bathroom home he'd rented on a month-to-month basis until he could find something he could afford to purchase.

She didn't seem to notice the house. Or him, either, for which he was thankful, considering the day-old jeans... and beard...he was sporting.

He wouldn't have been caught dead looking like this outside his bedroom in Boston.

"He's back here," he said, leading the way to the spare bathroom that was now completely taken up by the kennel.

As soon as they got close, the puppy started to howl again, saving Josh from the need to make conversation with the woman whose plain black sweater hugged her breasts. He was pissed at himself for noticing.

Maybe once the dog was settled he'd head into Phoenix for the night, find a club and a willing woman. Even without the Redmond money backing him, he shouldn't have any trouble finding someone to hook up with. "Oh...my..."

Dana Harris was kneeling in front of the kennel door, unlatching the hooked closure. The puppy—drenched in pee again, judging by the whiff of air Josh caught as the demon hurled itself at Dana's chest—squealed with delight when he saw his visitor.

And then Josh caught a glimpse inside the bathroom. The dog had done a number two in his kennel again. How could any being excrete waste so many times in one day? And he'd also reached through the bars to find the roll of toilet paper Josh had erringly left on the floor beside the kennel. It was smeared with puppy doo, ripped up into little

pieces and now…scraps of it were everywhere those flail-
ing, awkward paws could put it.

"Hey, Little Guy, what've you got going on here?" Dana
asked with a voice he wouldn't mind hearing directed at
him. The woman, who was obviously a lot more comfortable around animals than Josh was, held the squirming ball
of fur up and away from her as she lifted him from the kennel to the sink in one swift arc.

"I'll need a towel, some soap and a glass if you have
one," she said over her shoulder, already running water
lightly into the basin as the dog did everything he could to
claw himself away from the water and up her shirt. Somehow she managed to hold on to him—and keep him at bay.

Josh didn't need a second invitation to vacate the scene
of the disaster. Grabbing a couple of rolls of paper towels,
a bottle of dog shampoo and his travel coffee mug, he made
his way back to the bathroom. Josh wasn't a religious man,
but he prayed, anyway, all the way back to the bathroom
where he could hear his rescuer in a continuous monologue
with his new housemate.

He prayed, not for freedom from the demon, but for the
dog's very quick acclimation to the right way to live in a
home. Josh was on a personal mission to think of others,
to be aware of their needs and put them before his own, so
the dog was staying.

He was going to keep it alive and well if it killed him.

Which it might.

Hurrying back into the bathroom with his sleeves
rolled up and with every intention of getting dirty, he
found the puppy soaking docilely in the sink, a slightly
sad and bedraggled-looking thing, shivering as Dana held
him in place.

And for the first time since he'd rolled into Shelter Valley, Josh felt relief.

CHAPTER SIX

WHERE TO BEGIN?

Holding a wet and subdued but very clean Little Guy wrapped in paper towels in her arms, Dana stood in the hallway of the ranch-style home waiting while Josh Redmond cleaned up his spare bathroom. The man was a sorry case when it came to dog ownership. And almost equally inept at cleaning.

The kennel and floor he did on his hands and knees. Then he used the same sponge on the sink that he'd used on the floor and the kennel—and used up the rest of the roll of paper towels, too.

He was trying.

And for that, she was okay with leaving the puppy in his care.

Once they'd had a talk.

She might only be a pet-placement volunteer, but she'd been volunteering in the veterinary clinic at home in Richmond since she was old enough to drive herself to and from the facility, and Cassie and Zack were depending on her to make decisions regarding the animals' well-being and to report back to them if she thought there was a problem.

Knowing Little Guy as well as she did, she suggested that they have their first discussion outside, where the puppy could roam at will and not destroy anything.

Josh Redmond had no patio furniture. Or anything else in the six-foot-high block-fenced backyard with dirt and a few weeds for landscaping. Warm enough in her sweater, as long as she stayed in the sunshine, Dana stood on the small cement patio and watched the puppy as she said, "First problem, the kennel's too big."

Little Guy tripped over his front paws and rolled onto his head.

"I was told he was going to be a minimum of fifty pounds."

"Eventually, yes. In the meantime, you can borrow kennels from the vet's. It's part of the service we offer the Love To Go Around adoptive families. His kennel should only be big enough for him to turn around in. It'll help him feel more secure and dogs typically don't go to the bathroom where they sleep, so if the kennel is only big enough for him to sleep in, chances are he won't go to the bathroom until you come get him. And then, after he relieves himself outside, you praise him with great gusto so he'll know he pleased you. That's his goal in life, to please you."

She was rambling. Sticking to what she knew best so she didn't feel self-conscious and stupid. Dana had dated in high school. And had one serious boyfriend before Daniel had hooked her up with Keith, the troubled son of Daniel's best friend, and made it almost impossible for her to keep peace in the family unless she agreed to date him.

But this was different. Josh Redmond was beyond gorgeous. And she was alone in his house with him.

"Did you keep him in a kennel during the couple of days you had him?" Josh asked.

"No, I didn't have one. I locked him in the bathroom the first night. For about an hour."

"And then what?" He quirked an eyebrow as he stood halfway across the patio, hands in his pockets, watching her.

The puppy bounded across the yard, falling as he went.

"I brought him into bed with me."

"To pee on your sheets? And mattress?"

"He didn't pee. But if you're worried that he might, you could put down a puppy pad."

"What if he moves off from it?"

"If you're a light sleeper like me, you'll wake up and put him back on it."

He studied her as if she was from another planet. "You've done this with a puppy before?"

"Several of them. My mom raises poodles, breeds them and sells them all over the country. My sisters were never really interested in helping, but I was."

"Are they around here? Your family?"

He seemed genuinely interested, but she wasn't. Not in having this conversation with him. Or thinking about how second rate she always felt when she thought of her family. So she shook her head and said, "It also helps, if you're going to keep him in a kennel, to have some kind of rhythmic noise beside him. Like an old-fashioned alarm clock. Or maybe some classical music playing softly."

The puppy had his nose pressed into a weed.

"Have you ever had a dog keep you up all night?"

It sounded, at the moment, like a full night's rest would be more valuable to him than winning the lottery. And he'd only had the puppy one night!

What was the guy going to do if he ever got married and had kids?

Thinking of him as a father—and what he'd have to do to get to that point—brought her thoughts to a screeching halt.

"Mom gave me a puppy for my thirteenth birthday—and a little kennel, too—so that I could keep her in my room. She wouldn't be quiet in the kennel. And she wouldn't lie down on the pads and go to sleep, either. I was afraid she was going to be whisked away from me and back out to the climate-controlled kennels Mom had in the backyard so I moved the little kennel onto my bed. The puppy was only four pounds so the kennel didn't take up much room. I threaded my fingers through the bars of the kennel and the puppy curled up next to them and went to sleep. We slept like that for about a month, until she was house-trained, and for the rest of her life she slept curled up by my side every single night."

He shook his head, as though he'd been transported to a very strange and unknown land.

She wondered about him again. About where he'd come from. And why someone as obviously educated and gorgeous as he was had landed in a place as out of the way as Shelter Valley.

"For the rest of her life? She died?"

"Yeah, the life expectancy of a toy poodle is anywhere from twelve to fifteen years, though we had one live to be eighteen. My little girl made it to twelve and died of congenital heart failure."

"You got her for your thirteenth birthday?"

"Yeah."

"So how old are you?"

"Twenty-five."

"Then you just lost her?"

"This past summer. Right about the time I got the Montford scholarship."

He asked her about the scholarship. She told him the same thing she'd told Cassie Tate Montford. And then she said, "We've been out here fifteen minutes."

"About that."

"Has your puppy gone to the bathroom?"

He looked at Little Guy. It was the first time Dana had seen him glance the puppy's way.

"I… He's contained and amusing himself. I didn't think…I don't know—has he gone to the bathroom?"

"Probably not because he hasn't had anything to eat or drink since he made such a mess inside. But the first rule of house-training a puppy is that you watch him every second he's out in the yard and praise him immediately every single time he does his business. Either variety. And conversely, from this point forward, every single time he goes in the house, even if you don't think it's his fault, like maybe you forgot to put him out, or he'd been alone too long, you have to scold him. The sooner he figures out that you're not pleased whenever he goes in the house and that you are pleased when he goes outside, the sooner he'll start to hold his business until you put him outside."

She was rambling again. The guy was going to think she was a big geek.

And maybe she was. Mostly she was okay with that. So why not now? It wasn't like this Josh Redmond was anyone special.

"And another thing," she added, because she felt awkward, standing there gawking at him, "you need to schedule an appointment with Cassie or Zack to have him neutered."

"Neutered…"

"Yeah, it's free when you adopt a pet, and because he's a boy, you want to have it done as soon as it's safe to do so."

"You have something against boys?"

"Of course not." She concentrated on the dog, not the man. "He squats when he pees." She forced the words past the dryness in her throat. "Mature male dogs, if they aren't neutered early, lift their leg to pee. It's a territorial marking thing. You don't want that. Once a male starts spraying you can have a hard time keeping him from marking his territory inside as well as out."

"I'll call the clinic Monday morning and make an appointment to have him neutered."

"We don't know how old he is for sure, but he can be neutered at eight weeks so they should be able to do it."

She talked to him about feeding schedules and about establishing who was the boss from the onset.

The puppy went to the bathroom. Dana told Josh to praise him. And grinned when he did so. There was something very endearing about such a perfect specimen of manhood bending over and congratulating ten pounds of matted fur on the little pile he'd just dropped. If there was a self-conscious bone in Josh Redmond's body, he sure didn't seem aware of its existence.

Maybe that was what endeared him to her more than anything else.

And when, another couple of minutes later, the puppy peed, Josh congratulated him again and they moved back into the house. He invited her to sit at his kitchen table. He offered her some iced tea and she accepted. "Here," he said, drawing her attention to the can he held out to her.

"Oh, sorry," she said, feeling the heat rise up to her cheeks. She'd been busy staring at the arsenal of cleaning supplies on the kitchen table. "It's just—" she glanced back at the table "—laundry detergent, hand soap, liquid body soap, dish soap, dishwasher soap, bar soap, car wash, carpet detergent, upholstery cleaner…" They were all lined up, obviously brand-new, two brands of every single item.

"I…am on a mission to try the top two brands of each to find out which I like best," he said.

She had the distinct feeling that he was making up every word as he went along. Someone who liked to clean also had brand preferences for every job.

But it wasn't her business.

"Have you picked a name for him?" she asked instead,

pointing to the puppy who was sound asleep with his head flopped against Josh's chest.

He shook his head. "It didn't occur to me."

"The quickest way to teach him to come when he's called is to call him only by one name, and to say that name every single time you speak to him. When you feed him, say his name and then the word *eat,* and put his food down. He'll learn what *eat* means, too."

"You called him Little Guy."

"Because he's male and little and I specifically was not naming him as I knew I wasn't going to be able to keep him."

"Did you want to?"

He was getting personal again. This wasn't about her. Though...she kind of wanted it to be.

And while Dana was all about living her new life, about believing that she was just as good as everyone else, she wasn't so far along on her journey that she was going to pursue the guy who had to be the hottest bachelor in town.

"I didn't think I wanted another puppy, not anytime soon. I've got a kitten now. And my duplex is small. But after having Little Guy around for a couple of days...yeah, I'd like another puppy. A smaller one, though."

"You should get one, then."

Maybe. "Anyway, I recommend naming him. Soon."

"I like Little Guy. It's what he is."

"He's going to be huge."

"So...all the more reason to remind him that no matter how big he gets, I'll still be bigger, right?"

He grinned. She melted.

And got the hell out of there.

CHAPTER SEVEN

JOSH DIDN'T HAVE to wait until Monday to speak with Cassie
Montford. His cell phone rang shortly after Dana Harris
left Saturday, and he recognized the veterinarian's number.

"Josh? This is Cassie Montford."

Montford. Not Tate. She was on family business. He
stiffened. "I assume you spoke with your husband?" he
said, the Redmond in him coming out as he prepared to
take control of the situation. To take control and not give
off an iota of the emotion roiling around inside him. Getting his own way was all that mattered.

He didn't want to leave town. Didn't have any idea where
he'd go.

"I'm sorry it took me so long to get back to you," the
older woman said. "I spoke with Sam last night but by the
time we were alone and could talk it was too late to call
you back. And I just got out of surgery now—a dog was
hit by a car outside of town this morning...."

It had been less than twenty-four hours. Josh had expected their decision to take at least through the weekend.
In Boston, it would have. The pros and cons of upholding
a family secret would have been weighed very seriously.

"Sam and I will keep your secret for as long as we can
without anyone being hurt," Cassie said, her voice sounding even warmer than it had the day before at her office.

More personal.

"Sam has a request, though, Josh. He really wants to meet you."

Ready to respond with an unequivocal no, until he was a little more certain he could trust himself, Josh didn't get the chance.

"I've managed to rein him in for now, with a threat to tell his parents some things about his past that he doesn't want them to know."

It sounded like a stunt any number of wives in his Boston circle might have pulled. It was all about keeping up appearances.

"Not that I'd carry through with the threat, which he knows, but he got the point, anyway. Sometimes people need some space to work through their issues on their own."

He swallowed. "I... Thank you," he said.

He wanted to say more. To ask more. To find out more about Sam Montford's life. About the secrets that he didn't want his parents to know...the fodder that gave his wife some leverage.

But he was determined to stick with his promise.

He asked about Little Guy's surgery, set a date for the week after Thanksgiving and started to ring off.

"Josh?"

He put the cell phone back to his ear. "Yes?"

"I can't promise that Sam will wait forever," she said. "My husband has a bit of a wild streak. When it gets ahold of him, he's apt to do something off the wall."

"Has he had run-ins with the law?" he asked. He couldn't imagine his mother being gung ho about claiming her Arizona family if he had.

"Absolutely not. Sam's never been in trouble with the law. Have you?"

Too late he saw what his question had implied. He

quickly said, "No. I don't have a criminal record." It was the truth. He'd never even received a speeding ticket.

Hard to believe, when a woman had lost her life because of his carelessness. He'd walked away without paying any price at all.

"Sam's just a bit of a social rogue," Cassie said. "He says what he thinks, and when he believes in something he goes after it, regardless of what it costs him. He's just found out he has a new cousin in town. And having grown up as the only son of the town's founding family, he's anxious to make your acquaintance. All I'm saying is don't be surprised if you come home some night and find him drinking a beer on your back porch."

Something Josh might have done if the situation were reversed...

Stop. He implored silently. This wasn't going to work if he got in with the family. He'd fall back on his old ways. Become someone he hated.

"Also, just so you know, there's another cousin here in town. Ben Sanders. He's fairly new to the family, as well, but biologically, he's a Montford. Ben's married to Tory and they have two daughters."

Did Cassie and Sam have children, too? There hadn't been children in their family since he'd grown up...

And he didn't want to know any of this.

"One other thing," he said, realizing that he'd almost hung up without taking care of the thing he needed most from her. "Will you write to my mother? Let her know that all is well?"

He hated being beholden to anyone. For anything. To his way of thinking, if he needed something done, he paid someone to do it. Except he couldn't afford that anymore.

"Is she on email?" Cassie asked.

"Yes." He waited while Cassie retrieved a pen and took down his mother's email address.

"So she knows you're here already?"

"Of course. She knows where I am 24/7," he said. "She always has. It's about the only thing she's ever asked of me."

At least, the only thing she'd asked that he'd heard and complied with.

He wasn't ready to know about all the times he hadn't listened, wasn't ready to be accountable for all the hurt he must have caused his mother over the years.

But he was getting there. One day at a time.

LORI WAS BACK Sunday afternoon, but only to drop off a catnip toy she'd bought for Kari, a thank-you to Dana for letting her spend the night twice that week.

She also let her know that she'd be in town for Thanksgiving and would love to help cook if Dana's dinner offer still stood.

Sensing that the girl's feelings were hurt by her father's choice to go hunting instead of spending the holidays with her, Dana invited Lori in on the pretense of planning the menu for the holiday. She was planning to cook enough food for twenty people to come and go throughout the day. If she had lots of leftovers, all the better. She just didn't want to run out.

What she hadn't expected, while she and Lori were sitting at the kitchen table just before dark, was for the other woman to ask about Josh.

"Did you invite Little Guy's new owner?" Lori asked, tapping a finger on the edge of the tablet she'd been using to keep their list.

"No." She hadn't even thought about it. And she should have. She'd planned to invite everyone she came in contact with that she knew was alone. Or even might be alone.

"I thought you said he's new to town. And lives alone."

"Yeah, he is. And he does."

"Did you not invite him because he's not a student like us?"

"He's not much older than I am. Three or four years, maybe."

She'd seen a soiled Harvard shirt thrown on top of the washer when she'd taken her empty tea can into the laundry room to throw it away. Emblazed on it was a year four years prior to what hers would have been had she gone to college straight out of high school.

She'd asked him if Harvard was his alma mater.

And as he'd answered in the affirmative, he'd sounded slightly lost again.

"I think he went to college on scholarship," she said now, saying out loud what she'd thought at the time. His reaction to having been a student at Harvard had been odd. It had reminded her of how she'd felt working at the furniture store, bearing the same last name as the one written on the marquee out front, but not being an heir to the business.

She was a Harris, but the name had been given to her, not earned consequence of biology.

After she and Daniel had found out about the lie her mother had told them both about Dana's parentage, Dana had not only been taken out of Daniel's will, but shuffled to the back corner of the family.

She'd felt like a modern-day Cinderella. And Josh Redmond seemed to have the same reaction when asked about his alma mater.

"He's a nice guy," she told Lori, remembering how Josh had gotten down on the floor to clean up his dog's mess without a moment's hesitation. "I was afraid, when I saw the state his bathroom was in, and this after he'd already lost a night's sleep, that he was going to tell me to take

Little Guy back. But he never even hinted at wanting to get rid of him."

"I hear he's gorgeous. A friend of mine had to go to the business office Friday afternoon to see to something about her scholarship and he was there, introducing himself. She told me about him because he was so hot, but when you told me about Little Guy's new owner, I knew it had to be the same guy. I guess he starts work on Monday. He has an office upstairs in the admin building."

Dana wasn't going fishing for information. But she wasn't above listening to gossip.

"I can't believe someone as hot as he is doesn't have a girlfriend. Or a wife," Lori said.

"I know, right?" Dana agreed. And remembered the soulful look in Josh's eyes. The lost look. "I wondered if he was married and his wife died," she said. "I don't know that, so don't say anything to anyone. I honestly have no idea and don't want to start rumors. I just…like you, I find it hard to believe that he's way out here starting a new life all alone."

"Yeah, well, if this town's anything like Bisbee, I'm guessing it won't be long before we all know who he is and where he came from."

Which suited Dana just fine. The one thing she could not tolerate, on any level, was someone keeping their identity secret. Broken-heart secrets were fine. Everyone had a right to their privacy.

But not to lie about who they were. In a bigger town, like Richmond, a person could show up and claim they were anyone and no one bothered to look past the words. To know that they were lies.

Innocent people got hurt by those kinds of lies.

Lives were ruined by them.

Anyone who didn't believe her could just ask her stepfather. The man who'd once thought she was the brightest apple of his eye.

And, later, couldn't bear to look at her at all. Because she had another man's eyes.

SOAPS OF ALL KINDS had found their temporary home on the shelf above the washing machine. Lined up by type, they fit. One by one he'd try them out. See what was good or bad about the different kinds and land on the brand he liked.

And it was his own damned fault that he hadn't known what had worked until now. He knew who had worked *for* him: her name was Betty Carmichael. She was in her mid-fifties and had a family with children and grandchildren—he wasn't sure how many—and he liked her a lot. She'd come with the condo he'd received upon his graduation from Harvard.

It seemed so long ago now. Hard to believe that in eight years of working and flying around the world, taking on daring adventures and making life about his own enjoyment, he'd never once thought about making a home for himself.

Michelle would have taken care of that.

And he'd have been perfectly content to let her do so.

Just as he'd been content to let Betty do all of his shopping for him, to make his choices for him, down to what kind of toilet paper and toothpaste he used. Hell, he hadn't even had to find the pack of toilet paper and take out a roll, which might have given him a clue to what kind it was... maybe. No, there'd been brass cylinders beside every commode in the condo, each holding four rolls, and Betty had always kept them filled.

She'd worked every single day that he was in town. And was off whenever he was gone. The arrangement had suited him. And apparently it had suited her, as well.

He hoped her new employer, the couple who'd purchased the condo and agreed to keep her on, would be good to her.

Little Guy woke up. Josh turned as soon as he heard the movement in the kennel on the kitchen counter behind him.

Before the puppy could so much as stretch, Josh had him out of his cage and out the back door. He was getting this part down. Having been peed on during his way out the door twice in the past twenty-four hours, he was learning the hard way.

But he was learning and he had a question. Pulling out his phone, he easily found the number he needed from his recent call list and hit the send button.

Standing outside, watching every move the puppy made as he trampled over his feet in the dirt, Josh listened to the line ring. Little Guy had only been asleep for an hour. And he'd gone to the bathroom right before Josh had put him in the kennel. It was possible he didn't have business to do.

"Hello?" She answered on the third ring.

"Dana? It's Josh. I hope I'm not disturbing you…"

"Of course not. What's up? How's Little Guy doing?"

"Fine," he was pleased to report. The dog might be a little confused by an owner who seemed to know less than he did, but Little Guy was clean, all of his parts were still working, there was no blood, no broken bones….

"Did you get some sleep?"

"Yes. Plenty of it." As soon as he'd hung up from Cassie the day before, he'd purchased a new, much smaller kennel, come home and cleaned out the larger kennel, bathed the puppy another time, showered himself off, put the kennel on the side of his expensive mattress and slept until dark.

And then he'd repeated the process a few hours later when he'd stripped down and gone to bed.

He'd stopped at putting his hand in the kennel. He had to

be able to move in his sleep. And Little Guy hadn't pushed him that far.

"So what's up?" the woman asked again, and Josh wondered if he *was* interrupting something. And wished she had all the time in the world. He was tired of his own company.

His life was so out of kilter at the moment. Other than the family he'd sworn off, and the business associates he'd met but couldn't name, he didn't know anyone in this town except for Dana Harris. Hell, he didn't even know himself all that well at the moment.

"I was wondering about tomorrow," he said, still watching the puppy. The idiot thing was batting at a cricket on the patio and missing by a mile. "I have to work from eight until five. I figure I can come home for lunch, but it can't be good to leave this guy alone in such a small kennel for so many hours at a time."

"People have to work," Dana said slowly. "And puppies are almost always kenneled or in a box after birth. They're also kenneled when they're boarded. But then they tend to be a bit more rambunctious when they're set free," she said. "And if he's left too long and has to relieve himself in his kennel, that barrier is broken and he might go in his sleeping spot more regularly, and then it could take you longer to house-train him…."

How the woman fit so many words into one breath he didn't know. He'd never met anyone with so much to say all at once.

"I think I'd be stretching my welcome if I showed up the first day of my new job carrying a kennel with me," he said laconically.

Not that he'd ever actually worked a job where he had to answer to anyone other than himself—or his father, who pretty much let him do whatever the hell he damned well pleased.

"I could come by a couple of times during the day," Dana said while Josh was thinking about asking her, as part of her counseling position, to phone Cassie for him and see if she could arrange for some kind of day-sitting at the clinic.

He didn't trust himself to speak with his distant relative again, so soon. Her invitation to meet the family had been too damned tempting.

"If you trust me to be in your home without you there," Dana finished.

"Of course I trust you in my home." It wasn't as though there was a lot there for her to steal. He'd sold anything of real value. "But I can't ask you to give up your day for me."

This was his new life. He was supposed to be doing things for others. Or at the very least, not imposing on others.

"I'm not doing it for you," Dana said with a matter-of-fact tone. "I'm doing it for Little Guy. He needs a home and I don't have the space here to keep him."

That was all right, then.

"Do you really have time?"

"I've got breaks in between classes," she said. "It won't take anything at all for me to run out there. Besides, I miss him. I'd look forward to a little puppy playtime."

The woman was…intriguing. "What about work?" he asked her. Little Guy was chewing on his shoe. The pair he'd peed on.

"Just volunteer stuff," she said. "My scholarship provides for living expenses. And I worked for several years out of high school and have money saved," she continued, refreshing in her openness. Her honesty.

"What are you studying?"

"General business," she said and, muffling the phone,

said goodbye to someone. What had she been doing when he'd called? What had he interrupted?

He should let her go. "You don't seem like the business type."

That was his world. Cold and calculating and nothing at all like a woman who got excited at the prospect of helping pets find good homes—helping people become good pet owners.

"My dream was to be a vet," she told him. "But I couldn't… afford…college right away, and it takes grad school in addition to a bachelor's degree. When this scholarship fell in my lap, for a bachelor's degree only, and knowing that I'd be thirty by the time I was in the job market, I figured it would be best to get a degree in something that would provide a good living rather than wishing on stars."

"I don't think being a veterinarian is wishing on stars." Cassie certainly wouldn't think so. Josh's mind rushed ahead of him. Maybe he should talk to her. See if there was something she could do to help Dana with some kind of monies for graduate school when the time came. There he was, thinking like a Redmond again. So easy to give out handouts when you didn't feel, in any way, the loss. Hell, what it would cost Dana to go to graduate school he'd spent on a week's vacation. More times than he could count.

"Maybe not," Dana said with a chuckle. "But I'm too practical to commit to so many years without a steady income."

"What about your family? They can't help?"

"No."

When she didn't say any more, Josh didn't push, figuring that her parents were probably strapped for cash, like most of the nation.

Shoving his hand in his pocket, he itched to pull out a wad of bills. To trade grad school for pet-sitting help. He pulled out two twenties instead, and pushed them back in his pants.

They were going to buy him lunches for the week.

"Anyway, I can stop by around ten in the morning," she said, her voice infused with its usual energy. "If you're there around noon, and I'm back at two, we should have him covered until you get home."

"And you're sure that doesn't interfere with your classes?"

"Positive. Believe me, I'm not going to mess up this chance to finally get a college degree," she said. "Classes come first. Always."

He believed her. To a point. He figured that if someone was in need, she'd put her own aspirations aside to help out.

His landlord had given him two keys to the house. He offered to drop the spare one off to Dana later that evening.

And smiled when she gave him her address. He had plans for the evening. Life in Shelter Valley was looking up.

And if any of his old buddies could see him now, they'd laugh so hard they'd piss themselves.

CHAPTER EIGHT

DANA TOLD HERSELF to go about her normal afternoon and evening. Josh Redmond was going to be stopping by for the two seconds it would take him to drop his key into her outstretched hand. It amounted to almost nothing.

She cleaned the hamster cage and the kitty litter box, anyway. And then a shower and change of clothes was in order.

The yoga pants and long, form-fitting gray sweater she put on were comfortable enough for Sunday evening lounging around.

She made a salad for dinner. Listened to classical music while she ate it. Enjoyed the one glass of wine she allowed herself when she was drinking alone. Thought about calling her mother. And called a college classmate instead. Sharon was in her sixties, going to college for the first time and had just moved to Shelter Valley from Phoenix. She was in Dana's biology lab study group and was supposed to have completed a worksheet that they were all going to use in class in the morning. Dana's portion of the assignment had been during the original research phase. A third student was writing up the end report.

Sharon didn't answer. At least, not the first time Dana tried. She got her on the second attempt, but the woman, a widow who seemed to take things in her stride, sounded harried. There was a problem with her plumbing and she'd be without water until the morning.

Dana offered her the spare bedroom Lori had used Friday night, having just changed the sheets that afternoon. She told Sharon that it would be fine if she didn't make it over until after ten so the older woman could still attend her Bible study that evening.

After she hung up with Sharon, her mother called. She said she was missing her, but Dana could also hear a change in her mother's voice—a lessening of the tension that had become a member of their family from the night Susan had been presented with a report of DNA results and admitted that she'd lied to her husband about the paternity of their first child. From that moment on, Susan had had a tight-rope to walk. To appease the husband she adored—and still see that her oldest child knew she was loved and wanted.

The phone rang one more time that evening. It was Jon, a guy in her calculus class—a single dad she'd met when she'd overheard him talking about his two-year-old son, about some adjustment issues the boy was having. She'd mentioned pet therapy to him, told him about the club on campus. That conversation had taken place a good six weeks before.

"I was talking to my fiancée about the whole pet-therapy thing and she asked if I'd put her in touch with you," Jon explained as soon as he'd identified himself.

"I'm happy to speak with her, sure," Dana said, unaware, until that second, that the guy even had a girlfriend, let alone a fiancée. "She can come to the next meeting with me if she'd like. It's next Wednesday at four—"

"Lillie's not a student," Jon interrupted. "She's a child life specialist and wants to research the possibility of using pet therapy at the day care."

In the end, Jon put Lillie on and, excited by the prospect of using animals in an entirely different way than she'd ever thought of before, Dana offered to meet the woman for lunch the next day. And to speak with Zack Foster, too, about having Lillie observe their next pet-therapy visit.

She'd just hung up—and hadn't yet had a chance to put on makeup or brush through the hair she'd pinned up for her shower—when the doorbell rang.

The Suburban she'd seen in the parking lot at the clinic on Friday was parked behind her Mazda on her side of the duplex driveway.

So much for making a good impression. Which was just as well. It wasn't like Dana would have a chance with an administrator at the college she attended—not when he looked as good as Josh Redmond looked.

Or sounded as sexy as he sounded. A man like that could have any woman he wanted. He wouldn't have to settle for some too-skinny plain Jane from Indiana. And an overage college student at that.

"Josh, hi!" She pulled open the door with her emotions firmly in check and her usual smile on her face. So they weren't going to be an item—she could still like him. They could still be friends.

"Hi." Dressed in jeans, a long-sleeved black pullover and a different pair of leather shoes, he made her tingle all the way to her toes. Holding out a hand to her, he dangled the key.

She took it. "Thanks," she said with another smile. Too much of one. She was being too smiley. Definitely too smiley. She tried to stop.

"Would you like to come in for a glass of wine?" *What? What in the hell was the matter with her?*

"Sure. Just a second…" He turned and jogged toward the driveway. And returned, almost immediately, carrying a small kennel.

He moved as though to enter her house and Dana stood holding the door in one hand and his key in the other, staring at that kennel.

"You brought Little Guy with you?" It wasn't that big of a deal. But…

"Yeah. I wanted to ensure that I get a good night's sleep tonight. Figured it was best not to leave him alone so close to bedtime or he'd be wound up."

He'd brought his puppy to run an errand. It was quirky, maybe even overkill, and Dana loved it.

She practically tripped over her own feet as she stepped back too quickly, allowing him entrance. She hid her embarrassment by reaching for the puppy. "Let's get you out of there, shall we?" she said, and Little Guy whimpered, giving her his saddest look.

Except she had his number. "You're spoiled and you know it," she told the puppy as she cuddled him for a second before setting him free.

"He just went about fifteen minutes ago, but still, do you really think that's a good idea? He's going to mess up your floor."

"It's tile," she pointed out. "Easily cleaned. And besides, he lived here first, remember?"

The puppy went straight to the kitchen and Kari's empty food bowl, proving Dana's point that he knew his way around. Kari was nowhere to be seen at the moment, but Dana figured it wouldn't be long before she reestablished who was the boss around Dana's house.

"You want to play a game of cards?" Dana asked her human guest minutes later as she stood in the kitchen, pouring two glasses of merlot from the six-dollar jug she'd picked up at the big-box store outside of town. Josh had made himself at home at her kitchen table and looked as if he'd be content to stay awhile.

Giving her that eyebrow quirk that she'd come to associate with him, he tilted his head. "What kind of cards?"

"You name the game."

"Five-card draw, cribbage, five-card stud…"

Setting the glasses of wine on the table, she scooped Little Guy up to sit on her lap and pointed to the drawer at the end of the counter closest to Josh. "Cards are in there. You deal," she said.

Figuring he'd pick five-card draw, Dana was almost disappointed when he brought the cribbage board along with him. Daniel was a card man, and five-card draw had been his game. So Dana, in one of her many attempts to win back the adoration of the man she'd grown up adoring, had made it a goal to be as good at the game as Daniel was.

She succeeded at cards. Just not with Daniel.

And not with Josh, either, she found as he counted his peg around to the home lap while she'd barely hit third street. "By the way," she said, her tongue a bit loosened by the second almost-full glass of wine she'd consumed that evening. "I'm having a group of people over for Thanksgiving dinner. You're welcome to join us if you'd like."

"Sure," he said again, dealing cards as if he'd done so professionally at some point. Dana's stomach did a flip-flop.

And not because of the card-dealing.

She wouldn't let herself wonder what would happen if she asked Josh to take her to bed and have his wild way with her.

She'd hold her tongue on that one. She didn't want to scare him off.

Or scare herself, either.

Because if, by some miracle, she asked and he said yes, she wouldn't have the foggiest idea how to follow through with the wild sex.

Strictly boring, missionary-style was all it had ever been for her.

Still, it didn't hurt to fantasize....

JOSH HAD A SECOND GLASS of wine at Dana's on Sunday night, staying until her houseguest showed up just after ten. At which time he went home to go to bed so he could wake up early for his first day on the job the next day.

He'd made it through his first official weekend as a regular guy.

L.G., as he was beginning to think of the puppy, had curled up in his kennel as soon as Josh settled it on the bed.

Which left Josh with absolutely nothing else to do except go to sleep.

Stripping down to his briefs, he turned off the light. Lay down. Closed his eyes. And thrummed a drumbeat on the mattress with his right hand. Until he noticed what he was doing and stopped. His toe took over the beat, tapping against the sheet.

Da. Da da da. Da. Da da da. Da.

He turned the kennel a bit. So he could see if L.G. moved. The puppy didn't seem to notice.

Ten-thirty. Half-past midnight at home. His buddies would be at the club. Some who had wives would have them along. Others who had wives would be out alone. Everyone just understood that was how the world worked. Their world, at least.

Da. Da da da. Da. Da da da. Da.

He didn't have any buddies in Shelter Valley. No one to call.

His Harvard buddy, Drew, might be home. His wife was expecting any minute now, unless she'd already had the baby. He'd been staying close to home. And didn't always join them on Sunday nights, anyway. The guy had it bad for his wife.

Which was cool.

Da. Da da da. Da. Da da da. Da.

Picking up his smartphone, Josh scrolled through the lighted contact window on his LED screen.

And, too late, remembered he'd deleted the list when he'd deleted his old life.

He and the guys had visited an online chat room for hooking up when they'd been in high school. Just for kicks.

With front-facing cameras and tablets and smartphones, he figured the experience was far more advanced these days than it had been back in the day when they'd had to gather around a webcam plugged into his computer.

The idea, while tempting for a second, was one he turned down almost immediately. He was a grown man, not some know-it-all, spoiled teenager.

Pushing speed dial, he listened to the ring on the other end and knew that his intended recipient would eventually pick up. It was part of what he paid her for, to take his calls, and keep him posted, too.

"Mr. Redmond?"

"Hi, Sara. Sorry to wake you."

"It's okay, I napped when Missy did this afternoon. And tomorrow morning Carol will be here."

One of the two other full-time caregivers on Josh's trust's payroll. One of the two who, unlike Sara, lived outside the facility.

"How was she today?"

They both knew he wasn't talking about Carol.

"Same as always, Mr. Redmond. Same as she was yesterday when you called, and the day before that, and the day before that, too."

He got the picture.

"Okay, well, let me know if anything changes. Call if she needs anything." As an afterthought, he added, "Or if you do."

"I will. I swear to you, I'll call. Now why don't you try and trust me to do my job, to call like I said I will if anything changes, and get on with that new life of yours?"

He didn't reply. And didn't hang up, either.

"How are you settling in?" Sara's voice came over the line a few seconds later.

"Fine. Good. Tomorrow's my first day on the job."

"You'll do fine."

"I'm not worried about it." But he was. Worried that he wouldn't know how to be a worker bee.

"You hook up with your family?" she asked next. He was surprised she knew about the Montfords. He must have mentioned them to her on one of his visits to Michelle.

"You did say you had family out there, didn't you?" she said into the silence that fell.

He must have. Probably so that if his mother stopped by to see Michelle, Sara would uphold his story.

"I did," he said.

"Well, that's good, then." She yawned. It was close to one in the morning in Boston.

"I got a puppy." He hadn't even told his mother that. He'd been afraid it would make her think he'd lost his mind.

"What kind?"

"A Lab mix," he said, repeating what he'd been told, as though he was as familiar as the next guy about the specifics of dog breeds. "He's a little over ten pounds right now, but he's going to be at least fifty."

"That's good to hear, Mr. Redmond. A dog'll be good for you."

He was glad she thought so. Sara yawned another time, and Josh rang off, promising not to call her again so late.

She'd told him not to call her again at all.

CHAPTER NINE

DANA LIKED LILLIE HENDERSON on sight. The child life specialist was only a year or two older than she was, although, because she'd already been established in her career for seven years, she seemed light-years ahead of Dana.

They met at the Shelter Valley Diner, and arrived at the same time, five minutes earlier than their agreed upon time. Lillie was the same height as Dana, but more filled out without being a pound overweight. Dana's boniness was something she'd learned to live with a long time before.

Walking together, they both migrated to the second available booth, not the first, and laughed as they both reached for the menu at the same time.

Lillie's hair—dark, like Dana's, but a rich chocolate brown, instead of the drab color of hers—fell forward as she bent over the menu. Dana would have to spend an entire night in bed with little sponge rollers all over her head to get curls like Lillie's.

They ordered salads, grilled chicken and iced tea.

"Let me guess," Lillie said as they waited for lunch to arrive. "You were born in February, right?"

"Nope, August."

"Well, then, we aren't twins separated at birth." The comment was offered with a smile, and Dana felt as if she'd known the other woman for years instead of minutes. Lillie had seen their similarities, too.

Nice.

"So, you know Jon?" Lillie asked, and Dana noticed that her left hand bore a very small solitaire diamond.

"Not really," she said. "He's in my math class, but we've only spoken a couple of times. I heard him talking about his little boy having some issues and butted in. I just thought that maybe pet therapy could help. And it's free. We've got plenty of student volunteers this year, all of them trained, and Cassie and Zack just donated another van through the clinic, so we have the resources to branch out."

There she went, babbling on again, like a brook that just couldn't stop flowing.

Nodding, her expression serious, Lillie sat back to allow their server to set their drinks in front of them. "I'd love to set something up at the day care on a Saturday if it can be arranged, at least for the first visit," Lillie said. "I'm afraid having pets there during a regular weekday might be too chaotic, but we only have one class of kids on Saturday, and I can invite in a couple of kids that I think would particularly benefit." She was obviously thinking out loud. And a plan was growing.

So was Dana's enthusiasm, as she envisioned little children who felt scared or misplaced or unloved, opening up to the unconditional love that animals brought.

"You'll invite Jon's son to join us?" she asked when Lillie paused.

"Abraham?" Lillie's smile changed when she said the little boy's name. "If I'm there, he'll be there. Jon works on Saturdays. Abe's actually the reason I wanted to see you. Alone."

"He's struggling?" Dana hadn't heard much of the conversation she'd interrupted in class, and it had been much earlier in the semester.

"Not anymore," Lillie said. "He was having some troubles, but it turned out to have a physical basis and that's been tended to. He's doing great, actually!"

Dana was envious. She wanted children. A houseful of them.

A picture of Josh Redmond on the floor cleaning up after Little Guy sprang to her mind. Did Josh want children?

"Jon and I are going to be married over the Christmas break," Lillie was saying, stirring sweetener into her tea.

Dana drank hers straight—the stronger, the better. "Congratulations!" she said, wishing she'd known Lillie longer so she could be invited to the wedding. And wondering if someone was giving her a bridal shower.

"Do you have family here in town?"

Lillie shook her head. "My folks died when I was a student at Montford," she said. "In a car accident."

Her heart catching, Dana could almost feel Lillie's grief. "I'm so sorry."

"Me, too," the other woman said.

"Do you have siblings?"

When Lillie shook her head again, Dana felt inordinately thankful for her two half sisters.

"Jon's an only child, too," Lillie said. "And an orphan," she added. "Which is why we're having a small ceremony here in town, officiated by the mayor. We'd have already gotten married, except that the folks in Shelter Valley decided we needed a celebration."

"I agree with them."

"Yeah, I do, too." Their salads were delivered, and, putting ranch dressing on her salad as she watched Lillie do the same, Dana wondered at the weirdness of having so much in common with the other woman.

It had to mean something.

What, she didn't know. But she was ready and waiting when the other woman said, "I need a favor."

"Of course."

"I'd like to get a puppy for Abraham for Christmas. Jon and I share a bedroom, and he sleeps alone, and I don't want him to feel lonely."

Dana's fork stopped halfway to her mouth. It was as though the other woman saw into her private life, knew things Dana had never told anyone.

In an instant, she was back in the Indiana home where she'd grown up. With Mom and Daniel's room. Rebecca and Lindsey's room. And hers. She thought of the little toy poodle, Angel, who'd shared that room with her for the past twelve years.

She blinked back tears. "I'm sure we can hook you up," she said. "What kind of dog are you looking for? How big? I'd recommend not more than twenty-five pounds, full grown, since Abraham's still so little. A cocker-poodle mix would be good. No shedding, and a gentle disposition…"

While Lillie ate, Dana babbled on, talking about the Love To Go Around program, already planning the call she'd put in to the clinic as soon as lunch was through.

And if all else failed, she'd call her mother. Susan would know if anyone had cockapoo puppies. And with it being winter, she'd be able to fly the puppy to Arizona, too, for the price of a plane ticket.

Dana remained at lunch until the last possible minute, fascinated by Lillie's profession as a child life specialist. She'd never heard of such a thing before, but could see where it was needed. And she wished, for a long moment, that she could pursue her own heart's desire, to be a veterinarian and really make a difference to the animals she loved, the animals that also contributed so much healing in the world.

And then, thankful that she was in Shelter Valley at all, that she had a chance at a better future than she'd thought, she rushed off to class. She had an hour of lecture to sit through and then it was on to Josh's house to play with Little Guy for half an hour.

Josh's scent, his presence, was everywhere in the house. And to her it seemed to be in the backyard, too. She couldn't get away from him. Even when he wasn't there. Even when *she* wasn't there.

Because he was something else she wanted, but knew she'd never have. And that was fine. She could lust in secret. There was no law against that.

She had friends. A home. People who needed her. Who valued her.

A mother, and sisters, too, who loved her.

Yep, she was one lucky woman.

JOSH MADE IT THROUGH his first day on the job. The work, overseeing the planning and implementing of fund-raising ventures for the university, while not completely up his alley, was still interesting. And he figured he'd ultimately be good at it, since it would include talking rich people out of money—something he'd been doing most of his life.

First with his parents and later with clients.

His biggest challenge on the new job was learning to take orders.

But compared to Michelle, who'd be spending the rest of her life tied to a chair, he figured his challenge was not even worth thinking about. He'd adapt. Acclimate.

He hoped to find ways to help the university that no one had ever thought of before. Find ways to help more people like Dana—people who weren't born with silver spoons in their mouths—get the educations they deserved.

He didn't see her at all on Monday, but he could tell she'd been in his home when he stopped in for lunch and when he arrived home after work. Her fresh, flowery scent lingered. It was nice. Light. Nothing like the heavy, expensive perfumes he was used to.

He thought about dinner. He really needed to shop for food. And wasn't sure what he'd buy. All he had at home was peanut butter. It had been his weakness, starting as a kid, to his mother's horror. She'd have preferred him to like hummus sandwiches. But their housekeeper back then, an older woman named Emily who'd died way too young, had introduced him to peanut butter when he'd been about two.

He'd been hooked ever since.

He could throw a frozen dinner in the oven. But who in the hell ate dinner out of a box?

Unless the box bore the emblem of a decent pizza place. Standing outside with Little Guy, he looked into the big brown pleading eyes, pulled out his smartphone and searched for pizza places.

A couple of choices come up on the screen. Touching the first link and pushing the call button, he ordered a supreme thin-crust pizza, and was told that it would arrive within the half hour. Then he noticed the puppy was rubbing his ear in his own shit.

This whole average Joe thing was going to be a lot harder than he'd thought.

SHARON HAD BEEN ABLE TO get back into her house Monday afternoon. Her eldest daughter, an elementary schoolteacher in Phoenix, had driven up to help her mother clean up after the miniflood she'd had in her bathroom.

Finished with her homework by seven, Dana made one of her favorite casseroles, split it into separate portions and froze them. She talked on the phone to a couple of classmates. Had a call from Cassie regarding a possible puppy for Abraham Swartz.

Then she made a ground-beef barbecue mixture, split

it into patties and put them in the freezer next to the buns she'd bought. Jerome, her short-on-cash, laundry-date classmate, usually came over hungry.

Lori missed home cooking, too.

She'd noticed Josh Redmond's refrigerator and freezer had been almost completely empty when she'd been there that afternoon. She'd been searching for the canned dog food he'd received from the clinic—planning to give Little Guy just a bite or two as a treat for being such a good boy—and had found a single jar of peanut butter.

And beer.

A fifty-pound bag of puppy chow stood in a corner of the laundry room. She'd scooped up a handful of the dry stuff and fed it by hand to the happy pup.

She knew the puppy wasn't going to go hungry.

She wasn't so sure about the owner.

Dana glanced at the clock. It was only eight o'clock.

She opened the newly packed freezer. Grabbed various containers, buns and a bag to put them all in, called out a goodbye to Kari and Billy the hamster and was in her car, headed back to Josh's place before she really thought about what she was doing.

CHAPTER TEN

EIGHT O'CLOCK AND Josh was at loose ends. He got out his tablet and, with L.G. under one arm, planted himself on the couch he'd moved into the living room by himself with the help of a furniture dolly.

That accomplishment had been four days ago. He'd taken the trailer back to a rental place in Phoenix before stopping in to introduce himself to Cassie Montford.

Now he'd saddled himself with a four-legged practice run.

L.G. plopped down on the sofa next to Josh and started to nip at his arm. They'd been through this on Sunday, too, before he'd headed over to Dana's place for an unexpectedly memorable evening of cards. Bending over, Josh picked up what had once been an expensive leather shoe from the floor and shoved it in L.G.'s mouth.

He leaned back into the couch, preparing to make a grocery list. And then the doorbell rang.

SHE SHOULDN'T HAVE COME. Or should have taken the time to pull on a nice blouse instead of the black sweater she'd worn with her faded jeans to go to class that day.

What little bit of makeup she'd brushed on that morning had long since worn away, but Dana wasn't out to gather catcalls.

"I brought you some food," she said, walking into his house as though she'd been doing so for weeks instead of a day or two. Heading for the freezer, she carefully and neatly stacked containers with their labels facing outward. "There's casserole, ground-beef barbecue and buns, chili, potato soup and some apple cobbler. I can bring more, but didn't want to take up all the space in your freezer. I didn't know when you'd be going shopping, and since you've been so occupied with Little Guy I thought it was the least I could do."

Stopping to take a breath, she realized he hadn't said a word since she'd walked in the door. She turned and saw him standing with Little Guy perched on his left arm—and a wide-eyed expression on his face.

"What?" She really shouldn't have come. She'd pissed him off.

"I just can't believe you did this."

He sounded incredulous. Good incredulous or bad incredulous, she couldn't tell.

"Did what?" Bring him something to eat to tide him over while he got settled in?

He sure looked good enough to eat. She'd never seen him in business clothes. And that body of his, the shoulders and thighs and…they filled out dress clothes like she'd never seen before.

He'd loosened his tie, but still had it on. At eight o'clock in the evening. What guy did that?

"The food…"

"You ever hear of the Welcome Wagon, Redmond?" she asked, feeling stupid again. And trying to play down the impact.

He frowned. "No."

Oh. She'd thought everyone had.

"Well, it's a neighborhood program. They're all over Richmond. Neighbors bring over packages to help welcome new people to the area. I brought a frozen-food package, is all."

Anyone else would have done the same. It had nothing to do with Dana's inability to stop mentally drooling over the man. As soon as word got around about him and the college girls took notice of him, she'd be relegated to the far back of the line.

"I just sat down to make a grocery list," he said. "How'd you know?"

Now she had to confess to snooping. She looked him straight in the eye as she apologized for poking around in his fridge.

"No! Don't apologize! This is great! I mean, what do I owe you?" He pulled a wallet out of his back pocket.

Dana stared and felt as if she'd been slapped. "You want to pay me for being neighborly?"

The wallet disappeared. "No, what I want to do is heat up one of everything and eat," he said, still holding the puppy, as though as long as he kept Little Guy between them, she wouldn't hurt him.

"I'll be going now," she said, folding up her bag and walking back through to the living room.

"Wait!"

She turned.

"I… Are there instructions?"

"Instructions?"

"For…you know…cooking stuff…"

"It's pre-made," she explained, wondering what part of her earlier exposition he'd missed.

"I know…and frozen."

"You put it in the microwave."

He nodded. Shrugged as if that was something he could handle. And stood there, unmoving.

"You do know how to use a microwave, don't you?"

"Of course."

Walking back into the kitchen, feeling him right behind her, she stopped in front of the built-in microwave above the stove and glanced over the controls.

"It has sensor reheat," she said. "Everything is in microwave-safe containers. Put it in on sensor reheat, push the button and wait. When it finishes, test it. You might have to run it through a second time since it's frozen. When you're finished, you can either keep the containers, or put them aside and I'll pick them up when I'm here to see Little Guy."

He nodded, and before she took a step he'd already pulled a container of casserole out of the freezer. Still holding the dog, he put the container into the microwave.

"Let me hold him." Dana took the puppy. He licked her nose. "You have to loosen the lid," she told Josh. "Unless you want pressure to build up and risk having your food explode all over the inside of your oven."

"Right. I know." He said the words and released the lid. Dana had the impression he had no idea whatsoever what he was doing.

"Do you have dog treats?" she asked, because she needed to know where they were so she didn't end up snooping again—and finding something else she could do to push herself on this man.

"No. I gave him the last package this morning when I left."

"You give him a whole package at a time?" She'd seen the stuff the clinic sent home with him. The packets of treats weren't full-size, but they should have lasted a week.

"I felt bad leaving him locked up all day."

Rubbing the warm spot under Little Guy's chin she said, "He sleeps, Josh. Puppies are like babies, they need extra sleep. And while some say an adult dog only needs about ten and a half hours of sleep a day, it's not uncommon for them to sleep fourteen or sixteen hours a day, sometimes more depending on activity level."

He stared at the puppy, who was falling asleep, leaning into her chest. It felt as if he was staring at her breasts.

Her nipples tingled.

He turned away. "I'll get more treats."

"And give them to him one at a time," she said. "It'll help with training if you use them judiciously, as praise. Like when he goes to the bathroom outside. Or sits when you tell him to."

"I don't tell him to sit."

"You will when he starts to get bigger and jumps up on you."

He glanced at the puppy again. She wanted Josh to notice her breasts. She'd never been so aware of her body.

And felt awkward as hell. Lindsey and Rebecca, her half sisters, would both know what to do; they'd have Josh tripping over himself trying to get their attention. They'd double-team him, playing him like a Ping-Pong ball.

Just as they'd been doing with all the cute boys in their town since they hit high school.

"You want to stay for a bit?" he asked as she continued to stand there.

She should go. But she didn't want to. He was watching her. *Her.* As though he actually saw her. And liked what he saw. "I'll stay if you answer a question for me."

"You want to know how I creamed you at cribbage three games in a row?"

No. She'd pretty much figured that her inability to concentrate on the game was the reason for her loss. She'd been too distracted by her opponent sitting close enough for her to feel his body heat and smell his musky cologne, to pay attention to the cards in her hand.

"I want to know how old you are."

"Twenty-nine."

Four years older than she was. "And how did you get to be twenty-nine without ever using a microwave?"

He froze. His hand was raised to the cupboard he'd opened to expose a complete set of very nice dishes. She counted three serving bowls, a platter large enough to hold a thirty-pound turkey and even a gravy boat.

"I'm an only child," he said then, almost awkwardly. "My mother spoiled me."

Dana's heart went out to him at his obvious embarrassment. "One of those moms who wouldn't let her son in the kitchen?" she asked.

"Yeah, something like that."

"She give you your dishes, too?"

"Yeah."

The microwave beeped. He tested the food and put the container back in the oven, pressing sensor reheat a second time.

"But you're twenty-nine," Dana said, hugging the puppy to her with his front paws on her shoulders and her hand bracing his bottom half. "Surely you haven't lived at home all of your life."

"No. But I traveled a lot with my job. And…paid for my meals."

She was pushing him into a corner. Told herself to let it go.

"So—" just to be sure she got it "—you didn't live with a woman, then? You weren't…like…married, or anything?"

Her need to know was more pressing than any fear of making a fool of herself.

"I've never lived with a woman. Other than my mother when I was growing up."

He stood watching the oven. Dana sat at the big table,

amazed at how beautiful it was. Having worked so many years in the family furniture business she recognized the quality. Wanted to ask him about it.

But figured she'd used up her allotment of questions.

DANA OFFERED TO check in on L.G. each morning and afternoon for the rest of the week, and Josh didn't argue. He didn't offer to pay her again, either.

On Tuesday night, feeling pretty good about his progress, he agreed to go out after work with a group of guys from the office. They were headed to Phoenix with box tickets to a Suns basketball game, compliments of an alumnus who'd been pleased with the year's fund-raising efforts, and they'd invited Josh along.

Leaving straight from the office, he was in high spirits with his vehicle once again filled with male voices, raucous jokes, laughter and a bit of in-depth business discussion, as well. Market analyses. Something he excelled at. They were all shooting questions in his direction by the time they pulled into the reserved parking outside of the stadium.

"Bank One Ballpark's right there," Ian, one of the younger guys in the group, pointed to a huge complex across the street from the basketball stadium. "In the spring we'll get great seats there, as well."

Josh nodded and grinned to himself. The Redmonds had had a box at every Boston team game since before he was born. He was the guy who handed out the complimentary tickets for jobs well done, or deals that he hoped to close.

He wasn't impressed by the VIP treatment they received from the moment they exited the vehicle—it was par for the course for him. But he had a great time. Downed a couple of beers.

And got to live it up like the old Joshua without compromising his current plans.

His phone rang as the Phoenix skyline was receding in his rearview mirror. His three passengers, all three of whom had consumed far more alcoholic refreshment than he had, were discussing player stats and arguing over potential strategies for the Suns' current season.

"Hello?" He held his cell phone to his ear. In his Mercedes he'd had a button to press on the dash that allowed him to have conversations through his six-speaker stereo system while driving.

"Josh?"

Dana. *L.G. Shit.* It was the nicest of all the expletives that ripped through his brain when he recognized the voice.

He'd been so caught up in the joy of being on familiar territory, he'd forgotten the damned dog.

"I'm on the road. I can't talk right now," he said. "Are you going to be up for a while?"

He was sweating. And pushed his foot harder on the gas pedal as they entered a stretch of deserted highway.

"Of course."

Promising to call her back, he rang off. And then called her right back.

"Hi," he said, knowing it was safest if he didn't talk on the phone and drive at the same time. But talking and driving was perfectly legal in Arizona. Everyone did it, and...

"Are you doing anything right now?" he asked succinctly, like the boss he'd been back east, a boss with an urgent matter on his mind that he needed someone to handle.

"Just homework," she said. "Zack Foster called earlier. There was a litter of puppies that had been abandoned, but we called around and got them all delivered to new homes," she said. "They're little, so finding homes for them was easier...."

She'd talk the rest of the way home if he'd let her. He wished he could. Talking to Dana was so different from anything he'd ever known. She wasn't after anything. She just talked to communicate with the other human beings in her midst.

"I have a favor," he said with less charm than he'd have liked. This wasn't about him. "I…kind of left L.G." He paused. He'd screwed up.

"Left him?" Now it was her voice that held the urgency. "Where? Oh, Josh! Is he okay?"

"Not *left him* left him," Josh said, slightly sick of himself. "I forgot about him and went to Phoenix after work." Aware of the silence in the car, hoping his colleagues had all passed out on him, but doubting the probability, he kept his gaze firmly on the road in front of him. He told her about the basketball tickets. The suite…

"You're telling me that Little Guy's been in his kennel since I dropped by at three?"

The question seemed easy enough, but he was sure the accusation was there. Couched in Dana style.

"Yes," he said. "Can you go rescue him?"

Take him home with you. He'd be better off there.

"I'm already on my way," she said. He heard her car start. "I'll stay with him until you get home," she told him.

"Thank you." He pictured the pup, the kennel, and swore silently again. "If the kennel's a mess just set it outside the door," he said. "I'll clean it when I get home."

She was going to wait for him. Would be there, in his home, when he arrived.

The idea shouldn't feel so good.

"It's probably going to be fine," she said. "He went to the bathroom just before I left. And he hasn't had dinner yet."

Way to rub it in. "I know."

"Josh?"

"Yeah?"

"It's okay," she said. "He's only been alone for a little

over eight hours. Some folks have to leave their dogs for that length of time every day."

"Not locked in such a little cage."

"Yes, some are locked in little cages. Now let me get off the phone so I can drive."

"I thought you were already driving."

"No, I've been stopped at the end of my street waiting to hang up. Drive carefully and I'll see you in a few."

Drive carefully. It was as if she cared.

For him. Selfishness personified.

The woman was a fool.

Josh was going to have to save her from him.

Soon.

Real soon.

CHAPTER ELEVEN

THE KENNEL WAS FINE. Little Guy, while rambunctious as heck, and gobbling his food like he was half-starved, was fine, too. Josh, on the other hand, looked as if he'd seen a ten-car pileup on the freeway.

All because he'd left his pup for an evening?

His concern was sweet.

She didn't really understand it. She stayed and talked to him—about the collection of dog treats she'd put together for him from the Love To Go Around stash, which was why she'd called earlier. She figured he could test out various ones, the way he was doing with his soaps. Soon he was grinning like the Josh she was coming to know, and she said she had to go home and get a few hours' sleep before class in the morning.

Josh insisted on following her home.

"That's crazy," she told him, standing in the doorway of his house, refusing to move.

"I'm not taking no for an answer," he insisted. "I won't come in. But it's late, after midnight, and you're out alone on my account."

"This is Shelter Valley. And besides, I've been going out alone at night since I was old enough to drive, in a city much larger than this little town."

He followed her, anyway. And it wasn't until she was inside her duplex and glanced out the front window to wave at him that he finally left.

ON WEDNESDAY, DANA came home for lunch to find a plant sitting outside her door. A live plant, not cut flowers.

The card read, "I figured you'd appreciate something that would live over something that would soon die. Thank you. Josh."

Dropping her backpack to the cement on the front porch, she carefully picked up the pot and carried it inside. She was not going to cry.

That would be dumb. He'd merely said thank you.

But she'd never had flowers sent to her before. Had never dated a flower-sending kind of guy.

She retrieved her backpack. And texted Josh's number.

The plant is wonderful. Thank you! She added a smiley emoticon, and then deleted it.

Sixty seconds later she received a text in return. Glad you like it.

Leaving the text on her phone, she went about her business. Made spaghetti sauce from scratch. Lori was coming over to spend the night—she had an exam the next day and was finding it hard to concentrate in the dorm—and had mentioned that she missed her mom's homemade spaghetti sauce. With the pet-therapy trip late that afternoon, Dana wasn't going to have time to make dinner before Lori got there, so she was doing it on her lunch break.

Understanding that the girl was having a hard time dealing with hurt feelings over her best friend's defection and her father's decision to bond with the guys over Thanksgiving, Dana accepted the exam excuse at face value.

Fifteen minutes after she set down her phone, the text message notification sound rang.

It could be any number of people texting her. Including her sisters, who texted her now and then.

L.G. just tripped and turned a somersault.

Grinning, she quickly and one-handedly returned:

Reminds me of his dad.

When did I ever trip?

The ground beef browning, she used a spatula with one hand and texted with the other.

Not the tripping part, the turning somersaults part. You don't have to work so hard to get things right.

Didn't know I was working hard.

Just quit trying to pay me off for helping. Or I'll stop.

Thought you liked the plant.

She had. Too much. He was wooing her heart and she was absolutely certain that he was not intending to do so.
But she couldn't—wouldn't—abandon him.

I do.

So?

She poured in tomatoes. A can of tomato soup. A quarter cup of cooking wine. A can of tomato sauce. Some spices. Added diced onion at the end so that instead of browning and collecting grease, the onions softened in the tomato sauce—and set it all to simmer, planning to leave the finished product in the Crock-Pot while she was gone. Lori could eat whenever she got there. She set the table and played with Kari when the kitten came running into the room with the new catnip toy Lori had brought for her. She looked over her calculus homework. Read the chapter from her biology book—twice because she didn't quite take it in the first time.

She skipped lunch.

And she did it all with a nervous edge about her. With tendons strung tightly, and not quite smooth movement, as if she'd snap in two at a sudden loud noise.

Then there was a noise. Another text notification.

Are you mad at me? Josh wrote.

No.

I'm just falling for you, which is ludicrous, and if you knew you'd be running for the hills, she thought but did not type.

She stirred the sauce. Little Guy needed her. She had to hold it together and quit thinking about Josh Redmond so much. She was absolutely not going to screw up her volunteering gig with the Love To Go Around program.

And… Oh, boy, did she have Love To Go around.

She wasn't going to read any more of Josh's texts. Not until she had herself better in hand.

Another text showed up. Lori. She'd just had a blowout with her roommate and wanted to know if she could come early and hang out at Dana's for the afternoon, as well. She was on her way.

You seem mad.

The text came through while she was reading Lori's. How did he know how she acted when she was mad?

How's Little Guy?

Had lunch and bath.

Why another bath? What did he do?

Nothing. He's sleeping in my bed, he has to bathe. Needs plenty of time to dry. Hates dryer.

As soon as he mentioned his bed, she was hot again.

Her doorbell rang, saving her from making an utter fool of herself with a man she'd known less than a week.

AFTER TWO DAYS of training, Josh's weeklong orientation was cut short. He was called into the boss's office for a consultation Wednesday after lunch. They wanted him to head up the alumni fund investment team as well as contribute to the university's fund-raising efforts as he'd been originally hired to do. He met Will Parsons, Montford's president. He liked the older man.

He received a bit of a pay raise to compensate for the extra responsibility. If he wasn't already a millionaire several times over, he'd never become one in his current position, but the salary was decent.

And the work was interesting.

Most important, he'd gotten a promotion after two days on the job. He left the early-afternoon meeting on Wednesday wanting to call Dana Harris to share the good news.

Josh glanced at his watch.

She was on campus. In class. And would be at his house in less than an hour to give L.G. a break from jail.

Unfortunately, he had to get back to work.

SHE NOTICED THE empty containers stacked neatly on the countertop when she went into Josh's laundry room to get a treat for L.G. Wednesday afternoon. Every single container she'd brought over on Monday. Empty and cleaned. Presumably ready to give back to her.

She'd put aside some spaghetti sauce for the freezer. Had more barbecue and casserole at home, too. And vegetable soup.

Clearly the man couldn't cook. And even if he was planning to learn, it could take a while. Judging by his lack of microwaving skills, he had a lot to learn.

Her afternoon class had been canceled—the professor was at a symposium in Phoenix, presenting a paper she'd published. Taking Little Guy with her, Dana ran home, checked on Lori, gathered up the food and stayed long enough to throw together a batch of chocolate chip cookies, too. To make up for her ungrateful acceptance of the plant he'd sent over.

Little Guy was back home, secured in his kennel, by four that afternoon. She'd done her neighborly duty, fulfilled her responsibilities for Love To Go Around and made it back to school for the pet-therapy outing. Lillie was joining them and she didn't want to be late.

It dawned on her, just before she climbed into the pet-therapy van, that she didn't even know if Josh liked chocolate chip cookies.

"HERE'S TO YOU, MAN!" Ian McDaniel raised a beer to Josh at a table in the campus pub Wednesday night.

Josh raised his glass—one shot of a lesser brand whiskey than he was used to. The first shot of whiskey he'd had since leaving Boston.

The liquid trickled down his throat, burning a bit more than he was used to, but still good. Familiar.

He talked business. And basketball scores. And thought of Dana Harris. She'd left cookies. Good ones. He'd had several when he'd stopped in after work to let L.G. relieve himself.

As he waited for his second drink, he texted her.

Thanks. Cookies are great.

She didn't reply.

WHEN HE CAME HOME during his lunch break on Thursday with a take-out sandwich from the school cafeteria, Josh set the sandwich down to let L.G. out and picked up the container of chocolate chip cookies to munch on while he watched the puppy play in the dirt.

L.G. peed. Stepped in his pee. Wagged his tail as Josh praised him, and carried on with his business.

Biting into another cookie, Josh looked up at the immense stretch of blue sky as he chewed. It was frigid in Boston right now.

Here it was warm enough to wear shorts.

He hadn't called Sara once since she'd told him not to.

Unclipping his smartphone from the case at his hip, he checked to see if he had any messages.

There was a text from his mother. And nothing else.

Opening up yesterday's text message window, he added a new message—You can learn a lot from a dog—hit Send, put his phone away and helped himself to another cookie.

L.G. didn't seem to be in any hurry to go back in his cage.

Josh wasn't in any hurry to get back to work, either, although he still had a number of things he wanted to accomplish that day.

But a break was good. Just ask LG.

Work hard, play hard.

One of his father's truisms. And as Josh stood there eating cookies, soaking up the sun's heat while he watched a little black runt nosedive in the dirt, shake himself off, and bounce around in glee, he re-formed his father's teaching.

Work well, play well.

His phone beeped with a text message, interrupting his thoughts.

Like what? it said.

Grinning, he fired back, Like people spend too much time worrying about what other people think, and hit Send.

Agreed. Glad you like the cookies.

He glanced at the container he had lodged between his elbow and his side.

Liked.

They're gone?

Yes.

There was half a container there this morning.

Lunch.

You ate half a container of cookies for lunch?

Yes.

It's becoming very clear to me that you need a keeper, Redmond.

Good thing no one could see him standing there in his backyard, grinning.

Got two.

Oh, yeah? Who?

L.G. and you.

Oh. Well, eat an apple, then.

Don't have any.

They sell them at the cafeteria.

You in class?

Yes. Now let me pay attention before I miss something important.

L.G. did both jobs.

Give him two treats. And I'm glad you liked the cookies.

He wanted to ask where she'd been the night before. But he knew better. He couldn't have her thinking that what she did mattered to him in any kind of a personal way. Even if it did. She'd only get hurt in the end.

CHAPTER TWELVE

LORI AND MARISSA were friends again, having spent several hours at Dana's Wednesday evening, after Dana returned from her trip to Phoenix with the pet-therapy club. That night the roommates had talked things over with Dana as mediator. It was Lindsey and Rebecca all over again.

Except that Lori and Marissa were a lot more open-minded than her spoiled sisters were.

Marissa had agreed to keep her boyfriend out of their suite. And Lori had admitted that she was jealous of Marissa's new relationship, and had been acting snippy instead of being happy for her friend. They'd both cried. Apologized. And laughed until all three of them had tears in their eyes as they regaled Dana with stories from their childhood—like the summer they'd decided they were going to walk from Alaska to Argentina and couldn't even manage the three miles to the bus station to find out the price of tickets to Alaska.

After class on Thursday—a class she didn't get as much out of as she should have because she'd broken her own rule and texted during the lecture—Dana had a call from Sharon, the widow who'd had the plumbing problem, inviting her to dinner. She'd accepted, but not without first wanting to refuse in case Josh Redmond called.

He wasn't going to call. He had his life. She had hers. And Little Guy was the only thing they had in common.

With her emotions firmly under control, she stopped at

Big Spirits, the senior citizen drop-in facility attached to
Little Spirits, the day care where Lillie Henderson worked
part-time, to chat with one of the female residents—a re-
ferral to the pet-therapy program.

She saw Lillie's car in the parking lot and decided to
pop into the day care, as well. Jon Swartz, Lillie's fiancé,
was there picking up his son. Lillie was in the back with a
preschooler whose father was terminally ill, and who was
having adjustment problems in class. Lillie had told her
about the child the previous afternoon when they'd shared
a seat in the pet-therapy van.

"So this is Abraham?" Dana said as she walked up behind her classmate.

The two-year-old with dark hair that hung just above his
big brown eyes stared at her from his perch on his father's
hip. And then smiled.

"Oh, hi, Dana," Jon said. "Yes, this is Abe. Abe, say hi
to Daddy's friend, Dana. She goes to school with Daddy."
He put his face right up to Abe's as he spoke.

"Hi," Abe said, and gave her another grin.

"Oh, my gosh, he's adorable!"

"Yeah, he's pretty great." Jon's grin wasn't the least bit
apologetic. Dana's heart constricted. A father who adored
his child…it was meant to be that way. Not like Daniel…

"…thanks to his ear tubes." She'd been so lost in her
own thoughts that she'd missed most of what Jon had said.

"Ear tubes?"

"Abe was throwing some major tantrums," Jon told her
as the three of them stood in the empty waiting room. "I
figured Lillie had mentioned all of that to you. It turned
out Abe was going deaf."

Dana sucked in air so fast she almost choked. "He… I'm
so sorry. I had no—"

Shaking his head, Jon interrupted her. "He's fine now.

Almost. There's still some fluid buildup that makes it a little hard for him to hear, but it won't be long now before he'll be hearing as well as the rest of us."

Lillie hadn't said a word about Abe's hearing problems the day before. They'd mostly talked about potential ways they could integrate pet therapy with supporting children who were going through trauma.

"Lillie was really excited about the plans you two came up with yesterday," Jon said. "And she told me about asking for your help in finding a particular Christmas present for this little man."

"She said you two moved in with her last weekend."

"That's right. So if you find a you-know-what for him, we can take him anytime. The backyard is fenced and we have plenty of room in the house."

The way Jon's face lit up as he talked about the you-know-what gave Dana the feeling that the puppy was as much for him as it was for his son.

The three of them made a perfect little family—one any puppy would be lucky to join.

Assuring Jon she'd do her best to find a you-know-what as quickly as possible, Dana asked him to give her regards to Lillie and left before envy could worm its way inside her.

If she wanted a perfect little family of her own, she would have one. When the time was right.

Until then, she had friends and school and volunteer work, a place of her own. And a dinner engagement she was going to be late for if she didn't get her ass in gear.

JOSH HAD PLENTY TO DO. Accounts to familiarize himself with. Markets to analyze. He hadn't gone so long without studying the market since he'd first become fascinated with Wall Street in high school.

He smelled Dana's flowery scent as soon as he walked

in the door Thursday after work. He heated up the vegetable soup she'd left, wishing he had some fresh homemade bread to go with it. And some cookies left for dessert.

He called his mother to assure her he was doing great and assure himself that she was fine, too. But he kept things brief. He wasn't going to get into a discussion with her. Didn't want to hear about life back home. And still hadn't mentioned L.G.

"I'm not going to be calling again for a while, Mother." He'd been toying with the idea and knew it was the right one. But cutting that last tie...

"You have to call, Joshua! All I have are your phone calls."

Watching L.G., who was twisted around, biting himself on the hip, or trying to, in between losing his balance and falling over, Josh weighed selfishness against saving self. He wasn't going to be able to change until he left his old world behind.

The basketball incident had shown him that. Give him something familiar and it was all too easy to fall back into old habits. But this was his mother. She'd done nothing to deserve being cut off from her only child.

"I'll text," he said. "Every day. And you text, too, so I know you and Father are well."

"But—"

"Just for a while, Mom."

"Will you at least be home for Christmas?"

L.G. was still biting himself, as if he had an itch or something. "I don't think so. Not this year."

Her silence tore at him.

"But we can Skype on Christmas Day."

"Are you happy, son?"

A picture of Dana sprang to mind, laughing as he beat her at cribbage. Holding L.G. against breasts that were surprisingly full and nice, considering how thin the woman was.

"Joshua? Your father tells me you're still taking your inheritance draw every month, and I'm glad for that."

He'd told his parents about putting his trust in Michelle's name for the duration of her life. But he hadn't told them that his current inheritance income was also going into the trust.

"I'm…adjusting," he said. "I'm doing the right thing. And will be better for it," he told her. His parents thought leaving Boston, his family and all of his friends was the extent of his sacrifice.

There'd been no point in telling them the rest.

"But you'll be coming home? Eventually? Your father can't work forever. He needs you here, ready to take over…."

The rope tightened around his throat. He couldn't listen anymore.

She was right. He had a duty. But he was right, too.

And was it so bad if Redmond Enterprises, a conglomeration of holdings that spanned the globe, liquidated at some point in the future? Was a legacy worth his soul?

Or was this just more selfishness on his part? Was his sudden interest in being a better person sincere or was he just running away from that which was most unpleasant to him?

The gossip. The whispers.

"I need some time, Mother. We've already been through this."

He couldn't make any promises for the future. Not until he figured out if he could trust himself not to live life as a selfish bastard.

It hadn't just been Michelle he'd callously hurt. Michelle's sister had told him, during those long hours at the hospital, about the other women he'd hurt. The hearts he'd broken. He'd called those women.

Her sister had been right.

"Tell me about the family, Josh. What are they like? Do you—"

"They're good folks and you promised we wouldn't do this, Mother. For now, this is my life."

"I'd hoped your relatives there would help you see that you're a great man, just as you are. I'd hoped you'd see yourself through their eyes and realize that gossip is gossip and it fades away. What happened to Michelle was a horrible accident—tragic—but not your fault. You would never have left her if you'd had any idea she'd had so much to drink—"

"You had a craniotomy and I didn't bother to come home," he interrupted her. "Should I tell the Shelter Valley Montfords about that?"

"The surgery wasn't dangerous, Joshua. A simple nerve procedure outside the brain. I was in the hospital two nights and then home and back to my normal routine."

He'd been told the procedure wasn't dangerous and, too busy living it up in the French Riviera, hadn't even asked what it was for. He'd barely remembered that she'd had it until they'd been sitting with Michelle's parents in the hospital and one of Michelle's neurologists happened to be the same doctor who'd performed his mother's surgery.

"He drilled a quarter-size hole in your skull and I didn't even know."

"I was asleep. Didn't feel a thing. Really, you're making far more of this than necessary. You would've been there if I needed you."

He'd like to believe it, but he wasn't sure. He probably wouldn't have bothered cooling his heels at a hospital all day, not back then. The world had been full of things to do and he'd wanted to do all of them.

"What about when Grandfather Montford had his heart attack?"

"There was nothing you could do. Only your grandmother and I were allowed in to see him. And you were in the middle of your first trip to Italy."

He'd been twenty-one. A college graduate.

"Father asked me to reconsider my position on that one," he reminded her softly. His father's way of telling him to come home. His mother had needed him.

"You just aren't good with medical situations, Joshua. There's nothing wrong with that."

Had his mother been doing this his entire life? Making excuses for him?

"I went mountain climbing instead of spending Christmas with our family and Michelle."

"You were soon to have a family of your own. When better to make the climb?"

L.G. was chewing on his left hind paw now.

"I forgot your fortieth anniversary party." He'd been in town, buying drinks for a new client, celebrating the deal he'd just closed. And had completely forgotten about his parents' shindig until the evening had been winding down.

Because he hadn't cared. If the party had mattered to him, he'd have remembered it.

"I didn't expect you to be there, Josh. The party was for our friends, not yours. You'd have been bored. Besides, you made it in time." To tell everyone good night.

"I have to go," he said into the phone. "I'll text you tomorrow."

"I love you, son."

"I know, Mom. I love you, too. Say hello to Father."

The old man wasn't speaking to Josh. Not since the day Josh told them he was leaving.

He'd hoped for his father's understanding but hadn't expected it. And hadn't gotten it, either.

"I will. He misses you, Joshua."

In his way, he probably did.

But his father's way wasn't Josh's way. Not anymore.

CHAPTER THIRTEEN

SHE HADN'T EXPECTED Josh to call.

He called. Just as she and Sharon were cleaning up after dinner.

"Excuse me," she said to Sharon, slipping out the older woman's sliding-glass door as she took the call.

"Is it normal for a dog to bite himself?" Josh's voice had that urgency to it again.

And still, it sounded so good.

"If he has an itch he can't scratch with his paws," she said, thinking of him in his business suit.

Did he still have on the tie he'd worn to work?

"He's biting all over. I hadn't noticed it before now."

"I'm on my way," she said.

She didn't give Josh a chance to tell her he didn't need her to drive out. In case he would have tried. She hadn't seen him in two days, and she missed him. And what did he know? He'd never owned a pet before.

"WHERE IS HE?"

He'd barely had the door open twenty minutes later when Dana plowed past him with a canvas bag hanging from her shoulder, along with the leather satchel she used for a purse.

"In his kennel. I didn't know what else to do with him."

She went straight to the corner by the patio door where he kept L.G.'s kennel.

"Come here, Little Guy," she said, grabbing up the puppy as he darted out of his cage.

"Are you sure you should hold him?" The dog obviously had a problem. He didn't want Dana to catch something.

"Of course! Worst case is he has fleas, which I doubt since they aren't prevalent in this part of the desert, due to the lack of grass... Or it could be an allergy, which isn't going to hurt anyone, but him." Holding the puppy up, she gave him a once-over and then sat down with him.

"Have you fed him anything different?"

"No."

She looked in the puppy's eyes. Under his arms. On his belly, and then, with L.G. still on his back, glanced up at Josh. "You didn't give him any cookies, did you?"

"No." But only because he hadn't wanted to part with any of them. "Why?"

"Chocolate is poisonous to dogs."

He'd almost inadvertently fed the dog poison. Probably would have if he hadn't liked the cookies so much.

"It's unlikely that chocolate would have given him skin issues," she said.

Josh watched her part the dog's fur with her long, slender fingers. And imagined them wrapping around his...

"I'm pretty sure he's just got dry skin," she said.

"What would cause that?"

"Too many baths."

Oh. Not surprised that he'd caused it, Josh asked, "What do we do about it?" He would have preferred to stand there and think about sex. Physical intimacy was something he was good at.

"See if he'll eat some fruits and veggies," she said.

"I don't have any."

"I do." Handing him the puppy, she fetched the canvas bag she'd brought with her and pulled out some apples and carrots. "I stopped in at home on my way here," she said, finding a sharp knife in a kitchen drawer, and slicing the apples. "Start with these," she said, handing him a bag of ready-to-eat baby carrots. "See if he'll eat them."

L.G. sniffed the carrot. Took it in his mouth. And spit it out. Josh didn't blame him. He wasn't all that fond of raw carrots, either.

"Put him down a second," Dana said, looking delicious enough to eat in the faded jeans and blue sweater coat she was wearing. "See if he'll take it."

The puppy picked up the carrot. Tossed it. Pounced on it. And sent it rolling a couple of inches.

"Try this." She handed him an apple slice.

L.G. was more interested in playing with the carrot. "What do we do if he doesn't eat them?"

"I brought some fish oil to put on his dog food." She put a Baggie of caplets on the table. "And for immediate relief—like during the night if he keeps you up—here's some vitamin E ointment."

He looked up from where he squatted on the ground next to the dog, and stared.

She tucked a loose strand of hair into the ponytail she always wore. "What?"

"You know a lot."

"Only about some things."

"Whatever the problem is, you seem to have a solution."

"Not always." She laughed. He was making her self-conscious.

He liked knowing he had an effect on her. His gaze met hers. She stopped laughing.

"You're a beautiful woman, Dana Harris." The words came from deep within him. Not the superficial place from which compliments for women usually sprang, but from someplace different. Untapped, until now.

"I'm just ordinary," she said, avoiding his gaze.

Picking up the puppy, Dana set him on the kitchen counter and opened the tube of ointment. She started rubbing the cream into L.G.'s skin.

"You're kidding, right?" he said. "There's nothing ordinary about you."

Michelle, and the dozens of other women he'd been with over the past ten or twelve years—they'd been ordinary.

"Don't, Josh." She frowned.

"Don't what?"

"Don't flatter me."

"You think I'm lying about how attractive I find you?"

Putting the puppy back down on the floor, she screwed the cap back on the ointment and faced him. "I know I'm nothing special in the looks department," she said.

From where he was standing, she was beautiful. Real. Curvy in the right places. With long hair that he could get tangled up in, rather than hair that was perfectly styled to only look like he could get tangled up in it.

She had skin that didn't need makeup to look milky and smooth. Eyes that were big enough to stand out on their own...

Eyes that had real pain in them.

He took her hand. "I'm not flattering you, Dana Harris," he said softly. "I think you're hot as hell. There's nothing artificial about you. Nothing. We haven't even kissed and I've never wanted anyone more...."

"You...want me?"

An alarm went off in his brain. He hadn't said that. He couldn't let anyone need him. Not when he was living a duplicitous life. Not when he was hurting his parents. And had an ex-fiancée confined to a bed in Boston.

But right then, as Dana's big blue eyes pleaded with him

for something he didn't understand, he knew he had to do what he could to give it to her.

This wasn't about him.

She gave so much. And asked for so little.

Acting completely on instinct, Josh pulled her slowly forward, until her body was touching his, holding her gaze the entire time.

Her eyes grew wide, but there was no fear there. Or hesitation, either.

She wanted him to kiss her. He'd been around enough to know.

So he did. Lightly. Touching his lips to hers. Just to say hello.

Mmm. A long hello. Her mouth opened, inviting him in. And he went. Sensation exploded throughout his entire body. Sexual desire. And more. His penis got hard, but he was driven to hold her as strongly as he wanted to make love to her.

His gut lurched. His chest got hot, from the inside out.

And he quit thinking at all.

HIS KISS WAS BETTER than any fantasy she'd ever had. Josh tasted different. Sweet and minty and…God he could kiss. The mastery with which he guided her tongue, the gentle way he explored her mouth…

He was her knight in shining armor. *The* one. He could ride away with her into the sunset and she wouldn't say no.

He took her into the living room instead.

She'd never been like her sisters, someone who took sex casually. But then she'd never had the most gorgeous man in the world interested in *her*.

When Josh led her to his couch and took her fully into his arms, she went willingly. Eagerly.

She wasn't going to have sex with him. Getting carried

away to the point of throwing caution to the wind wasn't her style.

But she couldn't resist the chance to connect with him. To know what his touch felt like. To feel him.

He pulled his lips from hers and that look in his big blue eyes, the one that had struck her the first time she'd seen him, grabbed her anew. The man had demons and was fighting his way out.

Leaning forward, she kissed him softly. Letting him know that he wasn't alone.

He'd said he wanted her.

And God knew, she wanted him.

JOSH KNEW HOW to please a woman. The shy ones and the bold ones. The experienced and the inexperienced. He could adjust his pace, his appetite, to fit. And he always enjoyed himself, even if he didn't finish.

He liked women and he liked sex.

Kissing Dana wasn't about sex. It was about needing to be as close to her as possible.

He was turned on, but that experience wasn't new to him. What was completely unfamiliar was that his libido wasn't the driving force this time.

He had no intention of having sex with Dana Harris. Or any woman who'd want commitment.

Holding her against him felt right. The first completely right thing he'd felt since the morning he'd been woken abruptly to be told that Michelle had been found comatose in her apartment.

He'd been the last person to see her conscious.

It was as though Dana was some kind of healing spirit and only by being in her presence, by touching her, could he find absolution. Peace.

Shifting, he lay back and pulled her down beside him,

meeting her gaze, and when he read the willingness in her eyes, he kissed her again.

The fact that they didn't speak didn't seem the least bit odd to him. There were no words to express what they were giving to each other.

For now, there was only feeling. Giving himself up to the new person he was becoming.

And being aware of the woman in his arms like he'd never been aware of anyone, ever before.

SHE HAD TO STOP HIM. She never had sex without a condom. Josh's arms had tightened around her. She was lying against him, resting all of her weight on his weight. And was so on fire she didn't recognize herself.

It was fantasy come to life but reality was better.

He kissed her again. Oh, God, she was losing it. Her body pressed against his and she liked it and pressed harder. Moved her pelvis along his thigh, her jeans rubbing easily along the fabric of his dress pants.

Her breasts pressed against the solid muscles of his chest and she slid her hands along his shirt, seeking warmth. His warmth.

It was nothing. Just touching. Like kids necking on the couch. And she was consumed in a way she hadn't been the night she'd lost her virginity. Or any other time she'd been touched by a man.

Josh wasn't really even touching her. Not in that way. He was holding her. And kissing her. His hands hadn't strayed from the small of her back.

She ached between her legs and she assuaged the agony with more movement. More pressure. His body rose to meet hers. And she moved a little more, turning sideways, rubbing her taut nipples against his shirt. Their hands were keeping a mutual safe distance from private parts.

She kissed him harder.

He kissed her back and their body movement increased in unison. Josh moved beneath her, pressing rock-hard maleness against her. Her breast brushed the flexed muscle on his arm and she almost cried out with a need to be touched there. To put some kind of finish to the sweet torture. In the midst of all the movement her sweater crept up and her stomach was exposed, her bare skin rubbing against the buckle on his pants.

Trying to pull her sweater down without breaking away from his kiss, she touched his stomach, still covered by his shirt.

Josh breathed in sharply and his kiss grew more dominant, more needy, and ignited a fire inside her that drove all thought away.

He rolled over, pinning her down on the couch with his body on top of hers, and then slid sideways. He undid her jeans, yanked them down over her hips, exposing her panties to the night air. To him.

She couldn't stop herself from reaching for his belt buckle. It was there and she needed to yank on it worse than anything in the world. Nothing mattered but getting that belt loose and those pants down.

With one hand still beneath her back, he used the other to pull her panties past her knees. And then to shove his own down midhip, freeing his hardened penis. With one quick thrust he was inside of her, moving much as they'd been moving on each other for most of the past hour.

It was over almost as soon as it had begun. She exploded. He exploded. A home run and they'd never even made it to second base.

Dana laughed out loud. She floated somewhere in between fantasy and reality, on a cloud of sensation. Her bra was still fastened, her breasts completely covered. He still had on his tie. He'd never laid a hand on any intimate part of her. Nor did she on him.

And...

They hadn't protected themselves against sexual disease. Or pregnancy. Thank God it was her safe time, but...was Josh free of STDs?

"Shit." His exclamation broke into her thoughts.

And Dana figured he'd just read her mind.

CHAPTER FOURTEEN

JOSH JUMPED UP. Turning his back on the half-naked woman on his couch, he pulled up his slacks and fastened them, pulling the belt a notch tighter than normal. By the time he turned around, Dana's jeans were back in place, as well. She was looking around the back side of the couch.

"Little Guy!" she said aloud. "We forgot all about him."

He'd just messed up another life and she was worried about a dog?

Oh, God. What had he done? What had he *done?* Dana wasn't the type of woman one bedded and walked away from.

But that was exactly what he had to do. He was in the midst of too much inner turmoil to be any good for anyone.

"Oh, there he is!" Her voice came from the kitchen. "Come look, Josh."

He moved forward because he didn't know what else to do. Lord knew, he couldn't go back. Couldn't undo the pain he'd caused Michelle, a pain so excruciating she'd had to poison herself with alcohol.

He couldn't undo what he'd just done to Dana, either. Couldn't keep those jeans up around her hips, couldn't hold her thighs together instead of separating them. Couldn't take back his orgasm.

Couldn't expect her to have no expectations.

L.G. was curled up asleep in his kennel, with the door

still open as Josh had left it when he'd come in from work...
when was it? Just two hours ago? Three?

It didn't take long for a new life to burn to ashes.

"You have to go."

She was going to need things from him. He could tell her
that he wanted to give her those things. That he believed
she deserved them. But then she'd have faith in him. Expect things. Hope for things.

"What?" The shocked expression on Dana's face was
his greatest fear come to life. No. His greatest fear come
to life was the pain that looked out at him from her wide
blue eyes. "This...you and me. It can't happen."

"It just did."

Hands in his pockets so that he didn't pull her back into
his arms, he said, "It can't happen again."

"You act like I'm going to force myself on you, Josh. I
didn't do this alone."

He focused on L.G., until the puppy immediately reminded him of Dana, and that became painful, as well.
Looking at the floor, he said, "I know that."

"And before you assume that I'd allow a repeat perfor-
mance, you might want to find out what I think of what
just happened, rather than just announcing your opinion
like it's the only one that matters."

That brought his head up. He'd never even considered
her opinion. How did she know him so well already? "You
don't want it to happen again?"

"You sound so shocked."

She hadn't answered his question. And he wasn't sure
the implication was false, either. She was right. It had never
occurred to him that she might have been disappointed.
Or as upset as he was by what had just transpired between
them.

"Did I hurt you?"

Sliding her purse on her shoulder, Dana glanced around, as though looking for something. "No," she said.

"I'm handling this all wrong."

Out in the kitchen, she grabbed the canvas bag she'd brought, leaving the capsules, ointment and food on the counter. "I don't disagree with you there," she said, walking by him without so much as a glance.

Josh reached for her hand. Pulled her to a stop. She didn't pull away. And didn't turn around, either.

"I'm sorry," he said. He had to do something. To make things right again. And remembered something his father had said to him years before when he'd been given a small deal to handle and lost the sale.

The only real failure is to accept failure.

"I mean it, Dana." He could tell her about Michelle. She might even understand, at least to some degree. She'd probably hold him responsible for Michelle's comatose state. And that was fine, too. Good, actually. Because she'd know the whole truth about him.

But then he'd be the old Josh Redmond again.

And he couldn't go back. To go back would be to accept failure.

Thoughts flew through his mind as she stood there, facing not him but the door. He couldn't take the easy way out, even if, in the moment, it seemed the kindest thing to do.

"Hey." He gave her hand a gentle tug. She turned then, and he could see the glisten of tears in her eyes. She wasn't crying, though.

"I'd repeat tonight in an instant," he said, looking her straight in the eye, "if I could know for certain that you wouldn't be hurt."

Her expression changed, and the peculiar energy that Dana exuded trickled back into the room. "Life doesn't come with that kind of guarantee."

"I know. But you need better odds than I can offer you."

She didn't ask what he meant. He almost wished she had.

"I have to go," she said, pulling her hand from his.

He stood where she'd left him and watched her let herself out.

JEROME WAS WAITING for Dana when she got home from Josh's place Thursday night. It was hard to believe it was only half past nine. It felt as if her whole life had changed.

It had gone from good, to incredible, to horrible—all in one day.

"You look kind of sick," Jerome said, walking over to open her car door for her. His beat-up little truck was parked at the curb. "I can come back."

She remembered—he'd asked her to help him iron a shirt. He had a job interview the next day. She'd told him to stop by any time after eight.

"I'm not sick and there's no way you're going to that interview with a wrinkled shirt," she told him, grabbing her purse and the empty bag as she climbed out of the Mazda. "Have you been waiting long?"

"Nah, just got here."

"Come on in," she said, unlocking her door and letting him follow behind her. "It'll only take a sec for the iron to heat up."

Company was far better than being alone. Once Jerome left she'd take a hot bath, soak in her favorite lavender-and-rose bubbles, take an aspirin and go to bed.

By morning, she'd be just fine again.

JOSH TEXTED DANA three times Thursday night, just to make sure she was okay. And when she didn't reply to any of them, he stopped. Who was he kidding? He was texting her because he needed her.

And because he needed her, he cared that she was okay. His concern was really about him.

He felt her pain as if it were his own, and that was because she was the only person that made his life feel bearable at the moment.

She certainly didn't need him. He'd known her a week and in that time she'd had at least two different people that he knew of spend the night at her place. She was hosting Thanksgiving dinner for at least twenty people. She had pet therapy and Love To Go Around.

She had it all together. And he was lucky as hell that he'd screwed up with her and not some lonely, needy girl who didn't have anyone in the world to lean on.

Dana was fine. And he had to leave her that way.

By all accounts, he was not a good relationship risk.

DANA MISSED MOST of her biology lecture Friday morning. She was physically present, but couldn't focus on the microorganisms that seemed so interesting to her professor. She was too busy fighting with herself over the advisability of making her routine visit to Josh's house that morning.

Lots of puppies were left alone in their crates or kennels for eight hours a day. Little Guy only had to make it until noon and then dinnertime.

But the puppy's well-being depended upon his owner's comfort. And Josh wasn't comfortable leaving the dog in his crate for more than a couple of hours.

Of course, he was going to have to at some point. Or wait until Little Guy was house-trained and then put in a doggy door for him to go in and out as he pleased.

Chances were Little Guy would be more rambunctious for Josh if she didn't go over to let him relieve himself. Part of the reason Josh was getting so comfortable around the puppy was because there hadn't been any accidents for a long time.

She was a pet-placement counselor. She had a job to do.

Her biology professor dismissed the class.

And Dana hurried to her car.

THE SECOND JOSH opened his door at lunchtime he smelled Dana's already familiar scent. And ached. Had she left him a note?

Surely, after the previous night, after having sex with him, she'd at least have something to say to him.

He looked everywhere. Even in his bedroom.

Nothing. She'd had nothing to say.

You get what you pay for. You want to win big, you have to pay big.

His father's words rang in his brain.

Remembering Michelle, Josh knew that he was getting what he deserved. And knew that, if he never got anything in life he wanted ever again, he would still not have paid off his debt.

HE'D BEEN HOME for lunch. She could tell, not only from the lingering scent of his aftershave, or cologne, or whatever it was. But because he'd left her a note.

As opposed to sending her a text.

Dana,
I am truly sorry for the way I handled things. Those moments with you meant a lot to me. I would give just about anything to undo what I did.

Little Guy's squeals reminded her that he was still in his cage.

With the note in hand, she released the dog, saw him

out the back door and stood on the patio, paying absolutely no attention to him at all as she read the note again. And again. Trying to decipher the few brief sentences.

She was no closer to doing so when Little Guy was back at her feet, waiting for his good-boy treat.

"'I would give just about anything to undo what I did,'" she read aloud as she juggled the growing puppy, the note and the door. "What does he mean by that?" she asked the dog, who was staring up at her with eager brown eyes.

Door shut and locked behind her, she grabbed two treats and, sitting with the puppy on her lap, fed them to him one at a time.

"Would he undo having…you know…with me? Or just the afterward part when he made me feel like a slut?" she asked. "He said it meant a lot to him.…"

Little Guy stared up at her, his head cocked to one side.

That's when the tears came. She'd made it out of there the night before and through the rest of the evening and night all without shedding a tear.

It wasn't as though she'd been a virgin. She'd been engaged to be married. And she'd had a steady boyfriend before that, too.

A few tears dripped off her jawbone onto Little Guy's fur. He sprinted up and licked her face.

Chuckling through her tears, stifling them as she'd learned to do so long ago, she said, "I know, you're right. Tears don't solve anything. They only make you wet and give you a stuffed-up nose."

Logic she'd come up with the day she'd turned fourteen and there'd been no celebration.

How could you celebrate the anniversary of the biggest betrayal of your life? She'd heard Daniel ask her mother the question that night, when they thought all three of the girls were in bed asleep.

Dana's tears had dried the instant she'd heard the pain in Daniel's voice. Because she understood his side, too. She also felt betrayed by Susan. Horribly betrayed.

And there hadn't been anything Susan could do to change things for any of them.

"So, what do you think?" she asked the puppy as she ran her hand down his back and, with her other hand, scratched his throat—feeling something inside of her settle at the contact. "What should I do now? Leave him a note? Text him? Or pretend like none of it ever happened?"

The puppy stared. Dana nodded.

"Right," she said. "He's probably just saying what he thinks he has to say to smooth things over."

Little Guy's head cocked again.

"I know, I know." She grinned and hugged the puppy to her chest. "Smooth what over? Nothing happened. But something's going to happen if I don't get you back in your kennel and hightail it to class. I am absolutely not going to lose my perfect grade-point average over this."

She cut herself off just as she was about to add, "He's not worth it."

Because one thing Dana could not do was lie to a dog.

CHAPTER FIFTEEN

FRIDAY NIGHT, DETERMINED to leave Dana alone, Josh spent time on the internet, learning about a host of household things, including how to sort laundry and how to get hard-water stains out of toilets. He stopped short of home repairs. Ian, at work, had mentioned a handyman he'd hired to lay tile on his back patio, and if Ian could afford to hire home maintenance on his salary, then Josh could, too.

When Josh's computer failed to be company enough to keep him occupied, Josh turned to L.G., who'd been hanging out on the floor by his feet.

"You want to go for a drive?"

The dog stared at him.

"You want to go?" he asked again.

Lying on the expensive leather shoe he'd adopted, L.G. didn't seem to know if he wanted to go or not.

He wanted to go, Josh decided. The puppy had already spent too long in his kennel that day. It would be cruel to stick him back in there again so soon.

Decision made, Josh was in his SUV and backing down the driveway in record time—with no destination in mind.

It took him twenty minutes to make it around the town and back. And another ten to find the huge house outside of town that, to this point, he'd managed to avoid completely.

Stopping the vehicle far enough away to avoid concerns of suspicious activity, he put it in Park and sat back, looking over the landscape lighting that hinted at the overall elegance of the estate.

"What do you think, L.G.? Can you picture yourself living like that?"

Sitting in the passenger seat, his front paws braced against the leather, staring straight ahead as though he could see out a windshield that was well above his head, the puppy calmly lay down.

Josh could picture it.

Was he a fool to turn his back on what was rightfully his? Not the Montford mansion, but the life it represented?

Was it his purpose in life to be a spoiled rich playboy? Was he fighting something he'd never be able to change?

Or was this truly his moment of truth? His chance to save himself from wasting the opportunities he'd been given to make a difference during his time on earth? Did he have it in him to contribute something good of his own to the world?

As he'd been sitting in the hospital, waiting for news on Michelle's condition, Michelle's sister had asked him what good works he'd done in his life.

He'd listed off his successful business deals.

Parties he'd thrown that everyone had loved.

Generous gifts he'd bought.

And she'd shaken her head.

Good works, she'd said. She'd listed some charity opportunities they'd had at Harvard. He'd been too busy to look into them. But he remembered the checks he'd written for Michelle.

Rather than impressing her, she'd just looked away, shaking her head.

Now, as he sat staring at the mansion that loomed in front of him, he felt something wet against the edge of his hand. L.G.'s nose butting up against him.

Glancing at the dog, Josh was hit by the irony of his current situation. How could he possibly expect himself to unravel the mysteries of life when he didn't even know if the dog was simply seeking companionship or telling him that he had to piss?

Josh wasn't ready to head back to the house. But taking the puppy's cue, he put the car in gear and drove straight to his real destination—and the real reason he had the puppy in the car with him.

L.G. would be his ticket in.

Once he got there, what he did with the admittance was up to him.

When he pulled onto Dana's street, he relaxed for the first time that evening. Until he saw the car parked behind hers in her driveway and the other two parked on the street in front of her place. Her blinds were still open, and as he slowed down in front of her house, he could make out at least three people inside.

Speeding up, Josh drove on past. Obviously Dana wasn't suffering over his less than stellar behavior the night before. She wasn't alone, grieving....

Hell, for all he knew she had a boyfriend. He hadn't even asked.

It was so typical of him that it hadn't even dawned on him to wonder about her situation.

Which was why he was going to do her a favor and leave her the hell alone.

Dana deserved better.

DANA HAD LORI, Marissa and Dillon—Marissa's boyfriend— over for pizza and cards Friday night. While she enjoyed their company, she also felt kind of like their parent as she sat there listening to them talk about who was talking to whom and who said what among the kids they knew.

She listened, laughed and joined in, usually with a piece of advice, and thought about Josh's note. It meant something that he'd written that note instead of just texting her.

Maybe she should have responded.

She hadn't heard from him all night.

Cleaning up after her guests had left, she pictured Josh arriving home after work earlier that evening. Had he looked for a reply to his note? Had his eye gone to the place where he'd left the note and found the spot empty?

Her heart lurched.

Had he even gone home after work?

Now that Josh was meeting people he'd have his pick of dates. Of invitations and places to spend his downtime. Guys like Josh Redmond. The kind with all the confidence in the world, with looks that would buy them entrance into any circle and, most important, a heart kind enough to take on a puppy simply because it didn't have a home, even though they knew absolutely nothing about dogs but were willing to let the puppy turn their home upside down, to clean up after him and never once consider giving the dog back... Guys like him had so many people vying for their attention that they didn't have time for girls like Dana Harris.

She was everyone's friend. Lori's. Jerome's. Now Marissa's and Dillon's. Lillie's and Jon's. Sharon's. The list went on. It had been the same at home, too. People came to her with problems, and usually she found a way to help.

Most of the time, she was completely happy with that.

Turning off the lights, she went to bed. And refused to think about Josh or those few brief minutes when her body had been joined with his.

She had to be up early in the morning for another pet-therapy visit to a nursing home in south Phoenix. Jerome was coming over to do laundry after that. She had calls to make in an attempt to find forever homes for three older rescue dogs that were in foster care. Zack had called, giving her jurisdiction over the placement and follow-up. She had her own "clients" and was excited about this new road she'd embarked on.

And she also had a couple of places to visit for a possible puppy for Abraham Swartz. Something else she was excited about.

She had homework to do, too. Because she was in college. Finally.

Life was exactly what she made it.

And that was fine.

IAN CALLED SATURDAY morning, inviting Josh to join him and his wife, Amy, and Amy's single, ex-cheerleader friend for an afternoon of golf followed by dinner at the country club.

He accepted the invitation. But only played nine holes and took a side trip home before dinner to let L.G. out for a bit.

When Olivia, the ex-cheerleader, offered to take him mountain climbing not far from the cactus jelly plant outside of town Sunday morning, he agreed to go. L.G. would only be locked up for about four hours. And then he'd be home with him for the rest of the day.

But the invitation he received for Thanksgiving dinner, the one that would give him reason to leave Dana Harris well and truly alone, he declined.

His mother had taught him a long time ago that once you accepted an invitation, you did not turn it down for another one that came along.

At least that was the excuse he gave himself.

DANA DIDN'T FIND a puppy for Abraham on Saturday. But late Sunday afternoon, she had a good feeling when she pulled up to the desert home a few miles outside of town. Puppies Free To A Good Home, the sign read.

The owner was a client at the clinic and, according to Zack, had been shocked a few months earlier to find out that her cherished, rescue dog—a poodle-spaniel mix—wasn't ailing as she'd feared, but was, instead, expecting pups.

The second Dana saw the four-foot-by-four-foot wired cage with newspaper flooring, filled with a slightly suspicious mother and four little pups, one white, one brown and two a mixture of the two colors, she knew she was in trouble.

"How soon can I take one?" she asked the owner.

"Today if you like," the plump mother of two young boys said, practically throwing the pups her way. "They've been wormed, had their shots and have been eating puppy food and drinking water out of the bowl since the beginning of this week." A holler sounded from the other room. "Excuse me," the woman said, while Dana held first one and then another of the puppies.

She'd find homes for all four of them, she promised herself. But for now, the little brown male would be perfect for Abraham.

Holding her choice, she looked back at the cage. To the brown-and-white female with the tiniest paws, who was climbing on her siblings' backs in an attempt to get back to Dana.

"What did you decide?" The harried dog owner was back.

"I'll take him," Dana said, holding up Abraham Swartz's new puppy. And then, with one last look at the cage, reached down and grabbed the little girl. "And her, too."

She might not be good enough for Josh Redmond, but she would do just fine as a human mother to a new pup.

JOSH WAS CONTEMPLATING taking another drive with L.G. Sunday evening, maybe to Phoenix to find some good take-out sushi, when the text message came in.

Are you still joining us for Thanksgiving dinner?

The holiday was still almost two weeks away.

Yes.

He waited. No reply. Grabbed his keys.

Is LG busy tonight?

He grinned.

No.

Can he come over to play? I have someone I'd like him to meet.

Someone.
Someone else, not him.
Josh had never been an emotional guy. And he didn't appreciate the surge of disappointment he felt.
He's going to Phoenix with me. Josh punched in the words, reread them.
Idiot. You just told her he didn't have any plans.
He deleted what he'd written, sent off a quick Okay and dropped his phone back into its holster.

CHAPTER SIXTEEN

TEN MINUTES AFTER she'd texted Josh, Dana heard a car out front.

He'd rushed right over. Grabbing up Lindy Lu, she went to greet Little Guy. She'd already promised her growing pet family that she was not going to make a fool of herself over Little Guy's father.

With them watching over her, she'd be sure to keep her promise.

"Come on in," she said, holding the front door open as Josh, wearing jeans and a white button-down shirt, came up the walk, Little Guy under his left arm like a football.

"You got a pup!" Josh grinned.

"I told you I had someone here who wanted to meet Little Guy."

"I thought…" He broke off as Little Guy, seeing Lindy Lu, squirmed to get down. "Doesn't matter what I thought," Josh said, squatting as he put his pup down on the tile floor in her living room.

Dana sat, inviting Little Guy to come closer, while she cradled the four pounds of fur she'd just acquired.

"Little Guy, this is Lindy Lu," she said gently, as though speaking with a small child.

"You expect him to understand English?"

"No, well, some words, yeah, but mostly I expect him to react to the tone of my voice. I want him as calm as possible so he doesn't scare her."

Why it was important to her that Lindy Lu and Little Guy got along, she didn't know. Probably because she felt a sense of ownership with both dogs. Cared about them both.

"You've forgiven me, then?"

Lying on his side, propped up on his elbow, watching the puppies circle each other, Josh spoke to her almost as gently as she'd spoken to the dogs.

"There's nothing to forgive," she said, wishing they could pretend the disaster between them had never happened.

Josh's gaze collided with hers. And held on. He studied her so long her throat got dry.

"Okay. So we're good?" she asked.

"That's up to you."

"Why is it up to me?"

"Because you got the raw end of the deal."

"How do you figure that?"

"Let's see, I've known you a little more than a week and you've cooked, advised and babysat for me. What have I done for you?"

"Made me laugh." His honesty drew the response from her before she had a chance to think about what she was saying. Sitting on the floor with him, their faces only a foot or so apart, Dana felt the weekend of hurt feelings fade away. "I've never spent time with someone like you, Josh."

She stopped. If he didn't see what a nerd she was, she sure as hell wasn't going to point the fact out to him.

Or, maybe he did and didn't care.

He could just be sparing her feelings.

He was staring at her. Which left her words hanging between them, making her uncomfortable.

Completely out of character, Little Guy was quietly watching Lindy Lu, creeping up on her one paw at a time.

In return, the outgoing little pup batted at the air with her front paw.

"You don't bore me," Dana said, because someone had to say something to break the silence. Josh's eyebrow quirked in that way that made her stomach dance. "I know that's probably a horrible thing to say, but I get bored easily and I don't with you."

She was making it worse, not better. "If it would make you feel any better, I could start asking you for favors."

"Like what?"

"I don't know." Other than to make love to her again, which she definitely was not going to ask. She wanted him to be so hot for her he couldn't control himself around her. To need her as badly as she'd imagined he had the other night.

What she didn't want was charity. Of any kind.

"See, that's what I mean."

"You could carve the turkey for me on Thanksgiving. I hate carving the turkey." Jerome had already offered. She hadn't responded to him one way or the other. And then it hit her...

"I know what you could do," she said, the idea growing on her.

"You name it."

He wanted to be friends with her. If Dana hadn't been flying so high at the realization, she'd have warned herself to take things in stride.

She told him about Jerome. About his family and friends far away in Missouri, and his financial situation. About letting him do his laundry at her place.

"I'm afraid he's developing...an attachment to me," she told Josh. It was something she'd been trying, with increasing difficulty, not to worry about. "He's coming over for Thanksgiving and I've suggested several times that he bring a friend or a date, but he keeps saying there's no one. He's been stopping by and calling more and more often lately, and I'm… I don't want to hurt his feelings, but he's a kid! And I know, if he is feeling things like I'm pretty sure he is, it's just because he's homesick and I probably remind him of his mother or something, you know a transference thing, but I don't want to hurt his feelings and…"

She was rambling again. What if Josh turned her down? Burning with humiliation, she stopped talking.

"You want me to pretend that you and I have a thing… to let him down lightly?"

He didn't sound horrified. And wasn't laughing.

"I was actually just thinking that if I could introduce you to him, say, Tuesday when he's coming over for me to iron his shirt again before his next job interview…"

"You iron his shirts?"

"He scorched the first one trying to do it himself. He's only got one more and he can't even afford to do his laundry right now, let alone buy a new dress shirt. He's the oldest in his family and I get the idea that his family is sacrificing a ton so that he can get a Montford education. He's really smart."

Josh was listening—his focus seemed to be one hundred percent on her. And she realized it always was. And that was one of the things he did for her. When she was around Josh she felt valuable. It was as though, when he looked at her, he saw someone different than she saw when she looked in the mirror.

It was probably just a talent of his. He probably made every woman he talked to feel like a million bucks.

"I just don't want things to get so awkward between us that he can't still come over to do his laundry," she said, finishing more slowly.

"What time is he going to be here on Tuesday?"

"We didn't set a time, but if things go as they have been, he's going to show up in time for me to invite him to stay for dinner."

"How about if you bring L.G. home with you after your afternoon visit on Tuesday and I'll just head over here after work."

Dana felt like her insides were smiling at his inference that she would still be caring for Little Guy. It was a good idea. At least until the puppy was house-trained. She liked the break in her day. And if she was going to be honest with herself, she'd admit that she liked visiting Josh's home every day. It made her feel closer to him. "Unless you were hoping I'd head off dinner," Josh added.

"No! Your plan is perfect," she said. "I don't think we'll have to say anything to Jerome—he'll get the message. Before he actually tries something and I end up losing him as a friend."

"Sounds to me like he'd be the one losing out. He uses your washer and dryer, you iron his shirts for him… What does he do for you?"

Hadn't she just heard him say pretty much the same thing a second ago? In reference to him?

Lindy Lu had curled up into a ball against Dana's thigh and was sound asleep. Little Guy lay just inches away, fully alert, watching the pup.

"I don't keep accounts with my friends," she said, hoping she didn't offend him. But if he didn't like her, then there was no point in caring what he thought. "I'm not used to that way of thinking, and frankly, I'm not even sure if it's healthy."

He blinked. But stayed on her floor, as though he was perfectly at home there. "If you don't pay attention, it's easy to blow through life only thinking of yourself. At least for some of us. Clearly you don't have that problem."

Things had just changed between them again. His tone of voice was different. Something important was happening. She just didn't know what.

"You think you have that problem, Josh?" The guy let a puppy turn his world upside down.

"Let's just say that I'm on a mission to *not* have that problem anymore."

He'd been through something pretty bad, that much was obvious to her. Had been from the first time she'd looked in his eyes.

"You want to talk about it?"

"No. I just want to make absolutely sure that you don't pay for my thoughtlessness. I won't be the guy who takes and doesn't give back. And the only way I can be certain that I keep my word is to keep accounts."

Made sense. In a guy sort of way. But she still thought he was missing the boat somehow.

"Doing for people comes naturally out of caring about them," she said aloud when she really thought she should have held her tongue.

He sat up. "Maybe that's the problem, then. Maybe I don't care about anyone but myself."

"You don't believe that." She watched as he stood, stretched and looked around the room. "Do you, Josh?"

When he turned toward her, she saw an expression in his eyes she didn't recognize. "I don't know what I think," he said. "But I know I had sex with you the other night without giving any thought to your safety or emotional state. And then I made matters worse by slapping you with the fact that, with me, there can be no commitment. I took zero care with your feelings in that situation."

"I can't argue with you there," she said. Because it was true, to a point. "But what happened Thursday night was as much my fault as it was yours, Josh. We equally allowed what happened between us."

"But you were giving more than I was, weren't you?"

"I don't know what you're asking," she said, when she knew full well. And she didn't appreciate him asking.

Josh sat back down on the floor, directly across from her, resting his weight on his hands behind him. "Yes, you do, and it's not a bad thing, Dana. It's a great thing. You are so much more of a person than I am, so far above me I can't hope to catch up. Because whether you're having sex or ironing a shirt, your heart is open and giving. I'm not sure I have a heart to open."

Someone had done a real number on this guy.

"Of course you do, Josh. Everyone does."

"My receptors are misdirected," he told her.

"Your perceptions might be a tad off," she rebutted.

"I had intimate relations with you without even asking if you were in a relationship."

"And if I was, that cross would be mine to bear as I would have been the one being unfaithful."

"So, you're not involved with anyone?"

"No. For the record, if I had been, nothing would have happened. I don't do that kind of thing."

"But you have had other guys…"

"Yes." He'd have been able to tell that, she was sure.

"Anyone here in town?"

"No," she said. And because she saw no reason to withhold the information he was so clearly fishing for, she said, "I dated a guy in high school. We met up again a couple of years later and were together for about six months. He was my first. It was quite uneventful, I have to say, which is probably why we didn't last long."

"My first time wasn't that great, either," he said with

a grin. "It was all about me, of course, and lasted about thirty seconds."

She was still envious of the woman. Whoever she was.

"I was only ever with one other guy," she told him now. "And I didn't sleep with him until after we were engaged."

"You were engaged?"

Rubbing Lindy Lu's ear between her fingers, she nodded. "Unfortunately."

"Why do you say it like that?"

"Because it wasn't right."

"What does that mean, it wasn't right? Why did you agree to marry him?"

"My stepfather and Keith's father were lodge buddies, you know the kind of friends who'd do anything for each other and always put each other first type of thing."

She'd make it brief. Give him just enough to understand where she was coming from so they could move on.

Because it sounded as if they were really going to be friends. And she wanted that. Badly.

CHAPTER SEVENTEEN

"YOU GOT ENGAGED because your stepfather was friends with the guy's father?" Josh asked. Nudging L.G. with the tip of his shoe, he moved so together they formed a diamond—his legs to Dana's legs—to keep the puppies contained.

"I know, it seems crazy now," Dana was saying. "Some days I can't believe it, either. But at the time..."

"At the time, what?"

"Life seemed much smaller then," she said slowly. "With fewer possibilities."

"So you settled?" It didn't sound like the Dana he knew at all. But then, maybe he didn't know her as well as he thought he did.

"No, I did what I thought was best."

"Best for you?" Somehow he didn't think so.

"Best for everyone."

Her puppy woke up and stretched. She seemed quite content, cuddled up next to Dana's thigh. The puppy trusted her.

And so did he.

"Best how?" He was pushing.

"My stepfather owns a chain of furniture stores in Indiana," she said. "I worked for the family business. My mom still does. My stepfather was a good provider, a loyal, responsible, reliable man."

There was a note in her voice he couldn't make out. "Sounds like a good man."

"He is a good man."

He wasn't sure he'd say that about his old man. "You're lucky," he said out loud, ducking mentally. Dana was the farthest thing from Boston society. There was no danger in speaking with her.

But after a lifetime of being taught that he had to keep up appearances...

"You don't get along with your father?" she asked.

"I got along with him just fine." Until they'd quit speaking a few weeks ago. "I just knew that to get along I had to provide certain things, stay within certain boundaries, and so I did."

"Isn't it that way with all kids and their parents?"

He shrugged. He'd already said more than he should have. "Probably. My father screwed around on my mother. Discreetly, of course, but I knew."

"Did your mother know?"

"I have no idea."

"You didn't tell her."

"It's not something we'd discuss."

"You weren't close to her, either?"

"I'm closer to her than I've ever been to anyone in my life." Still, he hadn't been there for her when he should have been. His closest relationship, he was beginning to understand, maybe his only real relationship, had been with himself.

"What about siblings?"

"I don't have any. How about you?"

"Two half-sisters. Both younger."

"Did you know your biological father?"

"Nope. Daniel's name is on my birth certificate."

"He adopted you."

She paused, and then said, "His name was always there.

He and Mom were married by the time I was born and he assumed responsibility for me from the start."

Josh felt as if he was doing research on a deal, and the pieces were all coming together.

"And you feel like you owe him something for that."

"Why do you say that?" Her response was razor sharp.

"Because you were engaged to his best friend's son and you didn't seem happy about that."

Her puppy stood, circled and half lay, half fell back down, tucking her head into her paws and going back to sleep. L.G. laid down his head, facing her.

"Keith was a spoiled ass," Dana said.

The comment hit home.

"I don't think I've ever heard you say anything bad about anyone before."

"I try to see the best in people."

"But you couldn't find it in him?"

"I tried. His father owns a string of car dealerships. Keith grew up thinking he was God's gift to the world. I don't think his parents ever said no to him."

He could relate.

"And he decided he wanted you."

"Not exactly. Keith spent his high school and college years partying and having fun. He'd been all over the world but never worked a day in his life. He was into drugs and drinking and gambling, and got into debt one too many times. I, on the other hand, missed college to go to work in the family business. I was managing the three retail stores and they were turning a profit."

He wasn't surprised to hear that she had a good head for business. The woman excelled at everything.

And Keith could have been any number of Josh's buddies. Other than the gambling and not-working part, he could have been Josh.

"I was twenty-three, living by myself, and Daniel and Keith's dad figured that I was just what Keith needed. His father told him he'd pay off his debt, but only if he settled down, married me and went to work—either for Daniel, or at the car dealerships. They wanted him where they could keep an eye on him."

"And he agreed."

"What choice did he have?"

But she'd agreed, too.

Dana's expression changed and grew pensive. She shuddered.

Tapping her sneaker with the tip of his shoe, he said, "You didn't marry him."

"I almost did. But then, out of the blue, I got a letter in the mail, telling me that I'd been chosen to receive a full scholarship, living expenses included, to Montford University."

"Out of the blue? You'd said you were on scholarship, but I assumed... You mean you weren't applying to colleges?"

"I knew before I graduated high school that there wouldn't be money for me to go to college. My sisters were both going, and while the economy had hit us hard, we were still showing enough profit at the stores to prevent me from qualifying for financial aid."

"Your sisters are older than you?"

"No, younger."

But they got to go to college over her. Anger churned in Josh. Surprising him. He'd never been one to get worked up about much of anything.

"Scholarships don't just show up on people's doorsteps," he said.

"I'm pretty sure my mother applied for it for me," Dana said, a sad light in her eyes, but a smile back on her face.

"She knew that I didn't love Keith. And I know she wanted better for me."

"She could have told your father that they weren't going to sacrifice you for the betterment of his best friend's son."

Josh hated what she was telling him. And understood, too. Family and money came with responsibilities.

"Mom…she doesn't cross Daniel."

"But wouldn't she have told you if she'd applied? Especially after you got the scholarship."

"Not if there was any chance Daniel would find out."

"Because you were running out on his friend's son?"

She didn't say anything, but she didn't have to.

Josh knew how unforgiving parents could be when their offspring no longer followed their dictates.

"DOES DANIEL STILL speak to you?"

With Lindy Lu cuddled up to her chest, Dana sat cross-legged, petting Little Guy as he jumped up and stood in front of her, staring at the new little girl in his life and wagging his tail.

"As much as usual," she answered carefully. She'd said enough. "Keith met someone else and has settled down."

"I'll bet the time you spent with him was good for him."

She didn't see how. The creep had been all about what she could and should do for him. He'd paid little attention to anything Dana wanted.

"How did he take it when you broke off the engagement?"

"He pretended to be upset." She'd never known, until that night, how good of an actor Keith could be. "I'm sure it was all show for his father's sake."

"I'm guessing he'd grown to care about you and knew what he was losing."

"I think having gambling goons in dark clothes knocking at his door scared him into changing his ways. Keith acted like a tough guy, but underneath, he was just a self-ish, spoiled, rich kid."

"I think you underestimate your own worth."

Her hand stilling on Lindy Lu's head, Dana glanced at Josh and then down. Her mother used to tell her that all the time. That she underestimated her own worth. Those same words.

"I don't," she said, telling herself not to read too much into Josh's statement. He was a guy and guys seemed to think that they were supposed to tell women what they thought women wanted to hear. "I know that I'm good at a lot of things and I make choices that work to my strengths. I'm also honest with myself. I know where my assets aren't as strong so I don't give myself false hopes or rely on things that probably aren't going to be."

She'd never put a lot of stock in her looks. Maybe be-cause Rebecca and Lindsey were both classically beauti-ful and she'd always been the plain one. Or maybe she just placed more importance on other things.

"What assets are you lacking?"

"That's kind of a personal question, don't you think?"

The floor was hard and cold and her butt was begin-ning to ache. Jumping up, Dana set Lindy Lu gently in the packing box she'd brought her home in, walked to the kitchen, pulled out an opened bottle of wine and poured herself a glass. "You want some?" she asked Josh, who'd followed her in.

"You ever try beer?"

"I hate it. Can't stand hard liquor, either. Much to Keith's disappointment."

"I'd like a glass of wine, thank you." He took the stem of the glass she handed him, holding it in front of him while she poured a second glass. "So is that one of the assets you lack?" he asked as she corked the bottle and put it back in the refrigerator. "You're not a drinker?"

Why was he doing this?

Turning toward him, Dana raised her glass to her lips.

"Wait!"

She pulled the glass back without sipping. "What?"

"I'd like to offer a toast."

He was making her nervous. But she held up her glass and waited.

"To you, Dana Harris, the woman who sees far more than she knows and is kind enough to share her vision with the rest of us."

His arm stretched forward, he held out his glass to hers, but Dana hesitated. Was he making fun of her?

Sincerity shone from the depths of his eyes.

"To you, Josh Redmond," she said in return. "A man who is confusing the hell out of me."

The clink of glasses broke her gaze from his and Dana sipped.

CHAPTER EIGHTEEN

THEY PUT THE PUPPIES outside and sat at the little black wrought-iron table on Dana's patio. Telling himself that L.G. and Lindy Lu were fine, Josh settled back against the cushioned chair and sipped his wine.

"I want you to know that I have had regular checkups my entire life and I do not, nor have I ever had, any kind of STD," he said, the cover of darkness working for him. "I also don't generally have sex without wearing a condom. I'm sorry."

All the women he knew used the pill to protect against pregnancy, but there was still the danger of passing on a virus.

"It's a bit late now to worry about it," she said. "Although I was upset with myself for not taking precautions. That was stupid. Luckily it was my safe time of the month."

Safe time of the month. Josh started to sweat.

"You aren't on the pill?"

"No."

He couldn't believe it. And had to stay calm.

"You sound pretty sure of your cycle," he said, thankful for the darkness that hid his panic.

"I am. Completely."

"Because you have to understand, I can't be a father." Blurting was so unlike him. And not calm at all. "There is absolutely no way…"

Grown adults couldn't depend on him. How could a

child? Slightly sick at the thought of such a horrendously cruel twist of fate, Josh shook his head. "You're sure?"

"Yes, Josh, I'm sure."

He'd irritated her. But he couldn't stop. "Why aren't you on the pill?" Who wasn't these days?

"No real reason to be, so why risk the side effects? STDs are more of a threat to me than pregnancy and, because of them, I wasn't willing to consider sex without a condom, anyway, so…"

She spoke with all of the calm he so desperately wanted.

"I'm assuming you've always taken precautions in the past?"

"I've never had unprotected sex. And I have regular checkups, too," she added. "*I've* never had an STD."

"You emphasized the 'I.'"

"My little sister had one once. She was sixteen, and while she was lucky and it was easily treatable, it broke my mom's heart. And scared the hell out of all of us. Which is why I wouldn't consider sex without a condom. I can't believe I took such a risk. It's not like me."

"Why did you?"

"Because I underestimated the power of physical attraction," she said. "I've never come close to…" She glanced down. "I had no idea I could lose my head like that. In the past, there was no problem remembering to use protection."

His palms getting moist as he thought of her "losing her head," Josh took a sip of wine. Even with the pill scare, he wanted her.

"You threw caution to the wind," he summed up.

"Yeah, I guess I did."

"A first for you."

"But not for you, I take it."

"As a matter of fact, sexually, it was. But I've done stupid things before. A lot of them." His voice dropped. "I'm still paying for some of the things I've done." He drew from the speech he'd rehearsed, and dismissed, more than once over the weekend. "Until I've paid my debt, and I'm not talking financially, until I find some way to atone for my past actions, I can't be relied on for anything."

Not as a lover, a friend...or a father.

"That's ludicrous."

Whatever reaction he'd been expecting from her, it wasn't that.

"I'm being honest, Dana. This isn't a conversation, it's a warning. We can be friends as long as you don't expect anything from me."

"Your awareness of your shortcomings is more than most people bring to a relationship."

This wasn't working. "If you can't accept that there can be no expectations between us, we can't be friends." There, he couldn't put it any plainer than that.

"What are you so worried about? The fact that I might ask you to do something you won't want to do, or the idea that I might think there's something between us, thus preventing you from exploring other avenues?"

"What in the hell are you talking about?"

Dana took a sip of wine and looked toward the puppies, but they weren't doing anything but lying there, lit only by the small security light in the back of the yard and the glow from the kitchen.

"Let me ask you this, Josh. Do you want to be able to uphold any expectations I might have of you?"

"Of course. But wanting and doing are not the same thing."

"Do you intend to do as you said you would and come over on Tuesday night to help me out with Jerome?"

"I said I would."

"And you always do as you say you're going to do."

"Pretty much."

"That's the definition of reliable," she said, sounding satisfied.

She just wasn't getting it. He finished his wine and stood up.

"I'm a selfish bastard, Dana. Just take my word for it." Picking up L.G. in one hand, he scooped up her little ball of warmth in the other and handed the puppy to her. "For his sake—" he held out the dog in his care "—I'd appreciate it very much if you'd still come check on him throughout the week whenever you can make it. I'll be here Tuesday after work."

And without daring to look back at her, to plant whatever expression she might be wearing in his mind, he left.

LILLIE CALLED JUST after Josh left on Sunday night, preventing Dana from giving in to the need to have a good cry.

"We've decided on a name and thought you'd like to know," the child life specialist said, sounding almost like a kid herself. "We're calling him Harrison, after you."

"Don't you think that's kind of hard for Abe to say?"

"Hold on a second."

Dana held on, happier than Lillie or Jon would know that they considered her enough of a friend to even call and tell her the puppy's name, let alone name it after her.

She heard rustling of the phone and then, in the distance, Jon's voice saying, "Who is this, Abe?"

"Harrryyy," Abe said in his childish slur, and Dana grinned from ear to ear.

She'd helped build another family unit. And had a new member of her own family, as well.

Life was good.

Damned good.

JOSH COULD BE FORGIVEN for looking forward to dinner at Dana's Tuesday night. Especially with her scent lingering in his house when he'd gone home for lunch, reminding him of…her.

Olivia, Ian's wife's friend, had phoned Monday night, inviting him to join a group at the country club for drinks, but he'd declined.

He didn't want Olivia getting any ideas about him. Nor did he really want to run with the country club crowd. It would be too much like his old life. And he would risk running into someone who knew him—and also knew Cassie and Sam. Someone who might try to introduce them.

He left work on time on Tuesday and made it to Dana's place before the kid who had the hots for her.

Dana was being modest about it. But Josh knew better. If the kid was male and had spent any time at all alone with Dana, he'd have the hots for her.

Which was why Josh stayed right by Dana's side, acting like a devoted boyfriend, the entire ten minutes Jerome was in the house.

"That's it, then," Josh said, scooping L.G. up under his arm the second the younger man left. "I'll get out of your way."

The house was too small, too intimate, for just the two of them. "I thought you were staying for dinner," Dana said from the kitchen. "At least take a container to go."

He was selfish enough to accept the gift. Then he got the hell out of there.

If he'd stayed, he'd risk giving her the wrong idea. Telling her she couldn't rely on him and then hanging out and letting her get more attached was making lies out of his words.

If there was one clear thing he'd learned from his relationship with Michelle it was that actions spoke louder than words. He'd never told her he was in love with her. But he'd bought her a ring and planned a lifetime with her. His actions had told her she could count on him.

Dana was far too important to him to risk leaving any false impressions.

It worked! Jerome asked about you in class this morning. And he's bringing a girl from the computer club to Thanksgiving dinner! Thank you.

The text arrived while Josh was sitting in the campus pub with Ian Wednesday night.

Glad I could help. No need for thanks.

"Olivia's called the house three times in the past week," Ian was saying, working his way slowly through a second mug of beer. "She wants to know what you thought of her."

"She's nice." Josh dropped his phone back into its case. He'd been home, heated up the last of the frozen barbecue and spent half an hour with L.G. before heading out again.

Too much silence wasn't good for a guy who wasn't used to any silence at all.

"She seems to have it bad for you, man," Ian continued. "I think you can pretty much call the shots on that one."

Josh shrugged. "I'm not really looking…."

The other man nodded. "You want me to blow her off for you?"

"Wouldn't be a bad thing if you could steer her in another direction. It's nothing against her…"

"Gotcha."

"And tell Amy—"

"Not to find anyone else for now."

Looking into his beer, Josh grimaced and glanced up. "Sorry to be such an ass."

"No, man, actually, it's cool. Much better to let her know up front so no one gets hurt."

Josh sipped his beer. "But if your wife doesn't mind a third wheel, I'd love to treat the two of you to dinner in Phoenix," he said. He was making a life here. He had to have friends.

"Hell, I'm never one to pass up a free meal. But only if you come for dinner Saturday night," Ian said. "Amy's making lasagna and wanted me to ask you."

Josh raised an eyebrow, and Ian quickly added, "Olivia has not been invited, and now won't be."

"You might want to check with your wife to make certain the invitation's still open," Josh said.

"No need." Ian grinned. "You were a hit with my wife, man. She really liked you, and not just as someone for me to hang out with."

"She's looking for someone for you to hang out with?"

"Nah, just likes to know that when she's working late, I'm not out gallivanting with a clod who doesn't know how to behave himself."

"What time's dinner?" Josh asked, motioning for one more beer.

"Depends on whether or not we play golf first."

Loosening his tie just enough to get the knot off his Adam's apple, he grinned. "What time's golf?"

"I can put us in for eleven if you want to go eighteen."

L.G. would be alone for five hours.

"You got a fenced backyard?"

"Doesn't everybody around here? Got to keep the coyotes out."

"Would Amy mind if I bring my dog to dinner? I can go eighteen if L.G. can come to dinner."

"Amy loves animals. She's been bugging me for a pup."

With a chuckle, Josh said, "*You* mind if I bring my dog?"

"Bring him on. I know when I'm facing a losing battle and I've learned not to fight them."

"And I know someone who can find you a puppy whenever you're ready."

"Better give him a call. I have a feeling I'm going to be ready any time now…." Ian broke off as the door opened and a guy wearing a pair of expensive-looking jeans and a tweed jacket walked in. At first glance, with the clothes and longish, disheveled hair, Josh thought he was a student. One of the many well-to-do kids that populated Montford's campus.

"Sam!" Ian called out. Josh could see some signs of aging on the man's features as he turned toward them. He was definitely not a kid.

He didn't put the pieces together, though, didn't realize the situation he was in, until Ian said, "You have to meet Sam Montford. He's one of the school's biggest supporters."

Shit. He'd known that the Montford family was one of the university's largest contributors, that there might be a time when, at a fund-raising black-tie affair, he'd have to arrange with Cassie to keep his distance from her and her husband.

"What's Sam Montford doing in here?" he said under his breath to Ian as Ian motioned for another beer. And how the hell did a regular guy like Ian know him well enough to call him over to their table?

"Sam's a great guy," Ian said. "Not the country club type."

Holding his hand out to Ian, Sam Montford stopped at their table. And Josh stared. If he didn't know better he'd swear that his Grandfather Montford had just emerged from a fountain of youth.

Josh took after his father's side of the family in looks, but the fact that he didn't look like a Montford wasn't going to protect his identity from this one.

Setting his jaw and flashing one of his infamous Redmond grins, he wasn't ready at all as Ian turned to him.

"Josh, this is Sam Montford. Sam, meet our new miracle worker, Josh Redmond. He's only in his second week and already freed up enough monies to…" Josh didn't hear the rest.

He was face-to-face with a blood relative he'd never met and wasn't going to acknowledge. Nothing in the social rule book to guide him on this one.

Sam was grinning at him and could blow his cover at any moment. If he'd had any idea at all that Montford ever set foot in the college pub, he'd have declined the invitation to be there. And to think that his concern about running into the Montfords at the country club had been unfounded.

After hesitating a long moment, Sam held out his hand. "Nice to meet you, Josh."

"You, too." *Shit. He should have tacked on a "sir."* He should have stood up. Showed the deference he was used to receiving.

The waitress delivered their round of beers and Sam Montford slid onto the third of the four stools at their high-top table, staring at Josh.

"So, you're the new miracle worker," Sam said, still grinning.

The man was his cousin, albeit a couple of generations removed. Still, he was his flesh and blood—and heir to the other half of the Montford dynasty. For so long, Josh had carried that responsibility alone. And, according to Cassie Montford, some guy named Ben Sanders fit in there someplace, too. He obviously hadn't been on his mother's genealogy report. She'd told him the only cousins were Sam and him.

"Not miracles, no, *sir,*" Josh said. "But I'm good at what I do and I'll do it well."

A picture of Michelle, drool at the corner of her mouth, played across his mind's eye.

"I find my way into every bar we've got in this town at some time or another," Sam announced. "This is the first I've seen you."

Sam was telling him he'd been looking. Josh got the message. And waited to see if Sam was going to keep the word he'd given Cassie.

"Don't let him kid you," Ian said, apparently unaware of what, to Josh, seemed like a hell of a lot of tension. "Sam's not a drinker. He's too busy being a daddy to do much drinking. He comes in here to check on that daughter of his."

Sam had a daughter in college?

He had more family here than he'd thought. College-age kids…

Sam and Cassie, picturing them with kids, made them so much more real.

And harder for him to resist.

When he noticed the narrow-eyed gaze Sam was giving him, Josh said, "Your daughter giving you problems, sir?"

"She's a perfect kid, getting perfect grades, and I'm going to make damned sure no one breaks her heart, is all," Sam said, the grin gone from his face. Josh pitied any man who messed with his cousin's daughter.

"Mariah's a freshman this fall. She's dating a freshman from California and Sam's not taking it well."

"You two seem to know each other well," Josh said. Leave it to him to gravitate to the one guy at work who was in with Sam Montford.

He just wasn't going to catch a break—had obviously used up his allotment in his past life.

"I was born and raised in this town," Ian said with a grin as Sam took a swig of beer. "You grow up here, you know pretty much everything about everyone else who grew up here," Ian finished, losing the grin on his face as he looked from Josh to Sam.

Time to go. Back to his rented house. If Sam blew his cover…farther than that.

"He's right about everyone knowing everything," Sam said.

A warning to Josh?

"Which is why I left town when I wasn't much older than Mariah," Sam continued. "Thankfully my daughter's a lot smarter than her old man."

"She takes after your wife, then?" Josh couldn't resist the jibe.

"Of course." Sam's expression took on a look Josh didn't recognize. "But she's not our biological child," he said. "Mariah's American-Indian. Her parents were two of my best friends in the world. They were killed in a terrorist attack in 2001. Mariah saw the whole thing. She was catatonic for months. It was Cassie, and her pet therapy, that saved that little girl's life."

"Cassie's his wife," Ian said. "And they have a son, too. Brian. He's eleven and takes after Cassie for sure."

Sam took a swig of beer at that and turned his grin on Ian. "Careful my man, I know your daddy and he's pretty proud of you at the moment. I'd sure hate to see that change."

The threat was nonsense, but Josh figured that Ian had just been told to keep his mouth shut.

Fair enough.

Sam was keeping Josh's secret, respecting his choice to

remain anonymous to the Montfords; it was only fair that the Montfords not be known to him.

But when he lay in bed alone that night, Josh wondered again if he was being a fool to think he could change who he was. Or could ever be anything but what he'd been born to be.

An image of Michelle confined to her bed flashed in front of his closed lids.

She was never going to be the same again.

And neither was he.

CHAPTER NINETEEN

ON THURSDAY, DONE at the university for the day, Dana stopped in at home after her one o'clock class before heading over to Josh's house. She'd made cabbage rolls the night before and had frozen a couple of containers. She grabbed them both. And Lindy Lu, too. The two puppies were good company for each other.

While she was at Josh's house, she pulled out her phone.

I'm an adult. It's up to me to decide whether or not I need more than I am getting.

Agreed.

Less than two minutes had passed.
Encouraged by his rapid response she thumb typed:

You've been honest with me. I accept you as you are.

Okay.

An instant response.
She wasn't reading him wrong. Josh cared. He just had issues to work through.
And if she could help him, then she wanted to do so. Just like she helped Jerome. And Sharon. And Lori.
And all of the dogs who needed homes.

Josh might have missed the dinner waiting for him in the freezer that night if not for the written heating instructions left on his counter.

While it was heating up in the microwave, he tossed a treat to L.G. and pulled out his phone.

You need to stop doing so much for everyone else. They'll take advantage, he typed. Feeling as if he was doing her a favor, Josh hit Send.

If I don't care if they take advantage, why should you?

Because he was trying to save her from him. Didn't she get that?

The microwave beeped and, fork in one hand and phone in the other, Josh took his first bite while the container was still in the microwave.

Mmm. Cabbage rolls. Thank you.

You're welcome. And I like helping people. If they take advantage, it's on their conscience.

Exactly. And he wanted it the hell off.

Saturday made it one week and two days since she'd had sex with Josh Redmond. Dana wasn't worried about STDs. But she *was* worried.

She was probably just feeling guilty for throwing caution to the wind, was making an issue where there wasn't one. Her cycle was regular. It always had been. And her small window of opportunity that month hadn't been the previous week. But just to be sure, she picked up a home-pregnancy test first thing that morning—the brand that claimed it could detect pregnancy as early as one week after

unprotected sex. At home in her bathroom, she looked between Kari and Lindy Lu, two little faces staring up at her
as though waiting to see what would happen next.

"Taking action is the only way to stop the worry," she
explained. Kari took a paw swat at Lindy Lu's nose. The
puppy blinked, lay down and looked up at Dana again.

She followed the directions on the box and sat down
to wait.

Jumping onto the counter, Kari went for the little stick
and Dana rescued it just in time. The kitten batted the
folded paper directions instead, and Dana grabbed those,
too.

Kari sent the box flying to the floor. It landed a foot
from the puppy, who stood to investigate. She smelled it.
Pawed at it. And then, picking it up in her teeth, dragged
the thing that was as long as she was to the corner of the
room where she plopped down to chew on it.

"You really shouldn't be doing that," Dana admonished,
to which Lindy paid no attention at all.

Glancing in the mirror across from her, Dana saw the
skinny woman sitting there in jeans and a short-sleeved
navy pullover. She looked so ordinary. Plain and whole-
some. Not at all like someone who'd be taking a home-
pregnancy test.

Dana glanced at her watch. "Another minute and then
we can get on with our day," she said. "I'm sure it's going
to be negative." She took a deep breath. Watched the kitten bat at a drip from the bathroom sink. "Which doesn't
really let us off the hook."

She had to be honest with them. "It's really early so
chances are, even if I am pregnant, I'll get a false negative. Gestation can take up to five days and then you need
another few days for the hormones to get flowing, and it's
the hormones that register a positive on that stick."

Kari licked her newly moist paw. Lindy stood and tried to shake the box, which whopped her upside the head instead.

"Yeah, you're right. Worrying is silly. It wasn't my fertile time."

The kitty landed in her lap, her wet paw leaving a mark on the bottom of Dana's shirt.

Five...four...three...two...one.

Time to look. She waited a little longer. Just to be sure she'd waited long enough.

Setting the stick on the counter without looking at the results, she scooped up Kari in one hand and Lindy Lu in the other. "Ready?" she asked, looking from one to the other.

Kari batted at Lindy's nose again. The puppy scrambled to get down. "Shhh. Both of you. It's fine," she told them, raising them to either side of her face. "We just have to stay calm, okay? You guys can do that for me. I know you can."

She kissed each of them, put Kari down and cuddled Lindy Lu between her jaw and her shoulder as she looked at the stick.

Okay.

Not what she'd hoped.

Like she'd told her housemates, all they had to do was remain calm.

JOSH WAS BARELY out of the sack Saturday morning when he heard pounding on the door.

In boxer briefs and a T-shirt, he stumbled out to the kitchen, leaving a howling L.G. locked in his kennel on the unmade bed. He looked through the peephole and saw nothing.

The pounding came again. On the sliding-glass door off the kitchen. He'd overheard someone mention that there'd been a string of break-ins the previous month in Shelter Valley by a burglar who always entered the premises through sliding-glass doors.

They caught that guy, though. A student who'd since been expelled and was now in jail awaiting trial.

Peeking around the edge of the full-door blind he pulled closed each night after putting L.G. out one last time, Josh saw a black-suited guy with a black ski hat standing in bright sunlight on his back porch, holding two travel coffee mugs.

The getup did nothing to disguise the man. Josh figured he wasn't going anywhere, either, and took his time grabbing a pair of pants from the hanging rack in the laundry room, pulling them on and fastening them before opening the door.

"Hold on," he said, and, closing the door so as not to invite the intruder into his actual home, he sauntered back to the master bedroom, grabbed a rambunctious L.G. out of his kennel and made a run for the door.

He was not about to face his long-lost cousin with dog piss running down his pants.

The puppy made it to the patio. And, seeing Sam, ran up to greet him, peeing on his shoe in the process.

Josh figured he couldn't have planned that one better. The man was trespassing, not just on his property, but on his life. Grabbing a couple of paper towels from inside, wetting one, he held them out.

"I'm not changing my mind," he said, guy to guy.

"No one's asking you to." Sam handed him one of the mugs in exchange for the paper towels and wiped his shoe.

Josh took a sip.

Not as good as his favorite brew back home, but better than a lot of stuff he'd had in expensive coffee shops all over the globe.

L.G. took a dump in the yard.

"What's with the garb?"

"I rode my bike," Sam said, no longer grinning, but looking too damned friendly for Josh's taste. "It's cold."

"For wimps, maybe. This is spring weather in Boston." What in the hell was the matter with him? He might be lacking in a lot of areas but basic manners wasn't one of them.

Cocking his head to the side, Sam perused him. "You ever ride a Harley?"

"Standing up." Not one of his brighter stunts.

The older man was grinning again, just like he had that night in the bar. "You wreck it?"

Shrugging, Josh took another sip. "I lived."

"How about the bike?"

"It lived, too." But he'd sold the powerful fifty-thousand-dollar custom toy for pennies on the dollar because it had had a scratch on it.

"When I first left Shelter Valley, before I joined the peace corps, I bought a custom-made parasail and jumped off a mountain."

"I see that you lived."

"Yeah, the parasail didn't."

When he caught back his own grin, just in time, Josh scoffed, "What's with the ski cap?"

Sam pulled it off, letting the long locks of his hair float down to his shoulders. "Can't stand to have strands of hair poking around under the helmet."

"I didn't hear a bike."

"You don't look like you'd have heard much of anything." With his head slightly cocked and his gaze narrowed, Sam Montford was making Josh uncomfortable.

"I treated myself to nearly a fifth of aged Royal Salute last night." He'd brought the expensive Scotch whiskey with him, in case of emergency.

"How was it?"

"Same as always." He should have been the one with a low tolerance for alcohol, not Michelle.

"How's the house look?"

"Like the housekeeper has already been here this morning."

Sam kept watching him. And grinning. "I parked the bike a few blocks over—at my son's karate school. People around here know me. And know my bike. I didn't figure you'd want them knowing I was here. The boy's going to be expecting me back soon."

"Does he know where you are?"

"No one does. I merely went for a walk in the desert."

Sam was honoring his request for anonymity. As hard as he was trying, Josh was having a hard time finding anything about the guy to not like.

And he couldn't afford to like him. He couldn't trust himself to stay true to his cause with the temptation of the life he'd always known so close.

"You jumped the wall," Josh said, making the words sound like an accusation.

"Your mother thinks you're celebrating Thanksgiving with us."

"Not from me, she doesn't." And she wasn't supposed to be in touch with the Montfords, either.

"I think she just assumed. At least that's how it seemed in her response to Cassie's email. The one you asked her to send."

"She's wrong."

Nodding, Sam said easily, "We'd like you to be there."

"I have plans."

Chin to his chest, Sam hid whatever he was thinking. And then said, with all seriousness, "I respect what you're trying to do."

"Thank you."

"I'd like to know why you're doing it."

"Ask my mother."

"I'm asking you."

Josh hesitated, looking the older man in the eye.

"I almost killed a girl." It was no secret back home.

"Knowingly?"

"No."

"How long are you planning to be AWOL?"

"I can't answer that."

"Can't, or won't?"

"Can't."

Nodding, Sam sipped some coffee, looked at his watch and put his mug down on the ground next to a porch support. "I just bought the mugs," he said. "They're yours."

He could use them.

Turning, Sam headed toward the back wall, stopping to pet L.G. in the process. Josh followed him.

"Thank you."

When Sam stopped, he wished he'd kept his distance. The emotion searing from the other man's eyes was painful to see.

"I killed my first-born," he said. "Not on purpose, of course. I didn't know Cassie was pregnant." He paused for a few seconds. "Your acumen is already obvious in the work you're doing at Montford. You're a natural at it. I wasn't. I hated business. This town. And everything associated with both. My family expected me to go to law school. Cassie, too. I skipped town instead. Was unfaithful to my wife, and joined the corps. My desertion practically killed Cassie. The baby neither of us knew she was carrying at the time was born five months later. She only lived a month."

Josh stared. Didn't know what to say. If he'd had the whiskey handy he'd have offered the bottle to his cousin.

"It took me sixteen years to find my way back," Sam said, apparently not needing Josh to say anything. "If you need to talk, find me."

Before Josh could respond, the man had gone over the six-foot-high wall and disappeared from sight.

CHAPTER TWENTY

FUNNY HOW LIFE COULD "crash on a dime," as Daniel put it, and still just keep on going like nothing had changed. Dana had a call on Saturday from a new rescue dog placement—they needed a dog-sitter for the following week and didn't know who to call. She immediately thought of Lori.

Lillie called and asked if she and Lindy Lu wanted to join them that night for a barbecue. Harrison could visit with his sister and Dana could meet their friends, Mark and Addy, and Mark's eighty-one-year-old grandmother, Nonnie. She wanted to decline. To hide.

But she knew better. She was staying calm. Putting one foot in front of the other.

And the first step she had to take was to get ahold of Josh. She was her mother's daughter, but she would not make the same mistakes.

No matter what the cost. Because she knew that the price of secrets was far more costly than she was willing to pay.

She drove by his house several times on Saturday, in between buying groceries, stopping in at the vet clinic, dropping by the home of a new Love To Go Around pet owner and spending an hour at Sharon's house with her biology study group. Josh wasn't home any of the times. But L.G. was. She could hear him howling. So she went in and let him out.

"I have to talk to your dad," she told the puppy. But she couldn't tell him why. She hadn't even told Lindy or Kari yet. Life was going on as normal. It was the only way she could manage. "But I can't call him. I can't do this over the phone."

It would be cruel to give devastating news over the telephone.

THE FIRST THING Josh noticed when he walked in after golf was that the empty containers he'd left on the counter were gone.

Dana had been there.

L.G. played him, though, acting as if he'd been alone for days when Josh let him out of his kennel. The goofball didn't know he should have peed the second he hit the ground if he'd had any hope of Josh falling for the charade.

"You had company," he said instead as he made his way to the master bathroom to shower off, L.G. following at his heels. He wasn't jealous of the dog. Not exactly. "What did she have to say?" he asked.

The puppy grabbed his shoe and carried it into the bathroom as Josh stripped, lying with it on the floor outside the shower.

A habit borne from Josh carrying the shoe in every morning, and locking the dog in the bathroom with him so he didn't have to worry about the rest of the house while he showered.

"Was she having a busy day?" he asked, stepping under the warm spray.

It didn't occur to him to wonder why she'd been there at all, until he was out of the shower and getting dressed for his dinner date with Ian and Amy.

Once he was all ready, he attached his phone holster to his belt—but held on to the phone.

You were here.

Not sure he'd get a response right away, he waited, anyway.

Yeah. I stopped by and knocked. You weren't there, but L.G. was howling so I let him out. I didn't figure you'd mind.

'Course not. Glad he had company. You need something?

She could have just been stopping by to say hello. It was the first time he could remember wishing he'd been with a woman rather than on a golf course.

I haven't seen you in a few days. You going to be around tonight?

The answer was no. "No." He told himself out loud. Shook his head. And typed, Later. L.G. and I are having dinner with a couple who might be needing a puppy.

What time later?

He hadn't asked her for anything. Hadn't contacted her at all. She'd come to him. Which meant that he was supposed to do this. Right? For her.

Nine.

Dinner was at six. He could easily be home by then. And he could talk to her about finding a puppy for Amy. Or about anything else she wanted to talk about. She wanted to see him, and his new life was about doing things for other people rather than for himself.

My place or yours?

She was being kind of pushy. Josh grinned.

You pick.

I'll come there.

Far more pleased than he should have been, Josh picked up his pup and headed out to the SUV, eager to eat and get back home again.

DANA LIKED MARK and Addy on sight. Almost as much as she liked Lillie and Jon and Abraham. But her favorite that Saturday night was Nonnie. The tiny, wheelchair-bound woman had claimed Dana as her date, and within thirty seconds of her arrival, Dana felt like one of the family.

Lindy and Harrison rolled around and pounced and slept happily in Lillie's gated-off kitchen. Abraham charmed everyone.

The evening would have been nearly perfect—if she'd been able to stop staring at Abraham and wondering what it would be like to have a two-year-old of her own. And still be in school. Panic was new to her and she didn't wear it well.

"What's eatin' ya?" Nonnie leaned over to ask while the two couples conferred over the grill in the backyard, trying to determine if the steaks were done to perfection, or merely done.

"I'm fine, why?"

"You ain't fine, but I know to mind my own business. You come find me when you're ready to talk."

Dana didn't even know the woman but heard herself promising that she'd do just that. And then pulled out her smartphone to add Nonnie's address and cell phone number to her contact list.

She watched the clock all through dinner, in between watching Abraham. Mark and Jon kept up a running repartee, but Dana couldn't get her mind to focus on their humorous attempts to one-up each other.

Lillie sidled up to her as Dana helped her carry the dishes into the kitchen after everyone had finished eating. "You okay?" the other woman asked.

"Of course. I'm fine." She was fine. Healthy. Able. Lucky, really.

"You seem off."

"I just…" She wanted to talk to Lillie in the worst way. But her problems weren't just her own. "I…slept with… someone…and I wish I hadn't." Not quite the truth, either, and yet, in tonight's context it was.

"You're allowed to make mistakes, you know," Lillie said softly, her gaze compassionate.

No, she wasn't. She had to be perfect in every way.

Abraham started to fuss and Lillie turned her head sharply in the little boy's direction, as Dana reflected on the thought that had just popped into her mind.

She had to be perfect….

"He's tired," Lillie said as Abraham came toward them rubbing his eyes. Setting down the dishes in her hands to reach for the little boy, Lillie continued, "You have my cell number. Call me tomorrow."

Nodding, Dana busied herself with washing the dishes while she reeled in her thoughts. She didn't have to be perfect anymore. She wasn't back in Indiana, in a family where she didn't fit. In Shelter Valley her existence wasn't a mistake.

By eight-thirty, when she couldn't sit still any longer, Dana excused herself.

"We're teaching Addy and Lillie how to play five-card

stud," Jon said to her. "I remember hearing you were pretty good at it."

She'd mentioned the game in math class one day, in response to a question the professor had asked. It had had to do with a calculus problem.

"I wouldn't want your wives to see me whup the two of you," she said with a grin, tucking Lindy Lu under her arm. Truth was, she'd be the loser at any game she attempted to play right then.

She'd been struck with a complete inability to concentrate—an inability that was increasing with every minute that passed.

If she wasn't careful she was going to burst into tears.

Calm. She just had to stay calm.

To put one foot in front of the other.

She knew two things for sure. She was going to get through this.

And tears wouldn't change anything.

SHE'D BEEN THERE fifteen minutes and Josh wasn't nearly as happy as he had been when he'd opened the door to her.

Something was different about her.

He'd told Dana about Ian and Amy, about the dinner he'd had at his work associate's home and asked her if she'd be willing to find a rescue dog for them.

"Are they particular about whether or not it's a puppy?"

"They were, but I took L.G. over with me and told them about the work you do, the Love To Go Around thing, and they said they're willing to take either an abandoned pup, like him, or any other dog that needs a home."

"Do they have children?"

"No, does it matter?"

She shrugged but didn't look at him. Didn't smile. "Some breeds are better with children than others. And some rescue dogs are timid and afraid around children. What size is their backyard?"

"Same as mine. And it has a block fence, as well."

"Have they ever had a dog before?"

"Ian has. I'm not sure about Amy."

"I'm sure I can find something for them," she said, heading out in the yard to scoop up that ridiculously small ball of fur she called a dog. "How soon do they want it?"

"They're ready now."

"I've got a fifteen-pound, short-haired mix that's about a year old in foster care. If you give me their contact information, I'll see what I can do."

Pulling out his phone, Josh texted her his contact listing for Ian as they headed back inside. She'd said she wanted to see him, but she sure wasn't acting like it.

"You mad at me?"

"Absolutely not." She walked in ahead of him and didn't turn around as she responded. "You want to go for a walk?"

"With the dogs?"

"I thought maybe we could leave them here." She'd brought a little kennel in with her.

Josh was happy to do anything she wanted to do. He was just glad to see her. But, stopping in front of her, he bent until she was looking him in the eye. "You sure you aren't mad at me?"

"What do I have to be mad at you about?"

He searched her wide-open gaze and couldn't find any subterfuge there. "I don't know," he said. But he wouldn't be surprised to find he'd pissed her off. "Maybe I should have done something I didn't do."

"I'm not mad at you, Josh," she said, her tone softening to one he was more familiar with.

"Let's go for a walk, then."

Taking a second to change into tennis shoes, Josh set off

with her. And realized he couldn't remember a single time in his entire life when he'd walked just to walk.

Hunched against the chill, Dana half buried her face in the thick black cardigan sweater she was wearing over her jeans and shoved her hands in her pockets.

"I stopped by today because I wanted to talk to you about something."

"Shoot," he said.

"Many years ago my mother slept with a guy she'd just met. Her mother had just died and she felt all alone in the world. She was in a bar, drinking—my mother never drank—and she told the guy all about her dad being killed in the army when she was a kid. He'd been empathetic and supportive, encouraging her to lean on him for as long as she needed. She ended up spending the night with him, but when she woke up the next morning, he was gone. He'd left no phone number or address, and when she looked him up, there was no listing for him. She figured that he'd lied about his name, that he was married or something. She met Daniel the next day through a mutual friend and they hit it off immediately."

He'd been perfectly warm earlier in the pullover sweater he'd worn in Ian's backyard. Suddenly, he was chilled. Dana was going to tell him she'd made a mistake in having slept with him. She'd met someone else. Someone she'd hit it off with immediately.

She stepped up their pace. He was fine with that.

The night air was nice. Walking just for the sake of walking was nice. He was going to do it more.

They turned a corner onto a street that was wider than his, with yards that were larger than his, homes with more square footage than his had, and no sidewalks. Dana started down the side of the street, walking close to the gutter.

"Within three months of meeting, Mom and Daniel were

running off to Las Vegas to get married. He had no immediate family, either, at least not that he was close to, and
they were eager to move into the same home and start a
life together."

Made sense to him.

And then he remembered what she'd said about Daniel
being her stepfather. And his name on her birth certificate.

Obviously Dana's father was the lowlife who had sex
with a grieving drunk woman and then ran off.

Daniel was one hell of a stand-up guy to have married
a woman pregnant with another man's child. He could see
why Dana felt beholden to the guy. But her conception
hadn't been her choice. Or her fault, either. She had to see
that.

"My mother knew she was pregnant when she married
Daniel, but she didn't tell him."

Whoa. "Did she think the baby was his?"

It was dark out. There were very few streetlights on
the road they'd taken. But he could still see the shake of
Dana's head. "She knew she was pregnant before she slept
with Daniel."

"That's rough."

"She didn't tell him after I was born, either," Dana continued, marching forward with her hands shoved in her
pockets, her head bent against the cold. "He thought I was
his."

"When did he find out?"

He was assuming the other man knew, since Dana did.
Maybe that was the problem. Maybe Daniel had just found
out...

"The same time I did." Dana put an end to his theory before it was even fully formulated. "I was thirteen. We were
on a father-daughter field trip with school. We'd gone to a

forensic museum and were the first ones to raise our hands
when they asked for volunteers for a DNA demonstration."

Holy hell. He knew what was coming and couldn't imagine.

"While forensic DNA tests take a long time because
of all of the steps involved, the test to actually compare
one sample to another only takes about thirty-five minutes
to run. That's a total of an hour and ten minutes for two
samples. They sent us off to lunch and told us that when
we came back after lunch they'd show us how our DNA
is connected."

They were up to a brisk walk. Josh put his arm around
Dana. She didn't settle into him as Michelle would have
done. But she didn't shrug him off, either.

"Instead, they came into the lunch room and found us.
They took Daniel aside and talked to him while I waited
with another technician in the lab. He was my best friend
in the world when he walked off. And a stranger when he
came back."

"He did not put that on you."

"No. He was kind. Just in shock."

"So who told you what they'd found?"

"My mom. Later that night. We finished the field trip.
The technician told everyone that the sample had been destroyed in the testing and they used that as an example
of how sensitive the tests can be and how expensive, and
moved us quickly on to the next exhibit. I couldn't tell you
what it was. I don't remember much else about the day except Daniel acting so weird. I couldn't figure out why he
was so upset that they'd destroyed our test."

"I respect the fact that he waited to talk to your mother
before saying anything to you."

"He's a good man," Dana said without any of the obvious affection he'd heard in her tone when she'd been telling the first part of the story. "And I love my mother, too," she said. "She made a mistake. And she's spent the rest of her life paying for it."

"Did Daniel divorce her? They'd have had your two sisters by then, right?"

"Yeah, and no, they didn't divorce. They love each other. But that day changed our lives completely. My sisters changed as soon as they found out. I'd always been the oldest, of course, but also the boss of them. They no longer listened to me like they used to. My mother's lie is there, like a member of the family. Daniel lost his ability to trust."

And maybe Dana had, too?

They turned another corner and were back on a sidewalk but the yards were still an acre or more in size, and the streetlights low. He pulled her a little closer so they could fit side by side on the poured cement.

"From that day forward, Daniel has been unsure if Mom married him because of me, because she was afraid to be a pregnant single woman, because she wanted a father for her child and a wedding ring for her finger when she gave birth or because she really fell in love with him like he'd fallen in love with her."

"I can understand that."

"I can, too. Completely. And ever since then, he's had this thing where he puts her in situations where she has to choose between him and me. She has to prove that she'd put him first. That he was the reason she married him, not me."

"You can't possibly ask a woman to choose between her child and her husband."

"Sure you can. It happens all the time. Especially in blended families. But it's not fair to anyone involved."

"You think they would have been better off if they'd divorced?"

"I can't make that call."

"You think you would have been better off?"

"I don't know that, either. I just know that my life changed that day. I wasn't really a Harris. And I didn't know what I was."

"Daniel loved you, though. That couldn't have changed."

"Yeah, I'm sure he did. But I was also a constant reminder of Mom's lie, of the fact that I was another man's child who'd been foisted on him without him having any say in the matter. And those feelings took precedence. He wasn't abusive, or neglectful, really. We just weren't close anymore. I'd ceased being his little girl. He made sure I was safe and had what I needed, but we never had another father-daughter date. And when he'd take time out to do something fun like play video games, it was always with my sisters, not with me. Same for attending school functions."

"And this is why your mother didn't stand up for you when he wanted to marry you off to his friend's son."

"Yep."

"And why you agreed."

"For her sake, yeah. Daniel used to go for a week or more without speaking to her when he was at his most insecure, when he'd put her in a situation where she had to make a choice and she'd choose me—like attending my high school graduation instead of this ceremony that happened to be on the same night when he was getting Richmond's business owner of the year award—and I'd see what that did to her."

"That's wrong."

She shrugged, but not enough to push his arm off her shoulders. Almost all of the houses they passed had lights shining through curtained windows. Josh had never spent a lot of time in middle-class neighborhoods, with real people who lived real lives.

He wondered how many of the people inside those homes lived happy lives. And how many struggled.

In the house up on the hill where he'd grown up, a hill populated by rolling estates and family mansions, love hadn't been a driving factor. Expectations. Appearances. Those had come first.

He'd fit in there. As long as he met his father's expectations, he could do whatever else he wanted. Wasn't required to be more than he was.

Would he trade it all for a year with a father like the young Daniel had been?

At the moment he thought so.

"But I also think I agreed to marry Keith to please Daniel. I guess maybe I hoped it would get me back into his good graces, that I'd be like the other two girls to him."

"It didn't happen."

"Nope. Nothing is going to change who I am. Or what I signify to him."

Josh chilled. Though she'd have no idea, her words hit a little too close to home. Was it true that nothing could change who she was? Or who he was?

Maybe the truth lay in her second statement. As far as Daniel was concerned, nothing was going to change what Dana signified to him.

He breathed a little easier.

"So you think that's when your mother applied for the scholarship on your behalf?"

"Yeah. When she saw that I was still getting hurt by Daniel's distance from me. And I also think that that's why she doesn't admit to having applied. Because then Daniel would know that she'd chosen to put an end to his ability to help his best friend out of a really tight spot, in order to tend to my future."

"So, she kept another secret from him to do with you. The secret of applying for the scholarship."

"That's what I believe. But I don't have any proof of that one."

She was quiet then, as though considering her theory. Enjoying their walk, enjoying the chance to be close to her without doing any more than keeping her warm, Josh was happy to continue for as long as she needed.

"I'm my mother's daughter, Josh, but I can't make her mistakes."

"If you're smart, you'll learn from them," he said, thinking as much of his own mistakes as her mother's.

"I'm pregnant, Josh."

They were halfway up the street and took a couple of rapid steps. His arm fell away from her. He quit walking. She didn't.

CHAPTER TWENTY-ONE

DANA WAS A GOOD FIVE STEPS ahead of Josh before she realized she'd lost him. Stopping, she waited for him to catch up. And when he didn't, she turned around to see if he'd left her completely.

He was where he'd been when she'd dropped her bombshell.

"I'm sorry," she said, backtracking. "That just came out of the blue. I practiced a bunch of different speeches and didn't use any of them. There was just no easy way to tell you. No way to make the news good, or even okay."

He was looking at her mouth, as though trying to decipher her words. "I've had a few hours to process this whole thing," she said, understanding that he was probably feeling as if he'd dropped into a black hole.

At least, that was how she'd been feeling for most of the day.

Or maybe he was doubting her. Maybe he was thinking that what had happened a week ago Thursday had been by design. Her design. A classic case of plain girl trying to trap the handsomest guy in town in the most old-fashioned way. "I want you to know that I'm having this baby on my own, Josh," she said, the words forming as though they'd been there all day.

Maybe they had. Or maybe they were just becoming clear. But she felt real conviction behind them. Not only did Josh not want to be a father, he didn't think he *could* be one. He'd made his feelings very clear the night he'd practically suffocated when he'd found out that she wasn't on the pill. He'd also made it abundantly clear that she couldn't rely on him for anything.

He'd been honest.

And honesty was the one thing she valued more than anything else on earth.

"Even if you wanted to be involved, at this point, I won't allow it." She wasn't giving him a chance to let her or the baby down. "I just had to let you know. This is a small town and you're going to see me pregnant at some point and after seeing what my mother's lie has done to my family, how much pain she caused, I had to be up front with you."

"And you think everyone in town knowing I'm the father and seeing me have nothing to do with the child is going to make me happy?"

"I wasn't planning to tell anyone who the father is," she said. "I actually never once considered doing so. I just had to tell you."

They started slowly walking again. Side by side. Not touching. She kept her hands firmly in her pockets and her body a good foot away from his. "I guess, if—or I should say when—I meet someone I want to spend the rest of my life with, I will tell him, too. He'll need to know." She'd have to find someone willing to take on another man's child. But in today's world, that wasn't as much of a stigma as it had been in her mother's day.

She thought about the future. To a time when her child was old enough to ask questions. She'd be honest with him or her, too.

But she and Josh didn't need to deal with that right now. If she could find him, she'd consult with him about that when the time came.

"Fair enough."

For a second she thought she'd been thinking aloud. And then she realized he was replying to her comment about telling her future husband about him some day.

She walked to the end of the block. And when he remained completely silent, she turned the corner again, heading toward his place.

Back at his house, she greeted the puppies with the effusiveness they deserved. She took Lindy Lu out of her kennel, but picked up the kennel in her other hand and walked toward the front door.

"Aren't you going to put her out?"

"I need to get home," she said. "It's been a long day."

She'd been feeling as if she was on the verge of tears all day and had a feeling the flood was going to break through any minute.

She wanted to be alone when it did.

THE FIRST THING Josh did after Dana left was throw away the rest of the bottle of Scotch he'd mostly consumed the night before. He was not going to make it easy on himself to escape—not into a bottle and not anywhere else, either.

With L.G. on his arm, he dropped down to the couch, sitting in the near-dark.

The lasagna sat like lead in his stomach. He wanted to puke, but couldn't.

He wanted to be angry. But wasn't.

He waited until Dana had had enough time to get home and then he called her. When she didn't pick up, he called her again.

And kept calling until he finally heard a very subdued and slightly nasal, "Hello?"

"You know it's me."

"Yeah."

She was finally on the line and he had no idea what to say to her. "Thank you for telling me." That much was good. "You did the right thing."

"I know."

"You've been crying."

"It's been a rough day, Josh. It'll pass."

"You just found out today, then?" He hadn't asked. Not about how she'd found out. Or how she felt about it.

She'd been so sure it was her safe time of the month.

"Yeah, I've known since this morning. I took a home-pregnancy test."

Letting go of a very deep breath, Josh sat upright, knocking L.G. off his lap. The puppy landed on his butt, shook himself and lay down. "They're not all that accurate, are they?"

"They're usually only wrong when they're negative," she said. "At least that's what I understand from all the reading I've done. The positive result means I have an elevated amount of the pregnancy hormone in my body. That happens when a woman is pregnant. A negative could have meant that I was pregnant, but not far enough along to be excreting the hormone yet."

"How far along do you have to be?" It had only been nine days.

"A few days. Some women just take longer than others to gestate."

She knew her stuff. Deflated, he sat back. *Face it, Redmond. There's no easy-out this time.*

"I'm sorry." Dana's voice sounded stronger than it had when she answered the phone.

"This isn't your fault," he said. "At least, no more than it's mine. We did this together, Dana."

Another truism that he knew he had to live with. That he was determined to live with.

"We need to talk."

She'd been way ahead of him on that one. And had driven over to his place for that express purpose. After she'd told him, he hadn't said a word. But then, like she'd said, she'd had a head start on him.

"I don't know about you, but I'm pretty tired." Dana's answer came on a sigh. "Can we just let this go for tonight and look at it again in the morning?"

"Of course." Was his relief as palpable to her as it was to him?

"Okay, well, good night."

"Night."

Josh hung up, grateful for the reprieve.

DANA SAT STRAIGHT up in bed. Her text indicator had just beeped. Josh? Was he lying in the dark awake, too? Needing her as badly as she needed him?

Feeling as though the world was settling a bit, she grabbed her phone.

Marissa's sick. Drank too much. If I take her to the dorm she'll be in trouble. Can I bring her there?

Lori. Not Josh.

She glanced at the information bar at the bottom of her smartphone. It was midnight. The girls were just making curfew.

Of course.

Climbing out of bed and throwing on sweats, she smiled, grateful for the distraction. It was much better taking care of someone else than worrying about herself.

HE SLEPT THROUGH the night and woke up early, ready to face the day. Throwing off the covers, Josh was halfway to the bathroom before reality smacked him.

He was going to be a father.

He was overcome by a wave of panic so great it stopped him in his tracks. What he knew about babies, or children in general, would take up less than a paragraph.

Continuing on to the bathroom, he peed. Put L.G. out to pee.

He couldn't think of one time when he'd ever spent a significant amount of time with a child.

So he made a cup of coffee, grabbed one of the mugs Sam had left and filled it, carrying it back with him to the shower.

The couples he knew who had kids only included Josh in their plans when a babysitter was involved. No one associated him as a guy they'd want to bring their kids around.

Or a guy who'd want kids around.

And they'd been right.

LORI AND MARISSA were still asleep when Dana got out of her shower. She jotted down a short note inviting them to stay as long as they liked, to help themselves to food and to lock up when they left, and left the duplex with Lindy Lu under her arm Sunday morning. She wanted to call Lillie, but she couldn't bring herself to do it.

She decided, instead, to take a drive to the mountains not far out of town. But after an hour of feeling sorry for herself, she drove back to Shelter Valley determined to find a way to be happy about the prospect of being a single mom.

Lindy Lu bore the ordeal with unusual equanimity, mixed in with some chewing on Dana's fingers with very sharp puppy teeth. Dana rewarded her with a stop at the big-box store for a bag of puppy-size chew toys. And left her in her kennel in the car as she made her next stop.

A mission for Love To Go Around.

She'd met Skyline, the fifteen-pound short-haired mix rescue pup, twice before and her foster family was sorry to see her go. They'd have kept her but they were only in Shelter Valley from October until April each year and couldn't take her with them.

And Dana knew it was important to get the dog in a permanent home. Skyline had had enough turmoil in her young life.

Thanks to Josh, Dana had a potential family for her.

As soon as Amy answered the door, Dana knew Skyline had found her forever home.

"Oh, look at you!" the woman said, making eye contact, not with Dana, but with the dog in Dana's arms. "Can I hold her?"

"Of course." Dana turned the one-year-old female over to her new owner. "Her name's Skyline. She's been spayed," she said. "She doesn't tolerate a leash. Or a collar, either, but I suspect that if you work with her with nonchoke collars, you'll be able to overcome that. She's had all of her shots and just passed her one-year checkup with flying colors. She knows her name so I don't recommend changing it at this point, but that's up to you."

"So you're Dana!" She'd been so focused on how the dog responded to the woman, she hadn't even noticed the wiry man who'd come up behind Amy.

"Oh, sorry." The woman glanced up and Dana liked what she read in her compassionate green eyes. "I'm Amy and this is my husband, Ian. We do have manners, I swear."

Smiling, Dana focused on the woman. "I'm thrilled that you're more interested in the dog than you are in manners," she said.

"You want to come in?" Ian asked, grinning at her with a familiarity that could only mean Josh had talked about her.

What would he have said?

"I think we're good here," she said. She'd been planning to ask if she could bring Lindy Lu in and stay with Skyline for a little while, to watch the family interact with the dog, but she'd already seen enough. The dog was comfortable.

And Dana was not. No matter where she'd been that morning, or how busy she stayed, she couldn't find an ounce of peace within her own skin. "If you want to keep her for a day, I can stop by tomorrow and—"

"I think we're going to be keeping her, period," Ian said, a resigned smile on his face, but a happy glint in his eye as he reached out to pet the dog nestled against his wife. "Is there paperwork we have to do?"

She had it with her. She filled out her part and left the rest. Taking a couple of minutes to go over the Love To Go Around brochure she was leaving with them, as well as the contract agreement, she said, "I'll be back tomorrow to see how you're all doing and if you still want her, we can finalize things then."

It wasn't like her to be so short and to the point.

But it wasn't like her to be newly pregnant, either.

CHAPTER TWENTY-TWO

JOSH NEEDED AN ADVENTURE. Something different. Something he'd never done before.

Surfing the internet for an Arizona day adventure, he shook his head again and again. He'd already been skydiving. Enough times to be instructor material. He'd flown his own plane. He'd climbed mountains bigger than any they had in Arizona.

He'd never dug for gold, but it didn't sound all that appealing. Not dangerous enough. Fishing was out for the same reason.

Drag car racing…been there done that. Maybe he should try tent camping in the raw desert, just him and the cacti and bobcat to contend with.

And L.G. He could take the pup out in the desert.

L.G. would probably get stung by a scorpion or stick his nose in a rattlesnake hole.

And then he saw it…hot-air ballooning over the desert. There was something he'd never done. Might not be risky enough. Or fast enough, though.

Beggars couldn't be choosers.

Apologizing to L.G., he gave the pup an extra treat, locked him in his kennel and headed out to lose himself in the excitement of trying something new.

SUNDAYS WERE DANA'S least busy days. It was still way too early to start cooking for Thanksgiving—the holiday was eleven days away. And she'd already done all of the shopping.

Lori and Marissa hung around for most of the afternoon, watching a movie with her and eating popcorn. And then they were gone and she was left with her pets for company, a list of completed chores, no homework and an empty laundry hamper.

She cleaned Billy's cage. And remembered something she'd read once about cat litter boxes and pregnancy, which sent her to her laptop. Toxoplasma gondii. The parasite commonly found in cat litter boxes could cause stillbirth or brain damage in an unborn infant if a pregnant woman became infected by it.

She read on. About gloves and masks and hand washing and blood tests.

"We'll handle this," she told Lindy Lu, who was sitting on her lap. Kari, thankfully, was blissfully unaware as she snoozed on the textbook Dana had finished reading early that morning. Putting the puppy in her kennel, she drove to the twenty-four-hour clinic in town and asked to have a blood test. Because it was Sunday the procedure was quick. Getting the results was going to take a few days.

Then she went to the store, bought gloves and masks and an extra container of antibacterial hand soap to set on the sink in the laundry room and went home.

She didn't call her mother. Didn't call anyone.

Life was what *she* made of it and she was going to make it.

JOSH DIDN'T ACTUALLY fly the balloon. Or even go up in it alone. But he learned how to fly it. And paid a guy extra to take him up without any other riders, to take him higher, farther, than the tour company would have taken him.

And then paid him again, to keep him up longer.

As long as he didn't have to return to the ground, he'd be just fine.

THE KNOCK ON HER DOOR at just after seven that evening came as a relief. Hoping Jerome had laundry to do, or Lori was at loose ends again, or someone else needed her help with something, she practically tripped over Kari and Lindy Lu on her way to let her visitor in.

The cat litter box was cleaned. Her schedule for the week was made out. She'd cooked and frozen portions of bean soup, chicken-and-mushroom-soup casserole and a ham-and-mashed-potato mixture. Enough food to get her, Josh and anyone who stopped by through the week.

She was doing just fine until she pulled open the front door.

"Josh…" She should have looked through the peephole first.

He stepped by her without a word, but judging by the brief glimpse she had of his face, he was not doing well.

"We have to get some things straight," he said, standing in the middle of her living room with Kari and Lindy Lu on his feet attempting to welcome him and get to L.G., who was tucked under his arm like a football again.

"Like the fact that this is my home and you are a guest here only as long as I allow you to remain?" What was she saying? "I'm so sorry," she blurted next. "I'm… Please, sit down. Stay as long as you like. What did you want to get straight?"

She was babbling again. She wasn't sure she knew who she was anymore. It was far too soon in her pregnancy for her to be snippy. *Her pregnancy.* Oh, God. Pregnant wasn't her.

"No, you're right," Josh said, dropping to the edge of

the couch, still holding his dog. "I have no right to barge in here and tell you how things are going to be. I just… It's been a rough day."

"You can put him down, you know," she said.

"He hasn't been out in a long time. I came home and grabbed him up and headed straight over here."

He'd been gone somewhere. Was that why she hadn't heard from him all day? Not even a text message? After he'd called last night to tell her they had to talk?

"Let's put him out, then," she said, taking the dog from him, scooping up Lindy Lu and carrying them both out back.

She took some deep breaths, trying to gather the bands of control back around herself. She could handle this. Because she was always the one who handled everything. It was just a matter of staying calm.

The door slid open behind her. "I helped myself to a glass of juice. And brought one for you."

She'd squeezed the oranges fresh that morning. "Thank you," she said, accepting a beverage she didn't want.

"I don't mean to be bossy or autocratic," he said, leaning on a porch support while she stood staring out into the backyard.

"You're fine."

"How are you feeling?"

"Fine."

"Not sick or anything?"

"Nope. If I get morning sickness, it won't come until a little later." Hopefully perfectly timed over Christmas break. Because she absolutely could not miss class and have her grades drop.

"Have you thought about school?"

What, he was a mind reader now? "What about it?"

"Are you going to take a semester off? You can't very well go to class if you're having a baby."

He sounded pained by the idea.

"Of course I can. I have to." Little Guy pranced around the yard as though he owned it. Lindy Lu was trotting right behind him, step for step.

"What do you mean, you have to?"

"If I drop out, not only do I lose the scholarship, but I have to pay back everything I've used so far. Tuition alone is more than I can cover. Add in the year's rent I paid in advance and the living expenses, and there's no way I can afford to quit school. And that's aside from the fact that I'd then lose this chance to get an education at all."

Her words came out stronger than she would have liked. Stronger than she was feeling them. But if she wasn't strong, she was going to fall apart.

"Besides." She softened her tone. "There's no need for me to quit school. While having a baby is definitely going to complicate things, I can make the timing work. I'll be due sometime in August. So my most uncomfortable time will be during the summer and I don't have to take summer school to maintain the scholarship."

"I hear that summers here are brutal. You'll be at your most uncomfortable state in one hundred and fifteen degree temperature."

If he was trying to make her feel better, he was failing. It wasn't as if she had any say in the timing.

"But I don't have to work and I don't have to go out during the day at all, if I don't want to. I can do my shopping in the evening when the sun goes down." She'd already worked through this.

She'd be fine. Was lucky, really, that she had all of her living expenses covered for the next four years. And health insurance, too, at least for her. She'd have to check on the baby, but she had time to figure that out.

Time to figure out day care and...

"Classes start in August," Josh said.

"But not until late August. I should be due at the beginning of the month. Besides, I can work with my instructors to make up the first week or two if I have to. Or take online classes in the fall. I looked this morning and there are at least six classes that I can use for my general business major that are offered online."

She was going to have this baby. And be a fine mother. But if he thought she was going to quit school he'd best think again.

"You're much better at this than I am," Josh said.

"Better at what? Having a baby? I'm no more experienced at it than you are."

"You're better at finding a way to be positive about it."

"I don't have a choice, Josh. The baby is growing inside me and it's going to come out whether I want it to or not."

"But you aren't falling apart."

"What good would it do?" Her stomach felt like a million little ants were crawling inside it. Moving up to her rib cage. She willed them into stillness.

"I don't have a choice, either."

"No one's saying you do."

"I'm glad you agree."

She'd told him he owed her nothing. That she'd do this on her own. He'd already told her he had nothing to offer. Whatever had happened to him in his past was still too fresh. Too raw.

"I've never given you reason to think differently," she said slowly, keeping her gaze on the puppies as the sun dipped below the horizon, surrounding them in the rosy hue that came just before dusk.

Shivering, she wrapped her arms around her middle. She should have put on a sweater with her blouse and jeans.

"Actually, you have," he said.

Dana swung around, ready to give it to him good, when he continued.

"You told me that you wouldn't accept my help, Dana, but I have no choice but to give it to you. And as the father of that child, I have a right, too. By your own admission, you're going to name me as the father. It's the absolute right thing to do. And I would take you to court for DNA testing to prove the child was mine if you didn't name me. I will not walk away from my child. Not now at the prebirth stage, and not later, either, after it's born."

Her ears were ringing. They felt plugged, as if she was in an airplane. Only worse. She'd spent the day preparing herself for her life ahead and he was messing it all up.

She wanted to argue with him. To tell him he had no right to do this to her.

But she couldn't. He was right. He did have rights.

"The baby is a 'he' or a 'she,' not an 'it.'"

She was nitpicking. Sounding stupid. But she couldn't seem to stop herself. He'd been very clear about his rules. He was changing them on her now.

"I intend to be fully involved in every aspect of this child's life," he said, his tone unequivocal. "I want to be involved with the doctor, with the prenatal care, with the birth and after the birth, too."

He was talking about her body. Her life. And *his* baby, too.

"I've only known you a couple of weeks." The argument was weak, even to her ears.

"Since you're the one who will be handling the physical aspect of the pregnancy, it's only right that I pay for everything. I'm working and have insurance through my job, so I'll provide the child's health insurance, and since the child will be living with you—because I absolutely will not take him or her away from his or her mother, nor take your child away from you—I will pay all of the child's expenses, not just state-mandated child support. I'm also planning to have a room for the child in my home and will expect to have visitation rights—"

"Stop!"

She couldn't do this. Couldn't take any more.

Turning, Dana walked back into the house, completely forgetting about the puppy she'd left behind.

CHAPTER TWENTY-THREE

NOT AT ALL SURE what had just happened, Josh stayed outside for a few minutes, in case Dana planned to return. When he saw her in the kitchen, putting things in a bowl, he figured she wasn't coming back out and picked up the puppies.

Hers fit in the palm of his hand. Amazing that something so small could actually survive.

"I'm sorry I upset you," he said, closing the sliding-glass door behind him and joining her in the kitchen.

She didn't turn around. Measuring flour and other things, she dumped the ingredients in a bowl. "It's my life, too, Josh. You can't just tell me what I am and am not going to do."

"I was telling you what I was going to do."

"But every single thing you said affects me, too."

He supposed it did. Of course it did.

Breaking eggs into another bowl, she added sugar and started beating the mixture together by hand.

"Don't you have a mixer for that?"

"Yes. I'm choosing not to use it."

"What are you making?"

"Chocolate chip cookies."

Dare he hope she'd share some with him? He knew better than to offer to buy some from her. Offering to pay her hadn't gone over well when she'd been in a good mood.

She whipped the sugar and egg mixture until it was practically liquid, and then dumped the other bowl of stuff into it, beating that to a pulp, too. When he started to wonder if the cookies would become pudding instead, she added chocolate chips and handed him a spoon.

"What am I supposed to do with this?"

"Follow me to the table," she said. Setting down the bowl, she reached into a cupboard and pulled out a long thin sheet like the one he'd found among his kitchen things.

He'd mastered the art of house cleaning. Knew all about laundry now. But he'd yet to tackle the whole cooking thing.

And now his nightly internet reading was going to be about babies. Pregnancy.

Cooking was going to have wait a while longer.

"Take dough on your spoon like this," she said, filling her spoon with a glob of dough from the bowl. "And drop it on here. We'll do five down and four across, spaced evenly."

That was all she said. Doing as he was told, Josh spaced his dough blobs in line with hers. His were a little smaller than hers at first. And then a little bigger. She didn't complain.

She didn't speak, either, until two sheets of cookies were in the oven.

"We've got eight to ten minutes," she said.

Dana brought over two more sheets and proceeded to fill those, as well.

"You told me that you couldn't be relied upon," she said as, with a quick flick, she dumped dough from spoon to pan.

"I..."

"After we had sex you were quite clear about the fact that we couldn't have a relationship. That I couldn't count on you. Not that I'd expected a relationship. And when you found out I wasn't on the pill, you said that you couldn't be a father. That you couldn't take on—"

"I know what I said." He wasn't as proficient at the flicking, but he was getting his share of cookies down on the tray. "And I meant every word. I'm not suggesting that you and I have a relationship. I'm telling you that I can't turn my back on my child."

"How are you going to be a father to my child and not have some kind of a relationship with me?"

"Obviously we aren't going to be strangers," he said. "I don't want to be. I consider you to be my closest friend in Shelter Valley."

He hadn't meant to say that. Shouldn't have said that.

Dana's spoon had stilled.

"You're suggesting that we have a platonic relationship whereby we are friends having a baby, but other than sharing the baby, we have no commitment to each other."

Maybe. He didn't know what the hell he was suggesting. "Right." He liked the no-commitment part. He could handle that.

She started flicking her dough again.

"What about if I meet someone I want to date?"

"While you're pregnant? I mean, dating, well, going out is one thing, but you aren't suggesting you'd have sex with someone else, not while you've got my child in there...."

He sounded like a two-year-old. Not like a man who controlled million-dollar deals in a boardroom filled with men twice his age.

"I agree. That's a bit much," she said. "So, since you're so set on doing this fifty-fifty, I'd like your agreement that you will also be celibate during the nine months of my pregnancy."

"I—"

"If you're going to go to the doctor with me, you're going to be seeing me in intimate situations. I can't agree to allow you that access if you are also, simultaneously, seeing another woman in intimate situations."

Cookies forgotten, he stared across at her. Was she as hot as she'd just made him?

Dana's tall lanky frame was bent over her cookie bowl.

"Furthermore," she continued, sounding like some kind of boardroom executive and turning him on even more in the process, "if you intend to accompany me to doctors appointments, then everyone in town is going to know that you're the father of my child instead of just you knowing. Likewise, if you intend to be the baby's father in practice in addition to on the birth certificate, then everyone in our lives is going to know that you fathered my baby. I can't make that knowledge known if you're stepping out on me while I'm carrying your child. That would be too humiliating and I am going to have enough to handle in the coming months without adding more strain. Afterward, we can have a mutual breakup, but I can't allow myself to be humiliated and pregnant at the same time."

She was talking so fast he could have been forgiven for hearing gibberish. But she made sense. Perfect sense.

"Fine," he said. "I agree to your terms."

He was hard as a rock and had just agreed to be celibate for nine long months.

THE COOKIES WERE DONE. Josh had consumed his share while they'd been cooling. She wrapped up Jerome's intended share for Josh to take home with him. Jerome would never know that he missed out on a batch of cookies.

He had Little Guy under his arm and Dana was pretty certain she was going to get him out of her apartment before she fell apart again…until Josh left his plate of cookies sitting on the counter rather than picking them up.

"Did you want kids?" he asked her.

She'd already finished the dishes. Wiped the counters. There wasn't much more to do to occupy her hands.

"Yes," she said. "After I graduated, fell in love, got married…"

He cocked his head and quirked his eyebrow, and she tried her best not to respond. The man had just agreed to celibacy, rather than counter her platonic proposition by suggesting that they have sex with each other during the next nine months. There was absolutely no point in salivating over him.

It had been ten days since they'd had sex and not once during that time had he given her any indication that he wanted to repeat the experience.

He didn't want her when she was thin and able—he sure as hell wouldn't want her once she was fat and waddling to get from point A to point B.

"What if you fell in love before you graduated?"

"I don't know," she told him. "I take life as it comes. There's enough to deal with every day without borrowing trouble."

He stood there holding his dog. She wrapped her arms around herself.

"I used to figure I'd have kids someday, too." His words dropped into the silence. She'd expected him to say more, but he picked up his cookies and left then, without making any definite plans to see her again, or discussing practical realities. He hadn't asked about a doctor's appointment, or the cost of vitamins, or if she was telling her parents about the baby.

Fair or not, right or not, she felt cheated when he walked out her door and left her standing there. She'd agreed to become a partner with him in the most magnanimous project she'd ever take on, to allow him to be by her side during the most miraculous and probably the most painful moments of her life, and then he'd just left.

She took a hot bath. Cried a little.

And told herself that Josh's visit had been a good thing. He had a job with benefits.

She no longer had to worry about providing health insurance for her unborn child.

EARLY MONDAY MORNING, before work, Josh called Sara, Michelle's caregiver. It was the first time he'd spoken with her since she'd told him not to call.

"Good morning, Mr. Redmond."

"Good morning, Sara," he said as though they still talked every day. "How is she?"

"The same. No better, no worse."

He'd known that would be the case. Sara would have called him if there'd been any change.

Michelle wasn't going to change. She wasn't going to come back to the world, laugh out loud, drink wine…or have children.

By what right could he?

"Let me know if there's anything she needs, Sara. Anything that I can do to make her more comfortable or—"

"The fresh flowers you ordered to be delivered every morning are nice. I really think she likes them."

So did he. On some basic level Michelle was still with them and she'd always been drawn to gardens.

And he had a thought…

"Sara, I'd like to call Dr. Humboldt and see what he thinks about an outing." Michelle's attending physician hadn't expected her to hold on long after she'd been released from the hospital. Plans had been made in the short-term. But it had been months and nothing had changed. "If he agrees, would you be willing to accompany her? I'd buy a

van and a chair and hire someone to drive and handle pushing the chair around. I'll give you money to hire a medical
technician to assist with her apparatus…."

He was making it up as he went along, considering what
the idea would entail, but knew that the idea was a good
one.

"Where would we take her, sir?"

"Gardens," Josh said, his mind whirling to all of the
places he'd been in the world, and places Michelle had said
she'd wanted to visit.

"She loved the Arnold Arboretum there in Boston," he
said. He knew because he'd attended a fund-raiser there
with her and had been impatient to get to the alcohol trays
while she'd been taking forever looking at plants from the
1800s. "It's open year-round."

And there was Boston Public Garden. "There's a garden someplace by Cape Cod that's known for daylilies."
He'd been too much in a hurry to get wherever he'd been
going when Michelle had mentioned wanting to stop there.
"I know winter is coming fast, but if she does well, you
can take her farther. Maybe even to Florida. Would you
be willing to go to Florida, Sara, if I hire enough people
to help you?"

"I'd go to Florida if it was just me and her and the
driver," Sara said. "But you don't have to do this. She's
going to be the same here, in Florida, or anywhere else."

"We don't know that for sure, Sara. Maybe she's more
aware than we think. And if you don't mind going with
her, what can it hurt?"

Unless the doctor said it wasn't a good idea.

"We thought she was going to be gone by now when we
first made our plans," he said. "It's clear she's got the will
to live and I want to make certain that she has as much of
a life as it's possible for her to have."

While he was across the country creating new life.

"You make the call to Dr. Humboldt, and if he's agreeable, have him call me," Sara said. "I'll need instructions from him. And I can take the plans from there, if you're sure you really want to pay for this."

"I'm positive." The money was there. And while no one seemed to believe him, he had no intention of using any of it for himself.

Or maybe he was, Josh amended his thought as he drove into work that morning. Maybe all of his money was being used for him. Because if, as they said, Michelle had no awareness of her surroundings, then all the money he was spending on her was only to assuage his own conscience.

To make *him* feel better.

CHAPTER TWENTY-FOUR

Can you get out of your lease?

SITTING IN ENGLISH 101 Monday morning, Dana read the text as it came through. She'd forgotten her tablet that morning, still not used to having one even though the scholarship money had provided for it three months before.

I'm paid up for a year.

Can you sublease?

I don't know.

Find out.

She didn't reply.

AT TEN AFTER TEN, she was standing in Josh's backyard with a very happy-to-see-her Little Guy, when another text notification came through.

You just have student insurance, right?

Yes.

Won't cover pregnancy.

Yes, it does.

She'd checked. In a moment of panic Saturday morning just before she'd rushed out of the house. There had definitely been a pregnancy section. Her insurance covered sixty percent of the doctor's bill and one hundred percent of any hospital stay. She'd figured she'd use her savings to cover the other forty percent of the bill.

Not until you are on it for a year.

She didn't reply.

Unless there are complications, then covered.

"Come on, Little Guy, this isn't playtime. That's this afternoon. I have to get back to class."

She still didn't reply to Josh.

Her eleven o'clock was a lecture that started right on time every time. She wanted her front row seat and didn't relish walking in front of everyone after class had started.

Or maybe she just didn't relish standing in Josh Redmond's backyard while he was busy poking his nose into every aspect of her business.

SHE WENT HOME at lunchtime to let Lindy Lu out and to have a salad. To spend a few minutes in the peace and quiet of her own space.

Did you check on your lease?

Josh would be home now, too, having lunch with Little Guy. The man was starting to get on her nerves. How could she stay immune to him if he was going to be bothering her all the time?

No.

Okay, when?

She wanted to know why he wanted her to check on her lease. If he thought he was going to put her up some-place, like some kind of kept woman, he had another think coming.

But if he was rethinking the whole relationship thing... if he thought that two people who were having a baby and were going to be raising it together should live together...

If he was thinking that living together would be a way to save money...

This afternoon.

Okay, thanks. Let me know.

She didn't reply.

AT ONE-FIFTEEN another text came through. She was in class, had the phone on Vibrate and couldn't make herself wait to get out of class to look at it.

Just met with HR and set autowithdraw to new bank ac-count you have access to, to pay doctor. Will give you details.

This time, her fingers were shaking so much she couldn't reply.

JOSH WAS AT HIS DESK just after two on Monday afternoon, getting through a pile of paperwork in preparation for a se-ries of meetings he was planning, while he waited to hear about Dana's lease.

He'd set her number to a specified text notification so he'd always know it was her and not miss any communication. Even when he was in meetings. The woman was pregnant with his child and all kinds of things could go wrong. He'd only just begun reading up on pregnancy the night before so he wasn't an expert yet by any means, but he'd set the ringtone before he'd gone to bed.

I need to be able to take care of myself.

Yes.

Just so you understand.

???

You can't do everything for me.

Can't do much of anything but doing what I can.

What aren't you doing?

Growing baby. Birthing it.

Damn, he'd called the kid "it" again.

Oh.

They needed to talk about baby stuff—he wasn't sure what items she'd want, but from the brief cyber stroll he'd taken the night before of the children's store that had the highest rating on Wall Street, he'd been able to add up well over two thousand dollars in items that appeared to be necessary and he'd only gotten as far as the first couple of pages into the website. He was going to have to buy a house sooner than he thought. He couldn't afford to keep throwing money away on rent. He'd need the equity in the home to use as collateral in case he needed a line of credit.

Don't forget the lease.

He was at a standstill until she got back to him. Unfortunately, she didn't reply.

JEROME WAS COMING OVER that night to do laundry. He'd missed Saturday to attend an all-day gaming play-off in the student union. And before that, she had to stop by Lillie and Jon's place. They wanted her to see Harrison's new bed. She needed to convince Lillie that she was fine. At least until she and Josh discussed when and how they were going to let people know about that baby.

Next, she was going to visit Amy and Ian and Skyline. Dana texted Josh to let him know that she'd be busy all evening.

She took Lindy Lu with her. As it turned out, Lillie wasn't even home—there had been an emergency at the clinic—so Dana didn't have to fight her urge to break down and tell her new friend everything. She also didn't stay long. Then she spent half an hour in the second couple's home, mostly watching the dog. Ian wasn't home from work yet and it was obvious to Dana that Amy was already the rescue dog's "mom."

"You're a natural," she said to Amy, who stood holding the big girl. "Are you still certain that you want to keep her?"

"I'm certain," Amy said without hesitation. "She slept in the bed with us last night. She's ours."

They talked as they watched the dog. She found out that

Amy worked as a nurse on the surgical ward at a Phoenix hospital. That she and Ian had both grown up in Shelter Valley, attended Montford together and had been married for four years. Amy wanted children.

"Ian doesn't?" Dana asked, honing in on the one subject she was trying so desperately to avoid thinking about.

"Ian says he doesn't want to have to share me," Amy said. "I'm hoping Skyline will change his mind."

"Sharing you with a dog won't be like sharing you with a baby," she said. Amy and Ian had a lovely home and, by all appearances, a lovely marriage. There were pictures of the couple laughing together everywhere she looked.

They seemed like perfect parent material.

"I know. I hope he'll relax about the whole thing."

And what if he didn't?

"We set Josh up with a friend of mine."

The words fell like rocks on her toes. "That's nice," she said.

He'd told her he would remain celibate. That he wouldn't humiliate her.

"We double-dated," Amy said. "Olivia really liked him...."

Clearly Josh had given Ian and Amy the impression that Dana was just the person he got his dog from, or just a friend. Amy didn't strike her at all as a cruel woman. "What does Olivia do?" she asked, to be polite. To prove to Amy that she didn't care.

"She's a licensed architect but focuses more on interior design. We all went to high school together. Olivia was the head cheerleader and I was the one who helped wrap sprains and rub down sore muscles."

Lindsey and Rebecca had both been cheerleaders. And dated guys like Josh.

She didn't begrudge them. She could do herself up like

they did, spend an hour in front of the mirror every morning. Her sisters had talked her into getting a makeover once. They'd taken her to a spa and then to the mall where they'd made her buy some new outfits.

And she felt as if she'd been unfaithful to herself as she trudged around the stores in her makeup and new hairstyle, feeling uncomfortable and awkward and wishing she could hide.

She'd hated the attention she'd received from male customers, from a guy she'd known in high school who hadn't given her the time of day then but suddenly seemed very interested.

Lindy Lu was chewing on her finger. She'd have to get in the habit of keeping one of the pup's little chew toys in her purse. At least until Lindy was past the teething stage.

Would that be in time to replace it with a synthetic teething ring? The human variety?

"…he said it wouldn't be a bad thing to steer her in another direction."

Dana realized that she'd missed something.

"Wait, what?"

"Josh told Ian that it wouldn't be a bad thing to steer Olivia in another direction."

"He didn't like her?"

"He said he liked her fine. He just wasn't looking for a relationship and didn't want to lead her on."

Wow. He'd told the cheerleader the same thing he'd told her. He'd been telling her the truth. Not blowing her off kindly because she wasn't his type. "Ian and I think it's because of you."

Amy's words were so ludicrous that she almost laughed out loud. "What makes you think that?"

"You're all he talks about. Dana said this. Dana mentioned that."

"I talk a lot."

"And he apparently pays attention to every word. You know how many times I have to repeat myself to get Ian to actually listen to me?"

"Guys like things in ten words or less," Dana said. "I've just never been good at expressing my thoughts in anything less than paragraphs. Maybe that's the trick, if you talk enough some of it eventually trickles in."

Amy laughed. And Dana stood, giving one last caress to the side of Skyline's face as she lifted Lindy Lu up to her chest.

"So there's nothing going on between you two?" Amy asked.

She was going to have a baby with him, but she couldn't say that.

"We're just friends," she said, not sure at all what she meant by that.

She got out of there before Amy could press her any further.

JOSH WAS READING, something he'd been doing a lot of since he'd come home from work and pulled another frozen meal out of his freezer. He'd signed on to the internet while the microwave did its thing. And had been on ever since.

While there really wasn't a rush for Dana to see a doctor, they still needed to make an appointment. Dana was going to need prenatal vitamins and the sooner she started on them, the better. For her and the baby.

Vitamins were just one of the things Josh had read about on the internet. Flipping between various pregnancy-related online articles and a spreadsheet he'd started, he made some more notations.

Earlier he'd left a message for Michelle's doctor, too.

It was after ten when Dana's text notification sounded, and he picked up his phone immediately.

I can sublet.

Okay.

Half an hour later, he got another text from her.

Why?

ttyl, he typed. *Talk to you later.*
He never presented a plan that was incomplete.
It wasn't until he went to bed sometime after midnight that he noticed Dana hadn't written back.

CHAPTER TWENTY-FIVE

HE'D SAID HE'D TALK TO HER LATER—*ttyl*. Dana read her phone again as she sat in class on Tuesday morning.

She'd waited until after midnight but he hadn't called. Or otherwise contacted her.

Should she call him?

For what? She'd told him she could take care of herself, and it was imperative that she do just that. She couldn't rely on others to make her happy.

She called her mom on her way to Josh's later that morning. Not to tell her about the baby. She wasn't ready to do that. Just because she needed to talk to her mom. Susan was in the office with Daniel and seemed a little distracted, but still happy to hear from her. They didn't talk long.

Little Guy started howling as soon as he heard her key in the lock. If she wasn't quick about it, the puppy would leave a present for her before she got him to the door.

She stayed outside awhile, enjoying the Arizona sunshine and balmy seventy degree weather, pretending that pregnancy and raising a child, being a single mother, would be a breeze.

Knowing she had to get back to school for her eleven o'clock biology lab, she called Little Guy over to her. Only as she turned back to the sliding-glass door did she notice the note propped up on the dining table. It was a piece of computer paper with color printing, a picture of a house on front.

Inside, the note simply read, "Can you come to my office at lunchtime?"

He'd added the building and suite number beneath his signature.

"Josh Redmond."

Not just *Josh.* Josh *Redmond.*

Like she couldn't keep track of all the Joshes she knew? Or didn't know the last name of the man whose house she entered every day, twice a day? The man who'd fathered the baby that, though she couldn't feel it yet, was currently growing inside of her?

Locking the puppy back up in his kennel, she hurried off to class.

She was glad that her lab partners were in charge of the experiment. Her job was the final write-up.

Later that night she'd be better able to focus.

Because it would be after she'd answered her summons to Josh's office.

HE WAS READY and waiting, keys in hand, as soon as Dana knocked on his office door.

"You just said lunchtime," Dana said, stepping beyond him and into the office, looking around as though there was actually a room there to see. In her usual jeans, tennis shoes and blouse, she looked as if she was ready to handle anything life presented her.

He hoped so. Because he had the presentation of his life ahead of him.

She sat down in the faux-leather chair in front of his desk. He was embarrassed by the smallness of his space. The lack of quality furniture. Of art. Style.

"It was either here or behind your desk," she said, motioning toward the chair in which she sat.

He was a regular guy now, he reminded himself.

"I thought we'd go for a drive," he said. Surely she'd see things his way. He knew he was right.

And she was reasonable.

He'd already closed one deal that morning. Michelle's outings were a go.

He had to get this deal closed today, too. There was so much to do and not a lot of time in which to get it done.

"Drive where?"

"I'll show you."

"I'd like to know where I'm going," she said. "I have class in an hour."

She wasn't cooperating. And he hadn't even begun his pitch.

"We're going ten minutes from campus," he said. "Can you trust me on this, just until we get there?"

"The only place I know that serves lunch within ten minutes of here is the Valley Diner," she said. But she was walking beside him down the hall on the way to his SUV.

Lunch. Hell. He'd missed a key detail. Where was his secretary when he needed her?

Back in Boston, that was where.

Not only had he missed the detail, but here he was telling a pregnant woman he was going to do his part, telling himself that he was going to be a good father to his child, and he couldn't even remember that the woman and his child needed to eat. Well, they'd have to make a quick detour to the cafeteria for a sandwich that they could bring back to his office after their drive. It would be a working lunch. He'd attended and hosted more of those than he could count.

DANA DIDN'T KNOW of any lunch spot in the direction Josh was headed. She'd been in town a few months longer than he had and considered telling him he was going the wrong way.

But he knew different people than she did. Local people. Maybe he knew something she didn't know.

When they pulled up to the house, she recognized it right away.

"That's the house on the front of your note." She pulled the paper out of her bag.

"Right. I need you to take a look at it." Opening his door, he got out and came around to open her door.

Dana's heart started to pound. Surely he wasn't... Was he going to *propose* to her? Was Amy right? Did Josh want *her,* Dana Harris?

It was like every romantic movie she'd ever seen. She was surprised she managed to get herself out of the SUV without falling.

Josh walked up to the front door like he owned the place and, typing in a code in the lockbox, accessed the key and let them in.

Like he did own the place.

Oh, my God. She could hardly breathe.

"It has four bedrooms," he said. "And sits on half an acre. I looked at full-acre sites, but they were more than I can afford."

He was proposing to her. Any moment he was going to pull out the ring.

"What do you think of the kitchen?" he asked, taking her there first.

"You've been here before?" Dana spoke for the first time since entering the house.

"With the Realtor. This morning."

They'd reached the kitchen. A dream of a kitchen. With granite countertops, an undermounted sink, tons of cupboard space and an island with an electrical outlet.

"What do you think?"

This was *better* than any movie. Somehow while she

hadn't been paying attention her life had gone from a disaster to amazing.

"You don't like it. Well, that's fine. We can—"

"No, Josh. I *love* it."

She wasn't going to ask questions, although they were practically burning her tongue. She wasn't going to spoil the moment.

"Good," he said. "The rest of it doesn't matter as much. There's a fireplace in the living room, can be wood burning or gas, but I'm told that there are often bans on wood burning fireplaces in the city to try and keep the air fresh and clean as much as possible, being this close to California."

Was Josh babbling?

She watched him as he moved quickly through the rest of the rooms, pointing out three full bathrooms and four bedrooms. He gave room dimensions, talked about wallboard thickness, insulation and flooring.

"It has both an evaporative cooler and central air," he was saying when he turned to face her.

He was nervous. Which made her all the more willing to be patient. It made her smile, too.

"You're smiling. Does that mean you like it?"

Like it? She loved him. So it had only been a little more than two weeks since she'd met him. She'd waited a long time for him to walk into her life. And just as she'd always imagined, her heart had recognized him immediately.

"Dana? Do you like the house?"

The house. Not the man. She was getting ahead of herself.

"Yes, it's a beautiful house, Josh."

When was he going to tell her it was all hers if she'd marry him?

"Good," he said. "Let's lock up, then, and get back to the office."

She'd kind of been expecting to see a tray with a bottle of wine and a ring in the master bedroom. Or a table set up on the patio with lunch waiting—and the ring.

Was he going to propose in his office?

It wasn't what she would've imagined, but she didn't think she'd be disappointed. And maybe now she'd hear what had happened in his past, what issues he'd had to overcome. Or how she could help him overcome them. People didn't usually just solve their problems overnight. More like over a lifetime.

Whichever way this went, she was going to be the happiest girl on earth as soon as Josh got over his jitters and asked the darn question.

He parked closer to the school cafeteria than he did to his office building. And told her to pick out a sandwich and a drink and paid for both of them.

Fine. He'd bought a house this morning. He couldn't have been expected to do lunch, too. It wasn't as if he had an entire movie crew at his disposal making sure everything was perfect.

Josh continued to talk about the house as they made their way through the throng of students to his office. She saw at least five people she knew, all of whom said hello to her, and took note of Josh by her side.

She'd hear about him later, she guessed. And imagined how it would feel to show them her ring.

They'd reached his building, and then his floor. Dana looked around for Ian, wanting him to see her there with Josh so he could tell Amy, but there was no sign of him.

Josh made a beeline for the chair behind his desk. Dana sank back into the seat she'd left, feeling an entirely different type of nervousness. Josh hadn't summoned her to blow her off, to let her down gently, as she'd half feared when she'd read his note.

And he only had so much time on his lunch hour. He'd done the important thing, the practical thing, in taking her to see the house that they would live in after they were married.

Unwrapping his sandwich, he bit off a corner of it. Too excited to eat, she held on to hers.

"Aren't you hungry?" he asked.

"Not really."

"Morning sickness, which doesn't always come in the morning in case you didn't know, doesn't usually start until the sixth week."

"I know. Remember, I told you it was too early."

He nodded. He was so attentive, and damned cute, but would he hurry up and pop the question already?

She wanted to talk about the house. Which room would be the nursery. They had to think about furniture and painting before she was too far along.

And she wanted to talk about the wedding. They would have to set a date.

Would there be anyone from back home he'd want to invite? Any family?

Dana's thoughts skidded to an abrupt halt. She knew next to nothing about Josh's family. She knew he was close to his mom, but had no idea what she or his dad did for a living. Josh had told her he was an only child.

Josh finished his sandwich and said, "You'll need to keep a stash of crackers or dry cereal by your bed, and to set your alarm for an hour earlier than you normally get up. Eat smaller meals throughout the day, and try to drink a glass of water half an hour before every meal. You might have to avoid cooking during the first trimester and it's good to avoid spicy foods at dinnertime. Bland foods are best...."

Dana chuckled. She couldn't help herself. "What did you do, read Dr. Spock?"

"I got all of that from the American Pregnancy Association website. But I downloaded Dr. Spock's book, too. It just seemed a bit dated to me."

The man was better than anything she could ever have dreamed up. And he might drive her crazy, too, by the time this baby was born. The best crazy.

Clearly she was going to have to help him along.

"I have a feeling you didn't invite me here to discuss morning sickness."

Throwing his lunch wrappings in the trash, he leaned forward to pull a file from the tray on his desk. "You're right, I didn't."

Her heart beating such a rapid tattoo that she was having trouble catching a full breath, Dana waited. Her sisters were never going to believe this.

He opened his folder. Took out some pages, what appeared to be a spreadsheet. Placing a couple of pages before him, side by side, he slid two more across the desk, side by side, facing her.

Dana felt as if she'd stepped through Alice's looking glass.

CHAPTER TWENTY-SIX

SHOW THEM THE END IN MIND. Josh was back in high school, sitting in on a deal his father was putting together. The elder Joshua Redmond spent a month of evenings in his home office prior to the big day, educating Josh on every aspect of the transaction.

That month had shaped his life. It had shown him what he wanted, what drove him. He'd hung on his father's every word. And known, even then, that there were ways to expand upon the old man's theories and practices.

He still remembered every step his father had delineated. He'd honed them. Improved upon them.

But number one remained the same. *Start with the end first.*

"Picture this," he said now, sliding a full-color, glossy picture of the house he'd just shown Dana across the desk.

Slide number one, he'd mentally labeled the photo in the presentation.

"You're in the kitchen, baking cookies, and you look out that window to the backyard and see Lindy Lu and, running behind her, a little three-year-old girl with your long hair, in just that creamy milk-chocolate color. Lindy Lu is barking to get the little girl's attention, and the girl, your daughter, laughs out loud, her blue eyes twinkling just like yours do when you laugh."

Josh looked from Dana to the photo as he spoke. Assessing client reaction, keeping his mental finger completely on the pulse of the client at all times was critical. Dana was frowning.

"What's wrong?"

"Two things."

"Okay, let's tackle them one at a time."

"First, since we have a choice in this scenario, let's not stick her with my boring hair color. She'll have your luscious dark brown hair."

She was kidding, right? He was selling the deal of his life and she was quarreling about fictitious hair color?

And then, relaxing, Josh smiled.

"Your hair is beautiful and you know it," he said. "It's unique. Not like every other woman who gets their hair color from a bottle. Yours is much more striking. And luscious. Our daughter will be lucky if she takes after you."

The compliments rolled off his tongue more smoothly than ever before. And he was admittedly a pro at it. Not until he heard the words aloud did he realize that, in Dana's case, every single word was true.

The woman stared silently at him with narrowed eyes. As though she was trying to see through him.

He couldn't afford to let her look too closely.

"What's your second problem?" he asked.

"Where's Little Guy?"

"He's at home, why?"

She shook her head, meeting his gaze head-on. "No, here," she said, pointing to the house. "You have Lindy Lu in the backyard. Where's Little Guy?"

He didn't mean to stare, but Josh did. Was she being deliberately difficult? They had very serious matters to discuss.

"L.G.'s with me," he said. "Now can we get back to this?"

Leaning forward, seemingly satisfied, she nodded.

Josh pulled out what he'd dubbed *slide number two:* a

picture of a midpriced nursery that he'd printed off the internet.

"This could be either the third or the fourth bedroom we looked at this morning," he said. He rattled off measurements, pointing to different walls in the picture he'd printed to scale.

"This crib breaks down to an oversize twin with rails and then to a twin bed," he said. "It's the most cost-effective solution I found for the relatively quickly changing sleeping needs of young children."

Dana's eyes were wide, so he passed over *slide number three.*

"This is a cost estimate if we need three separate beds, a crib, a toddler bed and a twin bed. In less than four years' time, this is the amount we'd be spending on average-priced beds." He pointed to the bottom of one column.

"And this," he said, pointing to the other side of the page with the tip of his pen, "is the cost of the all-in-one."

Taking encouragement from her nod, from the way she was studying the sheets he put before her, he continued on with comparison cost analyses for the rest of the nursery, down to paint and average-priced wallpaper.

He'd read about preparing the nursery and was pretty certain he had it all covered.

"The only thing I didn't take into consideration was ceiling decor," he said. "I wasn't sure if you'd be one of those people who'd want glow-in-the-dark stars on the baby's ceiling, or if you'd rather leave the ceiling blank for the baby's imagination to fill in. It's important not to overstimulate, but some kind of light in the darkness is comforting, without making it so bright that the child grows up afraid of the dark, or so that his melatonin confuses night with day."

Dana's mouth dropped open.

"What?"

"I can't believe you know all of this."

"I didn't. Until this weekend."

Shaking her head she smiled. And glanced at her watch.

"Oh, my word, Josh! It's ten to one. I have to go to class."

Damn. That trip to the cafeteria had cost him too much time. He'd had everything planned down to the minute, as usual. Busy people didn't like to be kept waiting. And everyone had schedules.

He'd adjust. Flexibility was a key talent of his. "Are you busy tonight?" he asked.

"Nothing I can't work around."

"You want to go out to dinner and finish this?"

"Sure."

"I'll pick you up at six."

"Are you asking or telling?"

He paused. *Slow down, son.* His father's voice piped up again. *They have to feel like the choice is theirs.*

"I'm asking."

Standing, with her satchel over her shoulder, Dana grinned at him as she headed toward the door. "Just checking," she said. "Six is fine."

He watched her open the door and walk down the hall, her long legs going on forever, reigniting his desire to have them wrapped around him.

He was going to close this deal. There was no other option.

DANA HUMMED ALL afternoon. Funny how life could seem hopeless in the morning, and by evening be filled with opportunity and possibility.

Pulling a couple of outfits from the back of her closet, ones her sisters had forced her to buy, she considered her choices. Sexy without feeling slutty was what she was going for. Josh was going to propose. And she wanted him to see the best side of what he was getting.

As soon as she'd let L.G. out after class, she'd rushed home to get to work. Her hair no longer bore even a hint of the highlights her sisters had talked her into having professionally done, but there wasn't time to do anything about that. The Arizona sun had streaked it the tiniest bit. That would have to do.

Still, she curled it, and then pulled a small section of it back, just as Lindsey had shown her to do. She clipped it with the black embellished flower Rebecca had given her for Christmas a couple of years before.

The worst part was next—the makeup. On days when she had to dress up she'd put on a little mascara and call it done. That afternoon she pulled out all the crap her sisters had had her waste so much money on—from the clarifying wash that prepped her skin to the eyeliner that made her eyes look vampirish to her but, according to her sisters, made her eyes pop.

She remembered how to apply it all. Dana had always been a quick study. She just didn't like the feel of it on her face. Or the fake appearance it created.

Still, Josh knew the real her. And he had the lovelies of the world vying for his attention. She wanted him to know he could have that at home, too, if it's what turned him on. If the trimmings were what Josh found attractive, she'd get up earlier every day and go through the same rituals her sisters went through.

At five-thirty, she pulled on skintight black jeans with a black, equally tight long-sleeved Lycra top and her thigh-length, black-and-silver lightweight sweater coat, which she left open but belted loosely with a thick leather belt. Silver hoop earrings went in both piercings in her ears. It hurt a bit getting them in—she'd stopped wearing earrings when she'd left Indiana.

Still, the finished effect was what she'd known it would be. If someone didn't look too closely, she could pass for any popular beauty her age.

Dana focused on the loosely knitted sweater coat. It was the only thing she honestly liked. The only garment her sisters had encouraged her to buy that she actually wore regularly.

At five minutes before six, after letting Lindy Lu out, she took a peek at the cat litter box. Still clean.

Only then did she slip out of the tie-up ankle boots that she loved, for the slightly longer spike-heeled boots that her sisters had insisted were much sexier.

She was ready one minute before six, according to her phone. Peeking around the front window blind, she saw Josh's SUV out front and had a hard time breathing. He must have just pulled up because he wasn't even out of the vehicle yet.

Her heart pounding, she debated running out and jumping in the vehicle before he could come up to the door, but she didn't want to risk falling off her spikes, short though they may be, as she ran over the desert landscaping.

This was going to be the night of her life.

Josh was better prepared when he walked up Dana's driveway on Tuesday night. Carefully chosen words were running through his mind. By the time dinner was through, Dana would be thinking that moving to a new home and letting Josh take care of her and their baby had been her idea to begin with.

The door opened almost as soon as he knocked.

For a moment he thought Dana had company. And wasn't particularly pleased when he realized the heavily made up, sharply dressed woman was Dana. She looked like Olivia. Or Michelle. "Just let me get Lindy Lu in her kennel and I'll be ready," she said, while Josh stood there digesting the fact that Dana was just like other women.

That body...he'd known she was curvy, but he'd had no idea her breasts were quite that voluptuous. Or her waist so curved.

That body was carrying his baby. He didn't want to take it anywhere dressed like that. Except to bed.

And bed was off-limits.

Standing with his hands in the pants he'd worn to work that day, his shirt wrinkled from sweating in his faux-leather chair and the knot of his tie not as tight as it had been that morning, Josh wasn't particularly pleased.

Emotion rose up inside him. Not the grief and shame that had besieged him at the time of Michelle's crisis and become his accepted constant companion since. He wasn't sure what it was.

But he sure didn't like it.

"What have they done to you?" The words burped out of him. *Shut up, man,* he told himself.

Excuse yourself to the restroom and find your way back when you've got yourself under control. His mother's words that time.

"Who?"

"Whoever talked you into doing that to yourself?"

At the look of horror on Dana's face, Josh knew he'd blown it. His father would have fired him on the spot if he had ever lost control like that with a client.

"We're just going to dinner," he said now. The business deal of his life and he hadn't freshened up. He had his jacket in the car, but this was Dana—the one person in the world with whom he felt comfortable just being himself.

Or the person he was trying to become.

She slung her bag over one shoulder, locked her door behind them, and folded her arms.

"I wasn't sure if we were staying in town or going to Phoenix."

He'd never considered taking her to Phoenix. Perhaps he should have. "I'd planned to grab a burger or something at the campus pub."

"The pub's fine. Good," she said.

Okay, he could still salvage this.

"I just…" He spoke slowly, choosing his words carefully because he wasn't sure he trusted himself. "I'm sorry if I sounded derogatory about your appearance." They were walking side by side to his SUV. "I was just shocked."

Her chin dropped.

"You look great," he changed course. "Like you just walked off the pages of a fashion magazine."

"Stop, Josh. I prefer your honesty to complimentary lies. I will never be fashion mag material."

He unlocked the SUV with his clicker and reached out to get her door, but she was there before him, opening her door and climbing in without his help.

Oh, hell…

"Look, if it's honesty you want, then here it goes," he said as he climbed in on his side of the car and turned to face her. "I shouldn't be admitting this to you, considering the circumstances, but I find the real you far more attractive." If he was going to screw up, at least it was going to be with an eye to getting what he wanted. "The world is filled with women trying to look like beach babes, or fashion magazine cutouts. Frankly, they're a dime a dozen. The first thing that attracted me to you was that you didn't need any of that stuff and didn't seem to feel self-conscious about not having it on, either. You've got beautiful skin that looks healthy and that makes it a pleasure to look at. Your body is more enticing because of the mysteries your clothes hide."

She turned away as if she didn't believe him. He'd been on nude beaches enough times to know what he was talking about. But he didn't think she was ready for that much honesty from him at the moment.

Her face turned back to him, and when he read the turmoil in Dana's eyes, he wanted to take her into his arms and kiss her until she was breathless.

"Can you wait just a second?" she asked him.

"Of course. It's not like the pub takes reservations."

"Or needs them on a Tuesday night." She was herself again, giving him that sassy tone of voice. As long as he had the real Dana back, Josh was willing to wait for as long as she needed.

His mother would be shocked.

"WHAT?" DANA HAD BEEN about to put a carrot stick into her mouth and stopped. Josh was staring at her rather than eating.

Maybe this would be the moment. *Before* dinner, not after like she'd been thinking.

He'd ordered a beer. She had cranberry juice. Until she talked with an obstetrician, she wasn't even going to drink diet soda, let alone the occasional glass of wine she'd read was permissible.

"I'm just so glad you changed. I'm not kidding, Dana, you're so much more beautiful this way."

The sincerity in his eyes was hard to miss, even for a disbeliever like her. He must really have it bad for her.

"I've been with a lot of women," he continued. "Women who spend more on their hair, nails and clothes than I've budgeted for my monthly living expenses."

Thinking about her sisters, she smirked and nodded.

"And you really have them topped."

"You don't have to sound so surprised," she said with a chuckle, but she understood him being perplexed. She was, too. They'd only known each other such a short time and yet it—them together—seemed so right.

Natural.

Or it would be as soon as he gave her the ring.

CHAPTER TWENTY-SEVEN

"So, YOU SEE, if you look at the facts, the best option for both us and the baby is for me to buy that house and for both of us to move before next month's bills are due. Sooner for you, if you can sublet now, because that's more income that will just be added to our monthly overage for extra breathing room."

Dana studied his sheets. The amount of work he'd done in such a short amount of time, including a column for "profit sharing," giving her a percentage of the money he saved by paying for one household instead of two, was mind-boggling. He'd already opened an investment account for the baby. Not a savings account, an investment account.

At the moment it only had five hundred dollars in it, but he'd shown why he was putting the money where he was and how it was going to grow. And she understood why Montford had promoted him his first week on the job.

"I have a question for you," she said, sitting next to Josh in the booth rather than across from him as she had over dinner, so that they could both look at his charts together.

"Sure."

His tone was confident. Obviously the man was in his element. Even with her own business success, she was kind of intimidated. She told him about the money she had in her savings. "Can you help me do this—" she pointed to the baby's investment page "—with it?"

"Better yet, I can teach you how to do it," he said. "You

already understand the basics. We can follow the market together, play around with it a little bit, and you'll get the hang of it in no time."

"Is that how you learned?" Their faces were only inches apart, and her stomach turned over. In a good way.

"I took a certain amount of money that could be lost without undue hardship and played the market," he said.

"How'd you do?"

"I got lucky."

She wasn't surprised. In spite of his need to come up with a budget to afford his plans for their family, Josh reminded her of someone who'd been born with the proverbial silver spoon in his mouth. He just had that air about him.

Motioning toward the spreadsheets before them he asked, "So, what do you think?"

"I think it all looks good," she said. He'd figured out a way for her to be able to afford to choose new furniture for the nursery. She'd been envisioning spending many spring days frequenting garage sales, hoping to score baby paraphernalia in good shape.

"Oh, one more thing," he said, putting another sheet in front of her. "Ian turned me on to this handyman guy who says he can build kennels in the back corner of that yard and have them climate controlled, so if you want to you can expand on Love To Go Around, you know, beyond what Zack and the clinic do—or in partnership with them—and have a place to house many more dogs. You could have potential families come to you rather than you taking dogs to them."

Staring at the picture, tears came to Dana's eyes. Her own kennel. A real kennel. Not for purebreds, like her mother had raised, but for pups like Lindy Lu and Little Guy and dogs like Skyline—animals with so much love to give, with healing capabilities, and no home.

It was better than the engagement ring she was still

waiting for. "Oh, Josh, I don't... No one has ever done so much for me... I..." She broke off. She'd almost told him she loved him.

"You can change it if you like," he said. "This is just a rough sketch based on what I thought you might need. Randy will work with you directly, when the time comes, and he's doing it for a price I can afford, so..."

"Have you already bought the house, then?"

"No. I was going to sign the paperwork this afternoon, but then we ran over and you had to go. I'm not going to sign anything until I have your okay."

She nodded. And waited. There couldn't possibly be anything else for him to do, or say, before he popped the question.

"So? Is it okay?"

"If you buy the house?"

"All of it," he said, sweeping a hand above the table. "The plan. Are you willing to share a house with me—platonically, of course, just as we discussed—and allow me to take on the expenditures I've outlined here as well as give you a percentage of the money I save to do with as you wish?"

She couldn't possibly have heard him right. "You want me to live with you."

"Platonically, like we discussed. I won't expect anything from you sexually."

Cold and hot at the same time, she sat there, unmoving, as a strange calm came over her, and heard herself say, "But you're not going to be having sex with anyone else," she repeated the other thing included in the conversation to which he was referring.

"Correct."

"You're going to be celibate."

"Yes." His response was unequivocal, without hesitation. Either the man was an amazingly practiced liar, or he was being completely sincere.

"Just for the time I'm pregnant or for afterward, too? This is a small town. I don't want to live in your home, raising your child, while you're out with other women."

"I understand and I wouldn't ask you to. As far as other people will know, we're a couple, for as long as you want to keep up that appearance. I can't birth that child, but I can give you the respectability and companionship you deserve as you do so. After the baby is born, if you want to pursue other men, you just need to come to me and say so."

"So if I meet someone, I'm supposed to come to you and tell you I want to start dating and you'll move out?" Was it her or was the man nuts?

"If it's after the baby's born, and depending on finances, yes."

"And if I don't, we just live together forever?"

"If that's what you want."

"Don't you ever want to get married?"

"What I want became unimportant the second I got you pregnant. But for the record, no, I do not see marriage in my future. Ever."

If she'd had any hope left, it settled quietly and died.

"Just to reiterate, during the time you're pregnant, I will expect you to be celibate." Josh spoke quietly, although they were the only couple sitting in the back portion of the pub that night.

His lips pursed as his eyes met her face.

As if she'd be off having sex with a guy while she was huge. But wasn't that exactly what her mother had done? She might not have been huge yet, but she had had sex while she was pregnant with another man's child.

She cringed when she thought of the choices Susan had

made. And yet, she understood why she'd made them, too. She'd wanted what was best for the baby she was carrying.

As did Dana.

And the baby was the only reason why, when Josh asked her again if he had her okay for the plan, she nodded.

JOSH WAS LETTING L.G. run unsupervised in the backyard while he was on the computer the following Thursday, a week before Thanksgiving, when Dana called.

"We haven't talked about when and how we're going to tell people about the baby," she said.

"Okay."

"Next week is Thanksgiving. I'm going to be speaking with my family and feel like I should tell them, since my address is going to be changing in a matter of weeks."

"Oh, sooner than that," he inserted quickly. "I forgot to tell you. I found someone to sublet your duplex yesterday. He's a young guy who was here in the office on another matter. He's been living in the dorm, but finding it hard to concentrate and his parents were more than willing to pay a third more than what you're paying to get him out of there."

"You mean, I'll not only be out of my lease, but making money on it, as well?"

Make them feel like the choice is theirs.

"I did it again, didn't I?" he said, the world slowing strangely. With the phone to his ear, he stepped outside to the patio, glancing down as L.G. ran up to him, jumping up on his pant leg.

"I should have called you before I finalized anything."

"Actually, Josh, I'm grateful."

Not the reaction he'd expected. He shook his head as L.G. cocked his puppy ears up at him. The woman was going to be the death of him.

"Anytime you overstep rights I care about, I'll let you

know," she continued when he was beyond trying to figure her out. "You have my word on that."

"Okay."

"In this case, I asked around at school and everyone I know of is set, at least until semester break. There were a couple of people interested at the break, though. I was afraid I wasn't going to be able to move before next month's bills are due."

"We're closing on the house within the week," he said. A phone call to Boston for instant approval on a line of credit and an overnighted check were all it took for him to be able to buy the home and close the deal.

He was putting the house in her name so if anything ever happened to him, the house was hers, free and clear.

A detail he'd ironed out that morning and had not yet shared with her.

"Wait a minute!" Her tone had grown shorter. "I just realized you said I'd be changing addresses within a week."

"The kid who's renting your place wants to move in over the Thanksgiving holiday," Josh explained. "His parents are flying in to see his new home and help him get settled. That way he'll be ready when classes start up again the following Monday."

"Josh! I can't possibly pack and move this week. *I* have classes. And twenty people coming to my house for Thanksgiving..."

Small details, all of them. Little wrinkles, more like it.

Thinking quickly, he said, "I'll hire packers and movers. And the personal stuff you want to pack yourself, we'll do together, tonight and tomorrow night if you're free. That way we can get you moved in by Sunday and be ready for dinner next Thursday. Just think how much nicer it will be for everyone to gather around my bigger dining room table in that bigger dining room and leave the kitchen and your smaller table for serving the food."

"You want me to move by Sunday."

He did a quick calculation and told her how much money they'd save—even after hiring a couple of college kids and renting a truck.

And hung up with her agreement and a smile on his face.

AFTER SPENDING THE ENTIRE hour of her one o'clock class forcing herself to concentrate on the words the professor was saying, Dana not only had a headache, she was a bit grouchy, too. She just didn't care all that much that she was interrupting Josh's work when she dialed his cell on the way to his place to let Little Guy out.

Truth be known, she was angry with him. For not loving her.

Or asking her to marry him.

"Hi, what's up?" he answered on the first ring.

"We never decided when and how we were going to tell people about the baby."

"What do you want to do?"

She'd been thinking about that. A lot. Pretty well the entire time she and Lillie had been sitting next to each other in the pet-therapy van to and from Phoenix the previous afternoon.

She'd needed to confide in her new friend in the worst way. Lillie had known something was up. The concerned look in her eye as she'd asked three times if Dana was okay was proof of that.

All three times Dana had opened her mouth to tell Lillie about the baby and the move, and then had stopped. Regardless of what her relationship was with Josh, or how much hurt he'd caused her, he was her baby's father and should have a say in who knew what and when.

"I'd like to tell everyone the same thing," she said now. "I don't want different stories going different places."

"I agree completely."

"That means your parents as well as mine."

He didn't say anything, which bothered her—probably more so because she was upset with him. But, dammit, even if they weren't going to be married, she had a right to know where he'd come from. "Your parents are going to be grandparents to my baby, Josh. They should know that. I have a right to let them know. And the baby, most particularly, has a right."

If it wasn't about love, then it was about rights. At least for now.

"It's complicated."

"I gathered, since the one time you mentioned them it sounded like you and your father clash. But you said you're close to your mother."

"My father and I aren't actually speaking at the moment."

"Your choice or his?"

"His."

He had issues relating to his past. He'd been honest about that fact. Just as he was honest about everything else, whether it hurt her feelings or not.

Josh's honesty was one of the things she loved about him. His honesty was allowing her to agree to this unusual plan of his, in spite of the tears she was trying so hard not to cry.

"Can you fix it?"

"Not now."

"But he still lives with your mother, right? They're still married?" He'd mentioned his father's philandering, but not a divorce.

"Yes."

"Do you still talk to her?"

He hesitated, and then said, "Yes."

"So tell her. She can tell your father."

He paused again for a long time, and she said, "Josh?"

"Just what is it I'll be telling them?"

"That we've been seeing each other and while we've only known each other a short time it was immediately apparent to both of us that we were meant to be together." She was good at fantasizing.

"They won't believe me if I say it like that."

"How would you say it?" She held her breath.

"That, though we haven't known each other long, I believe it is the right decision to make a life with you."

"That's fine, too," she allowed. "The guy version, I guess. We tell them that we'd already decided to buy a house together when we found out we were pregnant, and sped things up to accommodate the unexpected arrival. That we're in shock, but looking forward to the future. And, most importantly, that we want this baby very much."

No kid of hers was ever going to catch wind from anyone that he or she was unwanted. Period.

"My folks will find that hard to believe," Josh said. "They know me."

"Then convince them, Josh. You're great at that, as I've discovered. And this point is nonnegotiable. Either we convince everyone that this baby is wanted, or the deal's off."

His pause was long—and painful—to her.

"I will convince them that I want this baby," he finally said.

"Good." Sitting in her car in his driveway, she looked down at the list she'd made—nothing that was ever going to rival his spreadsheets, but it was bulleted. And she was going to get through every item listed. He'd managed to waylay her too many times in the past couple of days.

"So, do you mind if I start telling people now?"

"No. The sooner, the better."

As eager as he appeared to be to get to the part where they'd be living together, she could be forgiven for taking hope now and then that he really did care about her.

"Okay, fine. Do you want me to keep a list of who I tell, and report back to you so you'll know?"

"No, that won't be necessary."

She'd said it in jest. To poke fun at his uptight attitude. To get him to chuckle again, as he'd done so often before they found out they'd made a baby together. She glanced back at her list.

"Do you want us to do our laundry together? It will save wear and tear on the machine as well as utility costs."

"Okay."

"And grocery shopping?"

"Yes."

"Fine. What time will you be at my place tonight to start packing?"

"Are you cooking dinner?" His voice had lightened.

"I can." She had to eat.

"What time should I be there?"

"Five-thirty." That would give her time to make a casserole, pick up some boxes and stop by the clinic to meet some new rescues. "And bring Little Guy with you," she added to Josh.

If Josh wanted business, she could give him business. Her years managing three furniture stores were finally paying off.

And her years of living with the pain of Daniel's rejection were paying off, too.

CHAPTER TWENTY-EIGHT

"HEY, WHILE I'VE GOT the two of you here together, I wanted to let you know..." Dana's throat dried up as both Cassie and Zack turned from the puppies they'd all been looking at to give her their full attention.

She'd thought she'd start with them. They were business acquaintances, not personal friends, and she was anxious to tell them about the new kennels she'd soon have, as well.

She had an idea—it was only in the beginning stages, but maybe, with their help, she could start a business of her own, a larger-scale Love To Go Around. Maybe they could get some federal funding. And could charge prospective families a small fee, just to keep up with administrative costs. She was bringing together her love of dogs and her business degree.

But first things first.

"Don't tell me you're quitting school," Zack said.

"You aren't leaving Shelter Valley, are you?" Cassie looked just as stricken as Zack.

"No, of course not. What gave you guys that idea?"

"The expression on your face," Cassie replied. "You look like you're about to tell us you ran over a dog or something."

"To the contrary," she said, feeling heat rise beneath her skin. "I'm going to be moving in with my boyfriend. He just bought a house and is having a set of kennels built for me in the backyard to house dogs for Love To Go Around." This whole thing, lying about Josh loving her, admitting that she'd had unprotected sex with a man she'd only known a matter of weeks…

And Cassie would know that because she'd been present when Josh and Dana first met.

"Kennels?" Zack and Cassie chorused together, looking like kids at Christmastime.

"That's wonderful!" Cassie said. The two of them talked about logistics and ways they could assist Dana, making house calls to her backyard when necessary.

The rest of it, growing Love To Go Around, could come with time. After the baby was born and she got her degree. If everything worked out.

"That's great news," Zack said for about the fourth time. And Dana knew she was letting her window of opportunity slide by.

"I have other news, as well." She couldn't look at Cassie. "I'm pregnant," she said. "Josh and I are both really happy, excited about the future. We haven't known each other that long, but…"

"Josh?" Cassie said. The vet was probably doing the math right then, counting back to the day she'd brought Little Guy in to see her.

"Josh Redmond?" The woman clarified.

"Yes. I met him here, as a matter of fact." When there was an elephant on the table, it was best to acknowledge it.

"You and Josh Redmond are having a baby," Cassie said one more time.

At which point Dana looked her straight in the eye. "Yes." If people were going to be judgmental, that was their problem. If they thought she wasn't good enough for Josh, well, they weren't going to know the truth about that.

"He bought a house and you're going to be living together."

Aware of Zack standing there, watching the byplay, Dana said, "Yes."

The grin that split Cassie's face startled her so much she wasn't prepared when the other woman reached out and hugged her. "Congratulations," Cassie said, letting her go immediately. "I think that's wonderful." The woman was looking straight at her, smiling, so Dana couldn't be reading her wrong. "If there's anything I can do, anytime, you let me know. Here—" She pulled out a card and scribbled a number on it. "That's my private cell. If you need anything, you call me."

Promising to do so, Dana made a quick retreat. She'd survived the first telling. And if everyone in Shelter Valley was so kind, she'd definitely moved to the right town—and found a new permanent home.

She'd learn to live with Josh without being a recipient of his love. Just as she had with Daniel.

And hopefully, as the pregnancy progressed, her appetite for sex would wane, as well.

HE NEEDED IT ALL LOCKED IN. The home. Dana in the home. And him there, too, watching over it all. He stayed at her place until she kicked him out Thursday night. They'd made some good progress, even with L.G. and Dana's little ball of fur helping. He'd gone to work early on Friday and gotten the final stamp of approval on the first of many fundraisers that were going to net the university the money to open a medical school on campus; this was the initial phase of a five-year goal. He'd given his landlord notice for the end of the month, although he didn't plan to wait that long. As soon as the movers he'd hired had moved Dana into the house, they were heading straight to his rental to get him moved, too.

He was also looking into veterinary programs in Arizona. Dana wanted to be a veterinarian. He needed to be prepared to help her become one. Their child would be three by the time she got her undergraduate degree. Ready for day care and self-sufficient enough for his or her mother to attend grad school.

On Friday, he signed the minor paperwork required to buy a home when paying cash for it, took possession of the keys and was on his way to his rental place with the back of his SUV filled with empty moving boxes, telling himself he was going to be just fine.

Pulling into his driveway, he noticed the new Ford F250 King Ranch parked in front of his house.

Someone had paid a pretty price for the vehicle. He'd bet it handled as smoothly as his Mercedes.

Sam Montford stepped out of the truck.

"I've been waiting for you," the older man said, walking up the driveway in broad daylight.

"I thought we agreed you didn't know me." Josh couldn't afford to play games. He'd closed on the house, and was about to get the Dana portion of the deal done. Now was not the time for complications.

"That was before I knew that you'd fathered a child." Sam was grinning.

Dana had said she'd be telling the people in her life about the baby. He'd assumed she'd meant her family. And maybe a few of her friends.

Cassie… He'd been so busy planning Dana's life, he'd forgotten about Cassie. But anytime Dana mentioned her pet-therapy work she brought up Zack's name.

Dana had asked if he wanted a list….

"Dana and I met, hit it off and were moving forward with our future together when we found out we were expecting the baby." He scrambled to remember what he'd agreed to say. "I closed on our new house today and we move in this weekend. We both want the baby," he said, feeling pretty confident that he got it right enough to suit her.

And now he had to get rid of Sam.

The older man wasn't grinning anymore, but his gaze

didn't seem judgmental, either. "She's a student at Montford, I understand."

"She is, but she's only four years younger than I am." He wasn't knocking up teenagers.

"And now she's carrying a Montford."

Sam's words hit him in the exact same place Dana's had done when she'd told him he had to tell his parents about them. About the baby. He hadn't yet done so, preferring to get Dana moved in first, but he understood what was going on. Sam was going to expose him. And, in so doing, blow the whole deal.

Panic shot through him. Reminding him of the first few hours after he'd received the call about Michelle.

There'd been nothing he could do. No amount of money or power were going to give him control over the situation.

"If you tell her, you risk ruining at least three lives."

"I figured that you'd told her," Sam said, frowning as he slid his hands into the front pockets of his jeans. "I'm here to invite the two of you over for Sunday dinner."

He could feel the whole thing slipping away. *If there's trouble, stay calm and keep your eye on the win.*

His father's words sprang to mind.

"Dana knows me better than anyone has ever known me," he said. "She knows plain-old Josh Redmond. That's who I am now."

His gaze locked on Josh, Sam asked, "For how long?"

Having the answers to every possible question that could be posed was the key to success. Josh didn't have this answer.

And before he could come up with one, Sam asked another. "How do you figure finding out that her child is heir to over a billion dollars would ruin Dana's life?"

Clearly Sam didn't know Dana.

"If she finds out that I've lied to her, she'll have nothing to do with me. She'll take that baby and make it on her own." He was absolutely certain of that fact. "Believe me, the money won't sway her. Dana's not like any woman I've ever known."

"That child she's carrying is a Montford. He or she has birthrights. And family, too, both here and in Boston, who are going to want to be a part of his or her life."

"And if Dana chooses, she can just move back to Indiana, put 'father unknown' on her child's birth certificate and forget she ever knew any of us."

"She's not going to do that."

Josh wasn't sure enough about that to risk the chance.

"Clearly you don't know her like I do," he said, and cringed at the weak response. "She's going to turn her back on all of us if she finds out I've lied to her."

He was repeating himself. Which would tell any worthy opponent that Josh had already played his best card.

"So what did you think you were going to do? Live your whole lives together without letting her know she's married to one of the richest men on the East Coast?"

They weren't getting married, but Josh didn't muddy waters with that detail. "I am no longer one of the richest men on the East Coast," he said emphatically. "My money all goes into a trust that does not have my name on it."

Eyes narrowed, Sam seemed to ponder that one, and Josh breathed a little easier. "I'm living wholly off my salary here, and will continue to do so. We'll build our own modest portfolio."

"You have family money. You're the heir to your parents' fortune. And you're going to deny your child the right to the best of everything? The best schools? The best opportunities?"

Dana hadn't had the same opportunities he had and she'd come out far ahead of him.

"I'm trying to do what's best," he said, developing an ache between his shoulder blades as he stood there.

Was Sam right? Was he, by his own unwillingness to go back to the man he'd been, denying his son or daughter a better life?

He pictured his mother, alone in the mansion on the hill in Boston. She was a good mother. In spite of the staff who'd been available to take care of Josh, his mother had always been a part of his daily life. She'd seen him off to school every morning and been there to welcome him home. He pictured her with a newborn baby in her arms....

"Bottom line is, the woman deserves to know who she's moving in with." Sam's tone brooked no argument. There was no hint of a smile now, either.

Josh was going to lose this one. He wasn't coming up with the words to turn it around. Wasn't fighting hard enough.

Maybe because a part of him suspected that there might be truth to Sam Montford's words.

"I need some time." This, he would fight for. He had to get Dana and the baby she was carrying into their new home. Once she was settled in, had everything she needed, once he was a little more confident that she'd stay put, at least until after the baby was born, he'd tell her.

"Cassie also wanted me to invite you to Thanksgiving dinner," Sam said. "I can give you until then."

An invitation in the form of a threat. He recognized the tactic. Sam was giving him six days.

"Dana's hosting a dinner for twenty, mostly college kids who don't have anyplace else to go. I'm helping." Six days wasn't long enough.

"Then bring her over for dessert," Sam said. "Either way, you have until Thursday to tell her or I'll do it myself."

Josh didn't doubt the older man. But he respected him.

"Your time's up, son," Sam said when he should have been walking back down the driveway to his fancy truck and driving back to his beautiful life.

Clamping his jaws on the words he might have said, Josh remained silent.

"You know I've been where you are." His cousin's voice had changed, taking on a warmer note he'd never heard in his own father's voice. "I left the money behind, too. It's hard to see what life's really about when everything comes easy."

Josh was listening.

"Your point of return arrived much more quickly than mine did," Sam continued. "Mariah's parents' deaths, having the little girl in my care, brought me home. Dana and this baby are your orphan girl. Either you're going to be the man you want to be, live up to your own expectations, or you're not. But this I know—you can't take that girl, or her baby, down with you."

He didn't have a comeback.

"Unlike you, I had neither a mind for nor the desire for a life in the business world, and having Mariah didn't change that. I had to find a way to be who I am, the heir to a fortune and future Patriarch of the Montford family, and be true to myself, as well."

Josh wanted to turn his back. And couldn't. Like a little kid, kneeling at this man's knee, he asked, "What did you do?"

"I started a construction company, doing work that I truly enjoy. And…" Sam paused, gave Josh a long assessing look. "I'm going to tell you something that only Cassie knows."

Sam expected Josh's trust so he was going to give his own trust, as well? "Okay."

"You ever read the SNC comic *Burrough Bantam?*"

"The one with the worm? I am, I am, I am…"

"Yes."

"Hell, yeah, I read it," Josh said, frowning. He'd been

reading it for years, since he was a kid. But what in the hell did a comic have to do with any of this?

"I write it."

Josh was confused. "What?"

"I'm SNC. Sam 'n' Cassie. That series was born shortly after I left Shelter Valley. It's my view of this town, the good and the bad. The strip sustained me for the sixteen years I was gone, and has sustained me since I came back, as well."

"And no one in town knows?"

Sam shook his head. Josh felt like his was shaking. There was so much to take in.

"Cassie and I talked about telling people. I was afraid people here would think I was poking fun at them. Cassie thought they'd be honored, but in the end, we figured it would ruin Shelter Valley and everything that makes it unique if people started flocking here to be a part of Burrough Bantam."

He'd put the town's welfare first. The choice didn't surprise Josh. He'd like to think that he'd have done the same. And wasn't sure he'd even have had the foresight to think about the town.

Sam squeezed his shoulder. "Let me know about Thanksgiving. And no matter what happens, you're family and my door is open to you. Anytime. Night or day."

Without waiting for a response, Sam walked back to his truck, got inside and drove away.

In business terms, Josh had just been closed.

CHAPTER TWENTY-NINE

FOR ALL THE RUSH, the move went much more smoothly than Dana would have expected. She and Josh went shopping for groceries Friday night before separating to do some last-minute things at their respective places. And by noon on Saturday, having taken off the weekend from her volunteering duties, she was in the new house. By four that day, Josh's things were there, too.

He'd hired someone to clean both of their old houses, to ready them for new tenants, and was off overseeing the work, while she was supposed to be unpacking. Part of his economic plan was for them to share household items, and when she'd told him that she wanted to put things away so she'd know where to find them, he'd easily agreed.

"If he's going to be this agreeable, this whole living together thing won't be too bad," she told the kitty and two dogs, who'd been following her around all afternoon. She'd made a quick stop to visit with a family who was interested in adopting a rescue dog just after lunch, but she'd been home ever since.

A home that had been overflowing with people—none of whom knew about the baby yet. Lillie had been with her all morning, helping her direct traffic and choose where everything should be placed as it was brought in off the truck. And Lori, Sharon, Jerome, Jon and Abraham had stopped in that afternoon. Mark, who'd been in the truck with the Swartz men, got all their computer and television networking hooked up for them. Jon offered to replace the

sliding-glass door in the back with French doors. She grate-
fully accepted his offer.

She hadn't yet told her four-legged family that there'd be
a man living with them. Hadn't so much as gone into Josh's
room yet. As she'd unpacked, she'd left his boxes stacked
in the hallway outside his closed bedroom door. He'd be
lying in his own bed alone. He could make it.

Other than Cassie and Zack, who'd had to know in case
they were concerned about a pregnant woman having volunteer counselor duties, she hadn't told anyone yet. The fact
that she and Josh were moving in together was enough of
a shock to deal with. No one other than Jerome had even
known that she and Josh were an item. She'd needed to
keep the rest of her news to herself for a few more days.

Late that afternoon, alone in her new home for the first
time all day, she unwrapped plates and glasses and put
things away. "This is our home now," she told the motley
crew watching her. Her home. Her first home. She'd called
her mother. Told her she was moving in with her boyfriend,
a man she loved with all of her heart. Because she couldn't
move without letting Susan know her new address.

She'd cried for ten minutes after she hung up. She hadn't
told her mother about the baby yet, either.

She'd meant to. She'd meant to tell everyone else. And
then she hadn't.

At least she wouldn't be alone over the next nine months,
whether Josh loved her or not.

She had friends. And a man who was going to support
her and be a great father to her baby. So why in the hell
were there tears dripping down her face and onto the dishes
she was trying to put away?

SHE WAS IN THE HOME. Had turned over the keys to her duplex. His temporary rental was also empty. The first phase
of Josh's project was almost complete.

Maybe tomorrow, they could go shopping for baby furniture. Get the nursery set. So if Dana decided to kick him
out when she heard who he was, if she refused to take another thing from him, at least she'd have the basics.

Have you told your mother yet? she'd asked as they were
setting boxes outside his bedroom door. She'd been talking
about their moving in together.

Of course he hadn't. And the look on her face had been
reminiscent of an expression he'd seen Michelle wear more
times than he could count. He knew what it meant now.
Disappointment. Hurt.

On his way back to the house Saturday evening, he
pulled off to the side of the road and hit his mother's speed-
dial number.

"Josh? Is everything okay?"

"Fine, Mother," he said, sitting up straight in the seat.
"I bought a house...."

"Is that what the money was for?" she said. "When your
father came home and told me that you'd called Leonard
for a signature loan, I'd hoped maybe you'd found an investment."

He should have known Leonard would talk to his father.
"I've met someone, Mother. Her name's Dana...."

Josh spent a good five minutes telling his mother about
the woman who was, at that moment, unpacking their
things in the home they were going to share.

He was avoiding telling her the rest.

He was also smiling as he told her about the way Dana
had helped him with Little Guy, teaching Josh how to care
for a pet.

"You have a dog?"

Something else he'd failed to mention. Pets were forbid-
den in the Redmond mansion.

"His name's L.G.," he said, delaying telling her the real

news. "Short for Little Guy," he continued, telling her how he'd ended up with the dog.

"You always wanted a dog," his mother said, something that he'd forgotten. "But your father was so allergic there was no way we could bring an animal into the house…"

His father was allergic to dogs? Shouldn't he have known that?

Maybe he had. Maybe the information was something else he'd been privy to but hadn't bothered to note.

He had to tell his mother about the baby.

So he told her about the meals Dana had left in his freezer, and the cookies she'd baked.

"You love her," his mother said, her voice soft. "I…"

What had Dana said to say? He was quite sure she hadn't mentioned anything about love.

"She's the one, Joshua."

He didn't have time for nonsense.

"What one?"

"The woman I knew you'd meet one day. The one that would stop you in your tracks."

Dana hadn't done that. The baby had.

"I can tell by your tone of voice when you say her name," his mother continued. "A mother knows these things."

She sounded so pleased, he hated to disappoint her. But it had to be done.

"We're having a baby together, Mother."

"What? A baby! When?"

She must have been home alone. She'd never have allowed herself to lose control otherwise. He could imagine the look of horror on her face.

And his stomach took a dive. He'd tried to avoid this. Would have preferred not to tell his folks at all. At least not until after the baby was born when he would've had some time to prove himself to be a good father.

"We have to meet her, Josh. I'll fly out. Next weekend. We have to plan the wedding. I'm sure she'll want to have it before she starts to show too much, which doesn't leave a lot of time, but we can get this done."

"Mother." It wasn't often that he'd used that tone of voice with her. In fact, he'd only had to once before, when he'd told her he was leaving Boston. "We aren't getting married. I can't. Not with Michelle…"

"Of course you can, Josh. No one expects you to live your life alone."

It was what he deserved. "Dana and I are happy to have found each other." They weren't the exact words he was supposed to have said, but they were close enough. "We want this baby and are sharing a home. That's what I called to tell you."

"If you want to wait on the wedding, I understand, Josh. I don't like it, and you know your father won't, either, but I do understand. The world's a different place now. Young people have children before they marry sometimes. And I give you my word that I will do my best not to get ahead of myself, but…a baby! I—I'm just so thrilled, Joshua."

She wasn't drinking. He could always tell when she'd had a couple of glasses of wine. "I thought you'd be horrified."

"Whatever gave you that idea, Joshua? You know I want grandchildren."

"And you know that I'm the farthest thing from father material there is."

The silence on the line was telling.

"What I know, Joshua, is that while it's true you used to be a bit…unaware…when it came to other people, you are and always have been a decent man. It's time you quit castigating yourself for something that wasn't your fault."

"I'm a spoiled, selfish ass who's spent my whole life focused on me."

"You've spent your whole life being the only one in your crowd who remembered to call your mother on her birthday every single year. Who, at eighteen, canceled a poker tournament when his father had the flu so he could handle a critical business deal."

"I left a chain of broken hearts and wasn't even aware of having done so."

Michelle's sister had pointed out the truth to him that first night at the hospital, when they'd been certain Michelle was going to die. She'd been the one to tell him why her sister had tried to drink herself to death at her bachelorette party. Because she was marrying a man she adored, who didn't even remember if it had been her or her sister that graduated with him. He'd made the wrong guess at the party that night, in front of all of their friends.

And then, to fill the silence, some smart-ass had called out, asking him to name Michelle's favorite color. It had been her wedding color—filtered through all of the wedding preparations from the invitations to the place settings. He'd seen a purple ribbon and called out purple. There'd been one purple ribbon in contrast to the various shades of yellow everywhere. Her favorite color had been yellow, and he hadn't known.

Dana's was green.

"You were always a handsome boy, Joshua," his mother said. "It wasn't your fault girls fell all over you. You did nothing to encourage them, not that I ever saw."

"And Michelle?"

"You asked her to marry you." Her tone was still soft—not the least bit condemning. "I thought you did it because you were aware of how she felt about you. It wasn't until after she…got sick…that I realized you were only doing your duty—for your father and the firm. You are your father's son, Josh. He made certain of that from the day you were born. But you're my son, too. You've got his single-focused drive, but you've also got more compassion in your little finger than he has in his whole body."

Sitting back, Josh stared at the desert landscape on both sides of him, as though expecting to see a waterfall. Or something else that was equally out of place.

"I've never heard you speak ill of him."

"Because he's my husband and I love him."

"You mean to say you've lived your whole life with a man who doesn't love you back?"

"No, son. Your father does love me. He loves you, too. He's a good man. Just not a perfect one."

And neither was he. Josh caught the implication.

Telling his mother to wait on buying a plane ticket, Josh rang off without confessing to the lie he'd been living since moving to Shelter Valley.

But knowing he wasn't going to be able to put off his mother for long, and with Sam's threat looming at his back, he faced the fact that he was probably going to lose the woman his mother thought he loved.

WITH BOXES FILLED with packing paper lined up by the back door, and others broken down in a pile beside them, Dana faced the last packed box. It was one from Josh's garage that hadn't been unpacked back at his last place. He said it had come from his parents' house, packed by his mother, who'd given it to him the morning he'd left.

The box wasn't very big. He'd told her he thought it was a set of monogrammed table and kitchen linens. Something about his mother being superstitious. He'd also told her she didn't need to use the linens, or even unpack the box.

Josh's mother had wanted him to have them. Of course she was going to use them.

There were a couple of towels on top—thick, soft kitchen towels in ivory with a soft green *R* embroidered at one end. There were cloth napkins, too, and matching place mats in the most exquisite fabric she'd ever seen. She'd never use that fabric to wipe her mouth.

Pulling out the last items in the box—some quilted pot holders—she noticed a large envelope at the bottom.

Dana looked at the envelope and frowned.

Should she open it?

The envelope wasn't addressed. Or sealed.

Thinking that it was probably a receipt, maybe from the place that did the monogramming, she picked it up. And pulled out an official-looking piece of paper. Just one sheet, but not a bill of sale.

Not sure what she was looking at yet, not sure if she should put it back without looking, Dana noticed the crest at the top of the document. It was the same marking that was on all of the linens.

The crest was followed by a section that reminded her of the front page in the family Bible at home—the one that listed their family tree.

Daniel had crossed out his name as father on the line that connected Dana to the family.

The one in her hand connected Josh to someone named *Montford*. His mother's maiden name was *Montford?*

Like the university in Shelter Valley where Josh worked?

Dropping down to the floor, she fell back against the cupboard and stared. Surely this was just a coincidence. Josh was not a Montford. He couldn't be.

And then she remembered that first day she'd met him. He'd been at the veterinary clinic. A man who had never owned so much as a goldfish.

Filled with horror, Dana remembered that day in the clinic's reception area in slow motion. Josh had told Cassie that he needed a few minutes of her time.

To discuss a personal matter? Because they were related?

Other things fell into place—Josh's business acumen, her sense that he'd played in much larger business fields than she had. His promotion the first week of his job.

The fact that he was a grown man who hadn't known the first thing about menial, everyday tasks. Like how to heat up leftovers in a microwave.

What bachelor didn't use a microwave?

Obviously he'd done something to fall out of grace with the family or he wouldn't be working in a college business office, or living on a budget. Or maybe he was fulfilling some familial obligation, doing his time, so to speak.

She stared at his kitchen table—she'd noticed the exquisite beauty of the wood the first time she'd seen it. Everything he owned was nicer than the high-end stuff they sold in their stores in Richmond. She just hadn't put two and two together.

She'd accepted him as he'd presented himself. A working man on a budget.

The quality of these linens. A family monogram…

And Cassie's response when Dana had told her she was pregnant. Her hug. And invitation to call…

Reaching up to grab her cell phone off the counter above her, Dana scrolled through her contacts until she found the private cell phone number Cassie had given her.

Barely managing to get past hello, Dana dove right in as soon as the vet answered her line.

"Is Josh Redmond related to you?"

The pause on the other end of the line told her all she needed to know.

"Wait, Dana, please. Let me explain."

She couldn't wait. Josh would be back soon.

She had to get out of there.

SAM MONTFORD'S CALLER ID appeared on Josh's phone when he was still five minutes from the new home he now shared with Dana. It was as if the family was determined to ruin his life before it had really begun.

One night. Couldn't they give him just one night in the same house with her?

Pulling to the curb, he answered the other man's ring. "What?"

"Cassie just had a call from Dana. I assume you told her?"

"No." Dread filled him. And continued to grow. "Why?"

"She knows who you are. And sounded upset. Do you need us to come over?"

"I'm not even there," Josh said, pulling back onto the vacant street. "I'm five minutes away."

"If we don't hear from you in thirty, we'll head over."

Josh had missed being part of a world where there was always someone else to show up in times of trouble.

Thank God he had family close by.

CHAPTER THIRTY

WITH LITTLE GUY and Lindy Lu sharing the seat beside her, Dana barely waited for the automatic garage door to open before she tore out of the garage and down the driveway.

Dana had no idea where she was going. Or what she was going to do. Had no destination in mind.

She just had to go. Turning the volume off on her cell phone, she tucked it away in her bag and just left.

Driving aimlessly away from town, she made one turn and then another. She took roads that seemingly went on forever and went nowhere. Entered an Indian reservation and kept driving. Came to a dirt road and took that, too.

Eventually she stopped driving and pulled over to the side of the road. She took out her smartphone. Her screen showed four missed calls. Three from Josh and one from Cassie Tate Montford.

Clearing them all, she touched the internet search button and typed in the name Redmond, pairing it with the other names etched on her mind's eye from the sheet of paper she'd held in her hand earlier. It didn't take her long to find what she was looking for. The Redmonds of Boston were all over the internet if one knew what to search. And if she'd still been trying to pretend to herself that she was wrong, that Josh hadn't been playing her, that chance was dashed, too, as soon as a picture of him, with a beautiful woman on his arm, popped up on the screen.

The caption read "Heir and Heiress to Wed."

268 THE MOMENT OF TRUTH

No wonder Josh hadn't wanted to have a relationship with Dana. He already had a woman. An untouchable, perfect in every way, rich and beautiful woman.

She'd found life hard when she hadn't been good enough for Daniel. There was no way, by any stretch of the imagination, she'd ever be good enough for Josh.

He didn't even live in the same world she occupied.

And she'd thought, just four short days before, that he'd been about to *propose* to her?

She cringed just thinking about that. She started driving again, trying to convince herself she was numb. Trying not to think about the afternoon after Josh had shown her the house and the time and effort she'd taken to make herself look glamorous.

Ha! Compared to the woman she'd seen on her screen, she'd been laughable.

She drove, and she didn't cry. She didn't really even think all that much. Time, life, emotion were all suspended as the puppies beside her slept.

They were fine as long as she remained calm. Her baby would be fine, too.

And at least Josh didn't know she'd been thinking that whole day that he'd be proposing to her.

He had no idea how she felt about him.

She was still in charge of her own happiness.

"So why the hell does everyone else keep messing it up?" she said aloud as the sun settled behind the mountains, leaving her in a seven o'clock duskiness that had her glancing around for streetlights. Or signs of habitation.

She had no idea where she was, other than in the desert someplace. This was stupid as hell. And not like her at all.

Turning around, Dana decided the safest thing was to head back the way she'd come. A plan that worked fine until she came to the first crossroad that she couldn't remember. Had she turned there?

She looked at L.G. and Lindy Lu, who were cuddled up next to each other on the passenger seat. Both of them looked back at her.

They were calm. They trusted her.

She wasn't scared. She had her phone. But she wasn't comfortable, either. What if she had a flat tire? Was she still on the Indian reservation?

Her baby was a Montford. And a Boston Redmond. She'd never even been to Boston.

If Josh was so embarrassed by her, why had he bought the house and insisted that they live there together? Why had he opened a bank account for her and agreed to tell everyone in town they were a couple?

Why had he agreed to call his parents?

Her heart lurched at the thought. He hadn't done it yet. She'd asked just that afternoon.

But he'd agreed to be celibate.

Or had that been a lie, too? Was he putting her up as other rich men did, supporting his mistress in a small town while he lived his real life elsewhere?

She drove and drove, looking to the horizon for any sign of lights that would indicate civilization.

And, switching her phone over to the hands-free speaker, she called her mother.

"I have something to tell you," she said as soon as she'd determined that Susan was alone. Daniel was at his Saturday night poker game. As usual.

"Did you get moved in?" Susan asked. "I've been waiting all day to hear from you. Take pictures on your phone, sweetie, in every room and outside, too. Send them to me."

If Dana hadn't already known that Daniel wasn't in the room, her mother's open effusiveness would have told her so. It was that obvious caring, expressed whenever Daniel wasn't around, that had kept Dana going all those years she'd spent at home.

"I'm pregnant, Mama," she said, reverting to a name she'd used for Susan when she'd been little.

Silence hung on the line, and then they both spoke at once. Eventually Dana got her whole story out. It was what she'd told Josh to say, practically verbatim. Word for word.

Ending with, "Josh and I both want this baby. He already has an investment account set up for him...or her."

Pulling the car off to the side of the road, Dana barely got it into Park before her eyes were blinded by tears.

"Oh, Mama, he lied to me. He's not who he says he is. He's this billionaire guy from Boston and now I know why he won't marry me. It's Daniel all over again, only worse."

She shut up. She hadn't meant to say that out loud. Ever.

"I'm sorry, Mama."

"I'm not, darling. You're right. At least about Daniel and me. And you have the right to speak up about it."

"I don't want to hurt you. You've loved me so much and—"

"Not enough, sweetheart. I love you with all my heart, but it wasn't enough. You are the most beautiful person I've ever known and I let you live your life feeling like you weren't good enough. I knew. And I couldn't seem to do anything about it."

"You did, Mama. I've always known how much you love me."

"And I've always known I didn't do enough. If there's anything I can do now...anything...you let me know. I will be there for you this time, Dana, you have my word on that."

"Tell me about my father."

"You already know everything. When I finally made the right choice to be honest, I didn't keep any secrets."

"You really don't even know his name?"

"He said his name was Bill Birmingham, but I could never find anyone by that name who fit his description."

"It wouldn't have made a difference."

"It might have. If I'd been able to tell him about you. He might have wanted you, Dana. Who knows, maybe he never had children and would be thrilled to find out about you."

"Daniel is my father."

Even now. The truth rang within her. Perfect or not, Daniel had been the man who'd been there, paying her way, seeing that she had everything she needed. Protecting her in his own way.

"I should never have let him treat you like he did," Susan said, her voice stronger than Dana could ever remember. Or maybe she could—from back before that horrible field trip that had changed everything. Her mother used to be strong. And happy.

They all had been.

Her phone beeped, signaling a call. She ignored it.

"You did what you had to do, Mama," she said, not quite believing she and Susan were having this conversation. "You had the girls to think about."

"Not at your expense. And while their lives would have been different if I'd left Daniel, they would have been okay, too. Maybe even a little less self-absorbed."

"But it wouldn't have been fair to Daniel," Dana said now, understanding that her mother had been in an untenable situation. "He adored you. Had children by you, and then found out that you'd kept a secret."

Just like Josh had. She'd always understood Daniel's sense of betrayal. Had never blamed him. But now, now she didn't just understand with her head, she got it with her heart.

"He didn't love me all that much," Susan said. "Not

enough to try to understand why I did what I did. To see that what I did was out of love for him, as much as for my unborn child. I could have raised you alone. Would have done so without hesitation, except for the fact that Daniel and I loved each other so much. I just couldn't break his heart. And I couldn't deny you the chance to have such a wonderful man for a father."

"Maybe if you'd told him the truth back then…"

"He'd have left me," Susan said. "He's said so a hundred times."

"He doesn't mean it, though."

"Maybe he does, maybe he doesn't, but I can tell you for certain, Dana, that while I made a horrendous mistake, so did Daniel."

There was nothing to see but pitch-black all around her. Dana was getting a little nervous.

The pups were going to need to go out soon. And they had to be getting hungry.

"How do you figure?"

"Bad things happen in life, Dana. People make mistakes. Everyone does. And one of the things that defines what kind of human beings we are is how we deal with those mistakes. Daniel took my mistake out on an innocent little girl who adored him. Yes, I gave him a raw deal, keeping such a huge secret from him. I know that. I've paid the price and will continue to do so until the day I die, but you paid the price, too, Dana, and that didn't have to happen. He had a right to shun me. He didn't have a right to shun you."

A band around Dana tightened. And snapped. She was shaking. And angry. And sad and relieved, too. It was so much at once that she was glad she was on a deserted road in the middle of nowhere.

She started to drive again, very slowly, inching along the shoulder of the deserted road and crying.

"Dana, just promise me one thing, darling."

Her mother's voice came out over the speaker, almost as if Susan was right there in the car with her.

Dana so badly wished she was. "What's that?" She sniffled.

"Don't make the same mistake Daniel did. Don't be like him, sweetie. Give your Josh a chance to explain."

Dana didn't know if she had that much trust left.

"WE NEED TO CALL GREG, JOSH." Cassie's voice broke through the haze surrounding Josh's thoughts.

He had no idea where Dana had gone. Cassie and Sam had been all over town looking for her in Sam's truck. They'd called Lillie, who'd been distraught and was out with Jon, conducting their own search.

Josh had alternated between being at home, and out looking for her, the damned family-tree paper he hadn't known existed and that she'd obviously unpacked, on the seat beside him in his SUV. He'd had no idea his mother had slipped it into the box she'd sent from the mansion. A little piece of home to go on the road with him, she'd said about the linens. Which was why he'd left it packed. He hadn't wanted a piece of home to hang on to.

Because he'd feared it would hold him back.

Why on earth he'd given that box to Dana to do with as she wanted, he had no idea.

He called Lori, who knew Jerome's last name, which allowed him to find the kid's number. No one had seen Dana since about four o'clock that afternoon.

"Greg Richards is the best sheriff this town has ever had," Sam said, standing beside his wife on Josh and Dana's new driveway. "And he knows the desert like none other. He grew up here. Lost his dad out in that desert. If anyone can find her, Greg can."

"Fine. Tell him to spare no cost. Helicopters, all of it. I'll find a way to pay."

"Done. And you don't have to pay for it. We'd do the same for any of our citizens."

Standing there with his new family, Josh had never felt more alone.

Because the one person who mattered most was lost to him.

Cassie's fingers slid into his for a moment, squeezed, and he barely felt her touch.

He was praying to a God he'd long since abandoned.

DANA'S MIND WAS PLAYING tricks on her. She kept driving endlessly, certain that she was recognizing a home or a pole or a sign, a particular cactus, a roadside memorial, and then doubting herself.

Little Guy sat up, disturbing Lindy Lu, who whined and tried to get across the small console to her lap.

"It's not going to be that much longer, guys," she said. She couldn't stop out there to let them go. It would be safer if they peed on her seat.

She'd never done anything so stupid. And sure as hell wasn't going to call anyone and have Josh find out how stupid she'd been. How could she explain herself? *Oh, by the way, I found out who you really are and my heart has shattered in a thousand pieces?*

If they were just friends, his true identity would be a mild shock, not the impetus for an irrational drive out to the desert.

She'd make it out. She still had half a tank of gas. But damn, she'd had so much to do tonight to get the house ready for Thanksgiving.

Tears sprang to her eyes again, but she brushed them

away with an impatient hand. She didn't have time for tears. They served no purpose.

Josh was rich. So what?

He'd lied. She didn't know why.

She loved him. He'd been engaged to a Boston heiress who was ten times more beautiful than Dana would ever be. Engaged with no wedding date set at the time of the publication of the photo.

She'd neglected to tell her mother that part.

Dana was having his baby.

And what about the heiress? Josh had told her he'd never lived with another woman. Did that mean he was still engaged? Or that he'd lied about that, too?

There'd been no mention of a breakup in the little bit of looking she'd done on the internet. No mention of the heiress again at all.

She should return Josh's calls. And she would. Just as soon as she had something to say to him.

He'd know by now that she was on to him. She'd left the family tree on top of the box she'd found it in. And called Cassie, too. There was no telling how tight they all were.

And that hurt, too. So much.

Cassie, the woman she'd practically idolized, had lied to her by omission. She'd known who Josh was, but hadn't said. Even when Dana had told the older woman that she was expecting Josh's baby.

But then, her first loyalty should be to Josh. He was Cassie's family. She was just a clinic volunteer.

Cassie obviously knew why Josh had pretended to be something he wasn't. And if she understood…

Give your Josh a chance to explain….

Dana's phone vibrated against her thigh where she'd dropped it. Glancing down at the display, she didn't recognize the long-distance exchange.

As long as it wasn't Josh. Or Cassie.

She flipped on the speaker phone. "Hello?"

She made a turn, and another one. And passed a place she knew she'd seen before. Because she was getting closer to home? Or because she was going in circles?

"Is this Dana Harris?"

She glanced around, looking for anyone who might be out there, watching her. It was odd to get a call from a stranger out in the middle of nowhere.

But the voice was female.

"Yes, who's calling?"

"This is Barbara Redmond, dear. I believe you know my son?"

The car swayed to the side. With a jerk on the steering wheel, Dana guided it back to the center of the road. If she'd have been holding her cell phone, she'd have dropped it.

"Yes," she said. Had Josh called his mother? Was the woman calling to buy her out?

Oh, God.

Be calm, she reminded herself. She hadn't known Josh was an heir to a fortune when she'd had sex with him. She hadn't done anything wrong.

"Joshua is going to be furious with me," the woman said in a formal tone that left Dana feeling as if she was talking to royalty. "I've debated this call for several hours and believe that for once in my life I must interfere in my son's life."

She'd been right. Here came the buyout. Dana remained silent, prepared to let the scene play itself out.

She wasn't selling her baby. Or taking any money to disappear, either. She had enough problems without creating more.

"I am understandably prejudiced, but my son is a good

man, dear." The woman sounded as though she thought she had to justify her actions.

"I agree," Dana said. Because she did. She made another turn. Passed a dirt road she hadn't seen before. Other than some run-down shacks and a dark hogan or two, she hadn't seen any sign of life in miles. Every road in Indiana led someplace, eventually. These roads had to, as well.

"Yes, but the thing is, Joshua doesn't agree," Mrs. Redmond was saying. "His father drove him hard, you see. There were problems when Josh was born and we knew he was the only child we would ever have. From the time that boy came home from the hospital his father was determined that Josh was going to be the best at everything."

The trouble with being the best was that you were setting an impossible goal. She'd tried it herself. For so many years. To be the best daughter. The best student. The best furniture store manager. It had never been enough for Daniel.

"I should have stepped in sooner, but J.P., that's Joshua's father, Joshua Phillip II, Joshua is III…"

Her head spinning, Dana looked at the long stretch of empty road in front of her, and out to the darkness on either side. She'd heard there were mountain lions and coyotes and javalina and rattlesnakes and all kinds of other things in the desert. All of which came out at night.

"As I was saying, J.P. is very good at knowing how to get people to do exactly what he wants them to do. He pushed Joshua, but he gave him a lot of freedom to do as he pleased, as well. I told myself that the two balanced each other out. And then Josh showed such a talent for the investment business his father had groomed him to take over. What was more, he loved the business as much or more than his father did. They had that in common and I thought it was good. Maybe it made matters worse."

She liked Barbara Redmond's voice. And couldn't think

about the fact that the refined woman on the other end of the line was grandmother to the baby inside her.

She also appreciated hearing the truth about the father of her baby. Finally.

"Things were fine until Josh asked Michelle Wellington to marry him."

The Boston heiress. "I knew things weren't right. Joshua didn't act like a man in love. But I wasn't privy to their... private life. J.P. isn't a demonstrative man, either."

"Mrs. Redmond, I—"

"I'm sorry, dear, I know I'm going on, but I must ask that you humor me just a minute or two longer. I am getting to my point."

Dana wasn't sure she could take much more hurt at the moment. At least not while she was in the desert. In the dark.

"Michelle always had a thing for Josh. Since they were kids. He'd never seemed to notice, and truth was, he hadn't. He asked her to marry him because it was time. He was of an age when the business needed him to have a wife on his arm. A proper wife. Because Josh's duty to his father and me, to the family, had been engrained since birth, he didn't consider any other option."

So he hadn't loved her? Dana was confused now.

And then she wasn't. Josh didn't need to love his wife. He just needed to marry a woman who was "proper."

And buy a house for the woman who wasn't.

She thought she saw lights in the far distance. Another car? Hopefully a good Samaritan as opposed to someone up to no good.

Maybe she should instruct her baby's grandmother to dial 9-1-1.

"Michelle misunderstood Josh's proposal. She assumed he'd chosen her over all the other women because he was in love with her. No one but her sister knew how much Michelle loved him. But I should have known. Should have seen. The night of Josh and Michelle's joint bachelor-bachelorette party, Josh made some comment that showed her how very little he really knew her, and she had a bit of a breakdown. She drank everything she could get her hands on, mixing alcohols and consuming far more than her body could handle."

The lights were definitely coming toward her. It seemed like more than one car. After hours of seeing no vehicles at all.

"Sometime after midnight her sister found Josh, who'd been partying with some of his friends in another part of the suite, and told him he'd better take Michelle home. She expected Josh would know to stay with her. But as I guess was normal for them, Josh hadn't seen Michelle all night. He had no idea the state she was in. He knew she was drunk, but didn't think anything of it. He took her home, put her to bed and left her there to sleep it off, returning to the party. Her sister stopped by to see her the next morning and Michelle was unconscious."

The woman had died. Dana could hear it coming.

And had never ached as she did at that moment. What Josh must have put himself through…

All of the times he'd told her he couldn't be relied upon came crashing down on her as she sat there.

She knew him well enough to know he'd have seen Michelle's choice to drink so much as a failure on his part. A failure to do his duty. And, as his mother had just said, and as Dana had witnessed during the weeks she'd known him, duty was everything to him.

"Michelle lived." Barbara Redmond's words broke into her thoughts. The lights ahead were still pinpricks, but getting closer. The distance in the flatness of the desert was deceiving. She had no idea how far she was from Shelter Valley. Or the California state border, either. How far was Mexico? She'd been told only a couple of hours from Shelter Valley. Had she been driving that long?

"Did Josh marry her?"

"No, dear. She had alcohol poisoning, went without oxygen for too long. She's in a vegetative state, living in a long-term care facility."

Oh, Lord. Oh, my Lord.

"When word spread about what had happened, people talked. Everyone had opinions on whether or not Josh should have left Michelle alone that night. And about his lack of attention to her in general."

In other words, Josh thought it was his fault that the beautiful Boston heiress had lost all quality of life. So many things made sense. Except the lies…

"When Josh came to me to tell me that he had to leave town because he believed his presence there was bad for the company, for the family, and too painful to Michelle's family, I didn't believe he was making the right choice. Gossip happens. Especially to people with money—folks like to point fingers. But it also passes…. Josh is a rarity among our crowd. An honest man who tries to make business deals a win-win even at the cost of losing a few. His father is that way, as well. People know that. The talk would have stopped and life would have gone on. The Wellingtons, Michelle's parents, were distraught, of course, but they never actually blamed Josh. Because, ultimately, the decision to overindulge was Michelle's, not his. She's an adult and Josh was not her keeper. He wasn't even in the same room, where he could have seen her behavior. Her sister was, though."

She understood.

Everything but Josh's lies to her.

"Josh visited Michelle every single day when he was in Boston," his mother said. "He insisted on paying for her care, including the three full-time caregivers. And now, I hear, trips to gardens, as well, even though she doesn't appear to have any sense of being there. Michelle doesn't even recognize him. She's not aware of her surroundings at all. But Josh still went to see her. And didn't go out anymore, socially, at all. That's why I finally agreed it might be best for him to leave. Because I couldn't bear to see what being here in town was doing to him."

As Dana watched the lights grow closer, and made out at least four vehicles, seemingly all traveling closely together, she listened to Barbara Redmond tell her about having recently found the branch of her family that had settled in Shelter Valley, Arizona. She'd been at peace with Josh's leaving as long as she knew he was with family, and so he'd agreed that Shelter Valley was where he'd go.

They'd come full circle. She still didn't understand why Josh had pretended to be something he was not. Why, even after he'd known about their baby, he hadn't told her who he really was.

But Mrs. Redmond had done what she'd set out to do. She'd raised Dana's sympathy for Josh to the point where she was ready to agree to whatever his mother thought was best for him. At least in theory.

If the woman was determined to buy her out, she'd at least try to reach a compromise with her. Something that would serve all of them.

"You can't imagine how thrilled I was to receive his phone call this afternoon, telling me that he was going to be a father."

What?

Frowning, Dana pulled off to the side of the road. She kept the car running. And locked. She'd start moving again before the vehicles approaching in the distance got too close.

"Then he told me about buying you the house," the woman was saying. "And the other things, and I'm afraid that he's going to blow his one shot at happiness."

She didn't follow.

"And that's why I'm calling," Mrs. Redmond said. "I'm going to interfere just this once…."

And then it occurred to her. They weren't going to try to buy her silence. They were going to take the baby from her.

All of the blood drained from Dana's face, and it felt like her extremities, too. The Redmonds were richer than the city of Richmond. She'd have no chance in a legal battle with them.

Josh must have known. Which was why he hadn't wanted to tell them about the baby.

Or maybe he'd told them, but hadn't wanted her to know who he was, the power he had, until he had his custody arrangement all wrapped up.

"My son is in love with you, my dear. I assume you're in love with him because I've yet to meet a girl who didn't fall for him, and I just want you to know, right now, that he loves you, too. But he said he's not going to marry you, and I don't think you should settle for anything less."

Tears blurred her eyes again. The lights in the distance were growing so close they appeared as a kaleidoscope of colors through the tears. Dana blinked. She had to pull out into the road.

Had she heard the woman right?

"He's in love with me?"

And she remembered her insistence that Josh make his parents believe their story. As she recalled, her cooperation had hinged upon his ability to do so.

The tears continued. The cars came closer. The kaleidoscope grew. And then she saw part of the reason for the sudden rush of color—a police bubble on the top of the first car. It was almost upon her now.

Followed by a vehicle she recognized because it had been parked in the driveway of her duplex many times over the past couple of weeks. And had a spot in her new garage, right next to her car.

Give your Josh a chance to explain....

Or a chance to be free.

"Mrs. Redmond? Josh is here and—"

That was as far as she got before Josh was pulling her out of the car and into his arms, to the squealing chorus of two puppies who'd just peed all over the front seat of her car.

CHAPTER THIRTY-ONE

THE ROAD WAS ABLAZE with color. Headlights from at least six vehicles. The blue-and-red flashing bubble from the top of Greg Richards's car.

"If you *ever* do anything like this again…"

He held Dana's body up against him. Or perhaps it was she who held him up. His relief was so great he couldn't be sure who was holding whom at the moment. Leaning her back against her car, he pressed his body against hers, placing his shaking hands on either side of her face.

"Are you okay?"

"Of course I'm okay, Josh. I was lost. Not hurt. I have plenty of gas and would have found my way back. I always keep a bottle of water and some hard candy in the car, and I had my phone."

He had the whole blooming town out looking for her and she hadn't needed him?

"You've been crying."

"I was on the phone."

He wanted to ask with whom. "You didn't answer any of my calls."

"I didn't want to talk to you."

But she was holding him. And letting him lean on her. In front of the whole crowd gathering behind him.

They'd wait. He was Josh Redmond—and a Montford.

"I was engaged," he said. Knowing he might only have this one chance to explain.

"I know all about Michelle, Josh."

"I haven't told anyone here."

"Your mother called me."

His mother?

"She thinks you love me, and that you're going to get so caught up in your sense of duty that you'll blow things and lose your one shot at happiness."

His mother thought that?

Yes, he had a strong sense of duty, but he was also…

Without a lot of time.

"I asked you to convince them and you did."

Dana was so calm. Even with her cheeks still wet with tears. And he was like a blind man struck dumb.

"But you don't have to lie anymore, Josh. You're a good and decent man, just like your mother said. And from what I can tell, you're blaming yourself for something that isn't your fault. Michelle was a grown woman…."

In true Dana fashion, she was going on and on without pausing for a breath, seemingly unaware of the small crowd gathered behind them. They'd all agreed to give Josh however much time he needed. Before they got their turn.

"Michelle should have told you how she felt," Dana was saying matter-of-factly, as if she wasn't pressed up against a car in the middle of nowhere. "She also knew, which you didn't, how much she'd had to drink that night. Whatever problems she had might have been exacerbated by you, but not caused by you."

She and his mother had obviously been talking for a long time. And he could tell by the look in her eyes that he'd hurt her.

"I just want you to know, Josh, that I'm not going to hold you to any of this. Your whole plan, the money you're spending… We'll work something out, but you are not beholden to me, or duty-bound to give up your life to—"

Putting his finger to her mouth, Josh applied pressure. He couldn't take any more.

"I love you." It was the most honest thing he'd ever said. And as uncomfortable as the words were for him to hear, they also freed something inside of him. Something far bigger than any mountain-climbing high or multimillion dollar deal.

He hadn't needed to hear his mother say he loved Dana to know. He'd just needed to think, if but for a second, that he'd lost her.

"I…"

"The proper response would be 'I love you, too,'" he quipped.

When her eyes welled over, Josh took his first easy breath of the day.

"I love you, too." Her voice broke.

"But?" He heard it there, in the tenuous threads.

"Josh, there are at least a dozen people over there, watching us."

He glanced over his shoulder. "They're speaking among themselves," he said. "And you can bet every single one of them is going to be telling this story, one way or another, for the rest of their lives."

"What story?"

"The one where the billionaire begs the most popular girl in town to forgive him for coming to the party so late and asks her to marry him." He paused. His whole life rested on this moment. The deal he couldn't close.

He had to wait for her to do that.

"Josh—"

"You said you love me."

"And you lied to me."

He'd known it was coming. And knew that if he didn't get this right, he was going to lose her. He'd been thinking of how he was going to explain things to her for days. And had come up empty.

He was still empty. Of everything but the truth.

"I didn't come here to fall in love, Dana. I told you from the start that I couldn't be in a relationship with you. Or anyone. Because of the lie I was living. I had to make good with the life I'd been given. Had to find who I was without the money and privilege that had made me so insensitive to those around me."

"Not insensitive, Josh. Just unaware," Dana said, fresh tears in her eyes. But the hurt he'd seen there a minute ago was gone. "I know, not from what your mother told me but from what I've seen, that you are, as your mother said, singularly focused. And one of the most sensitive men I've ever known."

He dropped to one knee. "Dana Harris? Will you marry me?"

The road was quiet as though everyone behind him had heard his question. As though they were all waiting.

"Dana?"

Getting down on her knees, she took his face between her hands and kissed him full on the mouth. Because that was reality.

And then, when she'd tasted him, her world fell into place. "Yes, Josh Redmond, I will marry you."

Cheers broke out, and she heard the sound of voices as everyone started talking at once. L.G. barked.

It was going to be complicated.

They still had a lot of things to work out. A life in Shelter Valley that he didn't want to leave just yet. A family in Richmond for him to meet. And a family in Boston who was going to love her.

He had to take her to see Michelle. And soon there would be a new baby to help bring into the world....

He couldn't get enough of it—this life he and Dana were going to spend together.

"Hey, Josh! Come on, man. Share a little!"

"That's Jon Swartz," Dana said, and Josh remembered why the others were waiting.

Once again, he'd been focused on himself.

That wasn't true. He'd been focused on what mattered more to him than anything. Dana. Their children. Their family.

"Josh! Sorry, buddy, but she already agreed to marry you and…"

Standing, Josh pulled Dana to her feet, but he didn't let go of her hand when the other man threw his arms around her and hugged her as though he'd never let her go.

"Jon?" Confused, and slightly tangled up between Josh's hold on her hand and Jon Swartz's hug, Dana noticed that Jon's friend Mark and Mark's fiancée, Addy, were there, too. Behind them stood Lillie holding Abraham. She had tears in her eyes and a smile on her face.

Beyond them, a little farther in the distance, she noticed Cassie Tate Montford with a man she'd never met before. Cassie's husband? They were each holding a puppy in their arms and were standing with the sheriff, watching intently.

"What's going on?" Dana asked.

"I was doing some research on Mark's scholarship," Addy spoke up. The night air was cool, and Dana felt chilled now that the sun had gone down. "Cassie said she mentioned him to you that first day you met, when she asked you about your all-expenses-paid scholarship…."

She hadn't realized that Cassie's friend was Jon's friend Mark, but she remembered the conversation.

"I'm on one, too," Jon said, with one arm still draped around her.

She felt like shaking him off. They didn't know each other well enough for that kind of familiarity.

"Mark was certain that Nonnie had written to the scholarship committee on Mark's behalf," Addy continued.

"My mom applied for it for me," Dana said, because she believed it was true, and she couldn't figure out why they'd all followed her out to the desert to talk about her scholarship.

Surely this could have waited until Monday?

Or at least until she and Josh got back into town?

"No, she didn't," Addy said. "Your mother didn't write to them and neither did Nonnie. I've suspected as much for a while, but just received a letter today, a confirmation...."

"Which is why we were all coming to see you when we ran into Josh and found out you were missing," Mark interrupted softly. Kindly. With a compassion in his eyes that calmed the sudden, irrational fear that had sprung up inside her.

"She told Mark first, and then they came to find me," Jon piped in.

"You, Mark and Jon have something in common," Addy was telling Dana. Everyone, including Josh, was watching her now. Scaring her. They all knew something.

Even Josh.

"What?" she asked. If it was bad, she didn't want to know. Jon was smiling. But he was holding on to her, too, as if she might break or something.

"No father," Jon blurted.

"Except that we do have a father." Mark stepped forward, taking her other hand from Josh.

"We do?" Dana asked, completely confused, and wishing Josh would take her in his arms again. And then, "Wait, I do? You're talking about my birth father? You know who he is?"

"*We* do," Mark said again. "We know who your father is, Dana. You know Nonnie raised me. I don't know if you knew that Jon grew up without either of his parents."

She shook her head, not sure what anything meant. Lillie had said something about Jon's childhood, but…

Mark stepped closer, leaning in so that his eyes, the kindness there, was all she saw. "The three of us have the same father, Dana. Our scholarships are from him. You're our sister."

She felt as if she was frozen in a photo, could see it from a distance. "You and Jon are brothers?"

The two men looked at each other and then, simultaneously, at her. "Yes." Mark spoke for both of them.

Dana fell against Josh, who was directly behind her.

"Your father's name is William Birmingham," Addy said softly when Dana wasn't sure she could hear much of anything. "He's spent most of his life either drunk or in jail, and in between, he fathered three children across the country by three different women."

"Apparently he sobered up during his last stint in jail and started a dot com that matches former convicts up with jobs and support, charging a finder's fee that's paid only after the convict has been straight and on the job for a year," Mark said quietly.

"With all the years he spent in jail, he knew what it would take for a guy like him to get it right and found a way to give back to others."

"He's quite a wealthy man," Addy said, her voice less emotional than Jon's or Mark's, giving Dana something to focus on, a slim clutch of reality to cling to.

"Somewhere along the way he tracked down the people he'd wronged in the past—without their knowledge—and found out about the three of us," Mark added from beside Addy. "And that's when he created the Shelter Valley Scholarships."

"There's enough money in the fund to provide educations to students for the rest of our lifetimes as long as it's invested right," Addy told her.

"Is he still alive?" Dana asked.

"Yes, and now that he knows he's been found out, he wants to meet all three of you."

Dana looked from one to the other of the men at her sides. To Lillie and Addy—and she started to cry again. Forcefully. Sobbing. The torrent that gushed forth was completely out of control.

She had brothers. And soon-to-be sisters-in-law. And cousins. She had Josh, and she was having his baby.

Her baby had grandparents who would welcome her.

Her father wanted to meet her.

She wasn't the stepchild anymore.

Arms were around her. Holding her up. Supporting her. So many arms. A circle of them.

And she knew that whatever came next, whatever kind of man William Birmingham turned out to be, whether he loved her or not, she was not second-best.

EPILOGUE

IN THE KITCHEN, holding an expensive monogrammed pot holder to her face, Dana tried to control the tears that seemed to insist on sharing every single one of her days lately. It was one week before Christmas, one day before her wedding, and she had a houseful of people waiting to eat.

It was absolutely not the time for a breakdown. Tears served no purpose. They never had.

She jumped as hands slid around the green silk dress she was wearing to cup the small mound of her belly from behind. Dropping the pot holder, she clutched the arms, holding them around her. "It's okay to be overwhelmed, love." Josh's voice came from the crook of her neck and she tilted her head back to look at him.

"I'm being an idiot, Josh," she whispered. "I've been responsible for my own happiness for so long, I don't know what to do with all of these people making me feel so loved."

"What have you always done?" he asked, kissing her neck in a way that had her thinking of something very different. And feeling emotions that were definitely not appropriate with a houseful of guests waiting on them. "When you were teaching me how to survive L.G., what did you always say? When you thought you could never have everything you always wanted, what did you tell yourself?"

She smiled and pressed her lips to his. "One step at a time," she said.

Just as she'd hoped, her lips were enough to distract him completely and he had his tongue in her mouth before either of them had time for another thought.

"Hey, buddy, I've given you my blessing to marry her, but that doesn't mean I'm giving up getting to know her myself. I've got twenty-five years to make up for."

The voice came from behind them. Recognizing it, Dana jumped back and turned toward it, her face flaming. "Sorry, we were just, uh… Everything's ready. I just had to get the rolls out of the oven."

"Food's been on the table for five minutes," William Birmingham said. "The others sent me in here to get you two."

"They actually sent *me* in here," Josh piped up, and the sultry tone in his voice made her hot again.

"And now they've sent me." Daniel appeared in the archway leading from the dining room. "Actually, that's not quite true. But this is the first chance I've had alone with the two of you—" he nodded toward Josh and William "—and this girl." He came toward Dana, holding out a hand to her, which she took. "I loved her as my own from the day she was born," he said, his voice breaking. "And then I let her down. I lost the right to be her father. Dana, girl, I want you to know that I will regret my actions for the rest of my life. I love you so much. It killed me to know you weren't mine."

"But I am," Dana said, swallowing against another onset of tears. "I always have been."

William stepped back. And Dana stepped forward. "There was a day when I needed a dad and didn't really have either one of you," she said, taking William's hand, too. "And now I have you both. To me, that's fate making everything perfect."

"Hey, you guys, we're starving." Jon appeared in the archway, dressed in his new black jeans. After much coercion, Jon had rented a tux for the triple wedding that was going to take place the next day at the Montford estate with Shelter Valley's mayor, Becca Parsons, officiating.

"What Jon means is that we've been asked to come see what's keeping you all," Mark said, coming to stand behind Jon.

They'd had Thanksgiving together, the brother and sister and their significant others. At Dana and Josh's new home with a houseful of students. And then the six had headed over to the Montfords' for dessert.

But this night was different. This night, their parents were joining them....

"You need help, dear?" Barbara Redmond pushed past the two younger men and into the room. Without hesitating a beat, the society matron bent to the oven and, taking up the pot holders Dana had dropped, lifted the large tray of rolls out of the oven.

"Let me help with those," Susan Harris said, wiping the corner of her husband's eye as she grabbed a basket and spread one of the beautifully monogrammed napkins along the bottom.

She didn't even seem to notice William, who had eyes only for his children. Dana knew, from a conversation she'd had with her mother, that she and William hadn't even recognized each other when they'd met for the first time in more than twenty-five years the day before. Nor had there been any hint of a spark between them.

Whatever had occurred the night that she'd been conceived, it hadn't been about love. Comfort, maybe. Survival, certainly.

And a sense of survival was the gift they'd given to her, their only daughter. A gift she would cherish and pass on to her own child.

Or children, if the fates gave her and Josh their way.

"What are you all doing to that soon-to-be daughter-in-law of mine?" J.P.'s voice boomed from the table. "She spent the time to prepare a meal we could have had catered—I think we all owe her the respect of letting her eat it. That's my grandchild she's feeding there."

Somehow, while Dana had spent a good bit of her life unable to attract the love of a father, she'd earned J.P.'s affection—and protection—right from the start.

"Lillie said to tell you she's changing Abraham and will be right down," Addy said, pushing Nonnie's chair up to the table.

The old woman had yet to say a word to the man who'd knocked up her daughter and left her emotionally unable to handle the responsibility of raising a kid on her own. Mark's mother had eventually been killed in a car accident after she got drunk and wrapped her car around a tree.

Mark reached for the glass of ice sitting at Nonnie's place at the table, and then for the pitcher of tea that was among the other pitchers waiting to be carried to the table. He poured, and turned.

"That's for your grandmother," William said, letting go of Dana's hand to reach for the tea.

Mark held on to the glass. "I'll take it to her," William said, and after another pause, Mark handed it to him. Coming up behind Mark, Addy put her hands on his shoulders and rested her chin there.

"I love you forever, Mark Heber, and can't wait to be your wife."

The words were obviously meant for Mark alone, uttered privately in the midst of the cacophony, but Dana heard them.

And so did Lillie, who joined them in the archway, Abraham on her hip. "*You* can't wait," Lillie said. "I don't think I'll be sleeping at all tonight."

"Illie, 'eep," Abraham said, bouncing up and down on Lillie's hip.

"You're a drunk and a loser, William Birmingham."

Everyone in the kitchen froze as Nonnie's words rang loud and clear from the dining room.

"And you're nothing but a barmaid," William said. "It's what I always told you, and you know I'm right," the man returned, at which Mark took a determined step forward. But stopped as the man who'd fathered him continued.

"I loved her, Nonnie, even more than you did. I just couldn't get her to stop drinking. To calm down. I followed her, you know, when she ran off that first time. I wanted to marry her. She never told me about the baby. She just told me she didn't love me so I had to go make a life for myself."

"So you went and got yourself drunk and jailed."

"Yep, that about sums it up. I swear I didn't know about Mark. Not until last year, when I came home to see you. To tell you I was in jail when I heard she'd lost her life. To see if there was anything I could do for you…."

"You were the one."

"What one?"

"The one my friend Mabel told me was asking 'round town about me. She didn't recognize ya."

"No, she didn't. And, yes, I was. And as soon as I saw that boy, my boy, working in a factory, I knew what I had to do. I started the scholarship for him. And then got to thinking about other women I'd bedded and left. All of 'em, every one of 'em was because I was missing Mark's mama so much. She's the only woman I ever loved."

Dana's gaze shot to her mother, and to Daniel, whose hand she was still holding. The two of them had eyes only for each other.

Dana's mysterious father had been between them for so long. William Birmingham took that evil specter away.

"We gonna eat? I got a card game startin' online in half an hour," Nonnie said then. "Got ten dollars on it." When William asked if it was too late to get in on it, she told him, "You sit down here next to me, boy. We got some serious talkin' to do."

"I think William's going to be staying with us tonight," Mark said to Addy, and then glanced at Dana and Jon. "If that's okay with you two."

"Fine with me." Jon nodded.

And it was fine with Dana, too. While she and Josh had the biggest house, their parents were already taking up the two spare bedrooms. And her sisters were flying in later that night; she and Josh would be driving into Phoenix to pick them up from the airport. They were going to be staying on inflatable mattresses in the nursery.

Josh moved forward, making a circle of four, with the younger adults still in the kitchen. "I just want to thank you all for agreeing to the formal wedding," he said, lowering his voice. "My folks really do mean the best...."

"Hey, man, bring it on," Jon said, grinning, when, in fact, he'd been the one who'd struggled the hardest to accept the trappings of a wealth he hadn't earned on his own.

Pulling Dana and Jon aside, Mark motioned toward the table. "The rest of you go on in. We'll be there in a second."

She knew Josh would save her a seat beside him at the table. He and his mother, plus Susan and Daniel, filed out, baskets of rolls and drink pitchers in hand. When they'd left, Dana looked at the man who'd become so dear to her in such a short time.

"The three of us, we're new to being family, but let's make a pact that it's forever," Mark said.

"I'm in," Jon agreed, nodding.

"You two might think you have a choice," Dana told them, wrapping an arm around each man. "But neither of you ever had a sister and I'm here to tell you that you're never getting rid of me."

Glancing up, she saw Josh smiling at her. And as the three of them walked in to face their families together, Josh stood, the lights on the newly decorated Christmas tree reflecting off his suit as he reached out, pulling her into his side as he raised his glass in a toast.

"To Dana," he said. "A woman with enough heart to save us all from ourselves."

"To Dana," a chorus of voices returned as glasses clinked.

More embarrassed than she'd ever been in her life, Dana tried to slide into her seat, but Josh held her up.

"And…to the future Dr. Dana Redmond," he said. "This afternoon, as a wedding gift to my wife, I opened a tuition account with funds that will allow Dana to attend the veterinary school of her choice. Provided that's what she wants to do…" She hadn't thought she had any tears left, but in true Dana fashion, they rained down her face as she listened to the cheers of her family and turned to give Josh the most intimate kiss yet.

In front of all three of her dads.

Maybe, deep down, she hadn't really believed in happiness before.

But she did now. This Christmas was truly the beginning of her new life.

* * * * *

COMING NEXT MONTH FROM

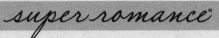

HARLEQUIN

super romance

Available December 3, 2013

#1890 CAUGHT UP IN YOU • *In Shady Grove*
by Beth Andrews

Eddie Montesano does what's best for his son. No way does he want his kid in special classes, regardless of what the teacher says. So Eddie will stand up to her...even if the teacher is one very sexy Harper Kavanagh!

#1891 A TEXAS CHILD • *Willow Creek, Texas*
by Linda Warren

Years ago, Assistant D.A. Myra Delgado betrayed Levi Coyote—but now she desperately needs his help. Will working together just make them relive past heartaches? Or will their commitment to finding a missing child bring them together?

#1892 THE RANCH SHE LEFT BEHIND
The Sisters of Bell River Ranch • by Kathleen O'Brien

Penny Wright has always lived up to other people's labels. But no more. She won't live on the family ranch, even if she's come home to help. Her little house in town is perfect for her...and so is the gorgeous man next door, Max Thorpe!

#1893 SLEEPLESS IN LAS VEGAS by Colleen Collins

Private investigator Drake Morgan would rather work with anyone than Val LeRoy. She's nothing but trouble. Still, he's learning to appreciate her *unusual* approach to investigating. Now all he has to do is control his attraction to her.

#1894 A VALLEY RIDGE CHRISTMAS by Holly Jacobs

Aaron Holder doesn't mean to sound like old man Scrooge. But Maeve Buchanan's bubbly holiday cheer brings it out in him. It's a sudden act of Christmas kindness that finally draws them together, though will they admit their true feelings even when they meet under the mistletoe?

#1895 THE SWEETEST HOURS by Cathryn Parry

Kristin Hart has romantic notions of Scotland, but she doesn't expect to find a real-life Scotsman in her Vermont hometown. Turns out Malcolm MacDowell isn't exactly Prince Charming when he closes the factory. To save her town she must go confront him...and maybe find a little magic along the way.

YOU CAN FIND MORE INFORMATION ON UPCOMING HARLEQUIN® TITLES, FREE EXCERPTS AND MORE AT WWW.HARLEQUIN.COM.

HSRCNM1113

SPECIAL EXCERPT FROM

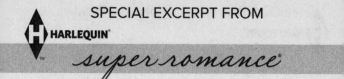

H HARLEQUIN®

™

super romance®

This might be the best Robbie Burns' Day ever
for Kristin Hart. Why? Because the gorgeous
consultant, George, who her company hired
joined her at her family's celebrations. And now,
the night is coming to a close.... Read on for an
exciting excerpt of the upcoming book

The Sweetest Hours

By Cathryn Parry

"I hope that you got all you need from us today," Kristin said,
as she walked George out.

He turned and smiled at her, descending two steps lower
than her on the stairs. His eyes now level to hers. "I did."

His hand touched hers, warm from the dinner table inside.
His fingers brushed her knuckles. Kristin was glad she hadn't
put on mittens.

"Kristin," he said in a low voice.

She waited, barely daring to breathe. Involuntarily, she shivered and he opened his coat, enveloping her in his warmth. It
was a chivalrous response, protective and special.

"Is it bad that I don't want this day to end?" she whispered.

"No." His voice was throaty. The gruff...Scottishness of it
seeped into her.

His eyes held hers. And as she swallowed, he angled his head and…and then he kissed her. He was tender. His lips molded gently over hers, moving with sweetness, as if to remember her fully, once he was gone.

The car at the end of the drive flashed its lights at them.

He straightened and drew back. Taking the warmth of his coat with him.

"I have to go." He looked toward the car. "Maybe some day I can tempt you away. To Scotland."

Maybe if she were a different person, in a braver place, she would dare to follow him and kiss him again…. But she wasn't that fearless.

"Goodbye, George," she whispered, touching his hand one last time.

"Kristin?" His voice caught. "I hope you find your castle."

And then he was off, into the winter night, the snow swirling quietly in the lamplight.

After this magical night, will George tempt her to Scotland? And if he does, what will Kristin find there? Find out in THE SWEETEST HOURS by Cathryn Parry, available December 2013 from Harlequin® Superromance®.